MURDER
by
FIRELIGHT

BOOKS BY MERRYN ALLINGHAM

FLORA STEELE MYSTERY SERIES

The Bookshop Murder

Murder on the Pier

Murder at Primrose Cottage

Murder at the Priory Hotel

Murder at St Saviour's

Murder at Abbeymead Farm

Murder in a French Village

The Library Murders

Murder at Cleve College

Murder in an English Castle

The Venice Murders

SUMMERHAYES HOUSE SERIES

The Girl from Summerhayes

The Secrets of Summerhayes

THE TREMAYNE MYSTERIES SERIES

The Dangerous Promise

Venetian Vendetta

Caribbean Evil

Cornish Requiem

Rio Revenge

The London Reckoning

MURDER
by
FIRELIGHT

Merryn Allingham

Bookouture

Published by Bookouture in 2025

An imprint of Storyfire Ltd.
Carmelite House
50 Victoria Embankment
London EC4Y 0DZ

www.bookouture.com

The authorised representative in the EEA is Hachette Ireland
8 Castlecourt Centre
Dublin 15 D15 XTP3
Ireland
(email: info@hbgi.ie)

ISBN: 978-1-80550-166-4
eBook ISBN: 978-1-80550-165-7

To J, a brilliant bonfire belle – with very many thanks.

1

THURSDAY, 5 NOVEMBER 1959

The sound of drums had grown louder in the cold, still air and the smell of smoke more pungent. Flora, standing on tiptoes, peered through the haze.

'Can you see? Are they coming?'

'I think they must be.' Jack Carrington's arm was wrapped tightly around his wife. 'It's becoming noisier by the minute.'

The percussive thud of the drums, insistent and almost tribal, was the backdrop to bursts of loud clapping, yells of encouragement and the boom of rook scarers.

The two of them were standing at a point halfway down School Hill, sharing the pavement with what felt like a thousand others, some jostling for position but everyone eager to see the magnificent procession when it arrived – the four bonfire societies of Lewes marching together from the top of the town to the bottom. Jack had been advised to find a spot on this part of the hill – from here, his colleague had said, they would have the best view of a celebration which, with few breaks since the late eighteenth century, had been staged every year.

Bonfire Night in Lewes was a huge event, he was beginning to realise, its purpose ostensibly to remember Guy Fawkes and his failed plot to blow up the Houses of Parliament, but a canny way for the town's residents to 'blow up' anyone against whom they had a grievance. Once the marchers reached the bottom of the town, each society would peel away, continuing on to their own fire site. Effigies of whoever or whatever a particular society had disliked most this year would be burnt on the enormous pyre that members had been building for weeks.

'Look!' Jack pointed ahead. 'They're here at last! We have fire!'

Over the brow of the hill the first of seventeen flaming crosses, one for each of the Lewes martyrs burnt at the stake by a Catholic queen some four hundred years previously, came gradually into view. One by one, the ten-foot fiery crosses breasted the rise, accompanied on every side by hundreds of burning torches held aloft, their flames terrifying the darkness into light. Flora caught her breath, stunned by a sight of such furious splendour. A sight of retribution, too, she thought, for the crimes of history.

'What do you think of the fancy dress?' Amused, Jack bent to speak into her ear. His attention had moved to the procession itself.

'Bewildering!' she told him, though her voice went unheard against the crescendo of noise.

An eclectic mix of Vikings, nuns and priests, Pearly Kings and Queens, Tudors and Native Americans had arrived. A regiment of feet marching determinedly down the hill, society after society, sped on its way by the cheers of onlookers who lined each side of the road, while spectators hanging over balconies and out of open windows toasted their good health.

'Who wants a beer?' a young reveller called from somewhere above, throwing a can to the thirsty spectator below.

'What an atmosphere,' Flora remarked in a suddenly quieter moment. 'Abbeymead has its own bonfire, but I've never seen anything like this.'

'You didn't come here as a child?'

'Can you imagine Aunt Violet bringing me?' Flora's much-loved aunt, dead for some years now, had been wedded to her village and rarely ventured to Lewes, a town some twenty miles distant. 'Violet would have hated the disorder! A burning guy and fireworks on the green each year is all I remember.'

'There'll be bonfires across Sussex tonight, I guess. Across England, in fact, but this is surely a world beater.'

'I'm glad we came.' Flora pulled her woollen hat firmly over her ears to fend off the cold that had been creeping slowly upwards from her boots. 'Even though it's likely to be our last time as well as our first.'

This was Jack's final term teaching at the local arts college, before he tucked himself away in their Abbeymead cottage and returned to writing crime full-time. For the last year, he had spent three days a week as a mentor to students keen to pursue their own writing dreams and it had been a friend there who'd urged him to make sure that this year he took his wife to the celebration, insisting it was a spectacular display that you had to experience at least once in your life.

As though to nudge people's memory of an event that was now over three hundred years old, an effigy rolled past of Robert Catesby, portrayed as a puppet master controlling a marionette Guy Fawkes, Catesby being the real conspirator while Fawkes had simply been the demolition expert. Blowing up figures you disagreed with was, of course, part of this evening's fun, and a giant inflated figure of Nikita Khrushchev had just now appeared at the top of the hill, the float drawn by men in a uniform of navy stars and grey stripes.

Jack pointed to the jumpers they wore. 'They'll be from the Harland society,' he said knowledgeably.

'How do you know?'

He tapped his nose. 'I have my sources.' Then laughed.

'Martin Winter, the history buff at college, has been giving me lessons.'

Immediately behind the float, two figures were dragging burning barrels of tar while at the same time trying to steady themselves as they approached the sharp incline of the hill. And, behind *them*, a line of bonfire *boyes* and *belles*, as society members were known, held aloft an enormous flaming banner, its proud slogan declaiming, 'We Wunt be Druv'.

'We wunt be druv?' Jack asked.

Flora, having spent most of her life in a Sussex village, explained the dialect. 'We'll not be driven. That's what it says.'

'We'll be contrary – is what it really means!' He pulled a face. 'In my experience, that sums up the county pretty neatly.'

'Not contrary, Jack – just a laudable refusal to bend to authority!'

'Well, you would say that,' he teased.

Several more floats had followed the platform bearing Khrushchev, most of them with figures that neither Flora nor Jack recognised. Figures of people who had evidently displeased one or other of the societies this past year: a council official who'd been difficult, an officious park attendant, the local police chairman, all destined for one of the four bonfires that would soon be raging.

'I recognise this chap,' Jack said, as another larger-than-life effigy hove into view, this time of Fidel Castro, and carried on a trailer attached to a tractor. 'That's unusual – the other floats have been pulled by hand. It makes Fidel seem top dog, doesn't it? A man of the people looking down at the masses. Is it ironic, do you suppose? I wonder what the... the Grove society, I recognise the jumpers... doesn't like about the Cuban revolution?'

'That revolutions disturb the peace, maybe?'

'And this doesn't? The whole town is a madhouse tonight.'

'But only for one evening and on a very small scale. The

Cuban Revolution was world news. But they've created his face perfectly.'

The large model of Castro, his face an elongated oval, complete with straggling hair and beard and a floppy beret perched atop, had been tied to the centre of the float and was wobbling somewhat precariously as the vehicle managed a slow roll down the hill. Unusually, too, there were figures surrounding the effigy – the bonfire boyes and belles guarding their trophy, perhaps?

As the float drew closer, Flora grabbed her husband's arm again. 'Masked Mexicans!' she said, pointing to the figures crowding the front of the float.

'More likely, masked Cubans.'

'OK, Cubans. But why the masks?'

'I imagine they're dressed as bandits.'

'And the others? Those at the back and walking behind – they seem to be in Tudor costume. All gabled hoods and embellished bodices and the men in velvet doublets. What an odd mix.'

Jack peered through the haze of smoke. 'I wonder if one of them is Leo Nelson. I saw him a few days ago on my walk round the Overlay garden and he mumbled something about the Grove society.'

For some years before he married, Jack had rented Overlay House and, though it was the least comfortable of places, he'd been happy there and, on occasion, found himself even now missing its shabby spaciousness. He'd called at Overlay shortly after they'd arrived back from their honeymoon in Venice, thinking he might have left behind a clippings file he was missing. Nelson, the new tenant, had seemed friendly.

There'd been no invitation into the house – there was no file, Nelson had assured him – but the man had told Jack that he was welcome to come to Overlay any time he liked and take a walk in the garden that he loved. A garden he'd worked hard to create. In the past, it had proved a sanctuary, often helping him think through whatever knotty writing problem was plaguing him.

On his first visit back, however, it had looked a sad sight: the grass unkempt, the beds choked with weeds and, what vegetables there were, left to rot. Knowing that young Charlie Teague, his former helper in the garden, had refused the chance to continue working there, Jack had asked Nelson's permission to go looking for a new gardener. The chap he'd found had, within weeks, brought the flower beds and vegetable patch back to life and, as Nelson was paying him well, the arrangement looked good to last.

'You know what Alice says.' Flora was laughing. 'What she suspects!' Alice was an old and dear friend from their home village. 'That Leo Nelson is a spy. She doesn't understand why he moved from Lewes to Abbeymead, and thinks it's highly suspicious that he doesn't work!'

'A spy in a Grove society uniform. That's a thought! I wonder if he *is* on the float and, who knows, standing in pride of place, right at the front!'

'That's important?'

'So I'm told. According to Martin, hierarchy rules. Families who've been in Bonfire for years march at the front. Those members—'

But Jack never finished his sentence. In that instant, one of the masked Cubans travelling atop the float keeled over and, for a second, seemed to hang in the air, his arms flailing, before he fell at Flora's feet, sprawled halfway across the small square of pavement and just missing a burning tar barrel.

Instinctively, she jumped back, but Jack had bounded forward, arms waving furiously for the driver of the tractor to stop. The procession collapsed in turmoil. A woman in Tudor costume – an ornamented French hood, low-cut boned bodice and dark blue kirtle – pushed past her fellows to clamber down from the float. Bending over the fallen man, she began chafing his hands and calling for water – it seemed he had been knocked unconscious. A few minutes later, she was joined by a rush of others, jumping from the float, keen to help but unsure what to do.

Two of the Cuban bandits, masks now abandoned, stationed themselves either side of the prone body, preparing, it seemed, to heave the man to his feet. One of them, Jack saw, was Leo Nelson.

Jack was swift to intervene. 'We should be careful,' he said, taking off the fallen man's mask and bending to feel for a pulse. 'He may have a head injury. It could be dangerous to move him. We should telephone for an ambulance – he needs expert care.'

Above the noise of beating drums and flying fireworks, one of the society members made his objections heard. 'We can't leave him lying there.' A burly man had pushed his way through the small crowd to appear at Jack's side. 'I'm Edwin Brooker,' he announced, 'and a former chairman of Grove. Been its chairman for years and I'm telling you we'll have to move him. He's holding up the procession.'

To Flora, the sentiment felt unnecessarily brutal, but Mr Brooker, a muscular figure in bright yellow, an ammunition belt slung across his chest, had evidently taken charge.

'Then we'll move him a few inches onto the pavement,' Jack conceded, 'but we do it very slowly.'

'You a doctor then?' Edwin enquired, sounding belligerent.

'I'm not, but in the past I've had to deal with severe injuries.'

Edwin Brooker gave him a long look, then nodded his agreement. '*You'd* better do the moving.' He turned to a man carrying a burning brand. 'Bring that torch over here,' he ordered.

In the flickering light, Jack bent down again to position his hands beneath the man's back, ready to lift the lower half of his body onto the pavement.

Flora, watching her husband, was startled, seeing his expression change from a quiet confidence to alarm.

'What is it?' She rushed forward.

Jack slowly withdrew his hands from beneath the man's body and spread them wide in a gesture of shock. In the light of the burning torch, every one of his fingers was coated red.

'Call the police – as well as an ambulance,' he said quietly, getting to his feet.

2

Flora was beside him, staring blindly into Jack's face, her own tight with shock.

'What?' she mouthed silently.

He fumbled for a handkerchief, gingerly retrieving it from his pocket, before wiping the blood from his hands.

'At a guess, I'd say he's been stabbed,' Jack said in a low voice, making sure he wasn't overheard. 'But that will be for the police to decide.'

'But... but...' She tried to speak, yet the words refused to come.

Jack gave her a swift hug. 'I've no idea how it could have happened, if indeed it has. And there's no point in speculating – we'll have to leave it to the police. Oh... here they are. That was quick.'

'They've a lot of officers on duty tonight. The constable was probably only a few yards away.'

'An ambulance has been called,' the policeman confirmed to anyone who was listening, 'but I'll need witnesses to the accident.'

He fished a notebook and pencil from his pocket as he

spoke, ready to write. His words, though, had brought an immediate thinning of the crowd, no one, it seemed, wanting their evening disrupted further. Jack stayed his ground. Like it or not, he had been closely involved.

'We'll get back to Cleve as soon as we can,' he told Flora, once the officer had noted his name and address and confirmed that the police would be contacting him shortly. 'But if you can bear to wait, I'd like to stay until the ambulance arrives.'

'We'll stay if you want, but it's not really your responsibility,' she said gently.

'I'm thinking Leo Nelson might need help. He's looking quite stunned.'

Flora drew her brows together and glanced towards the man Jack was nodding at. The new tenant of Overlay House was slumped against the wall, his sombrero having slipped halfway over his face and the coloured poncho he wore looking creased and torn.

'I know him a little and he *is* from our village.' Jack tried to explain. *And he's a loner, as I was before you rescued me.* But that was something he didn't say.

'He has a whole float full of help,' she pointed out, gesturing to a fresh flurry of Grove members who had joined the group. This time, it was Tudor costumes that swirled around them. By now, the float had been pulled to the side of the road, allowing the remainder of the procession to continue its march down the hill and on to their individual bonfires.

'I'd still like a word with him. Just to check he's OK to get home. I won't be long. Promise.'

Jack was back sooner than he'd expected. When he'd walked over to the drooping man, it was to see the ambulance crew arriving. They had made excellent time thanks to the town's main streets being closed to traffic and the procession having already passed.

At his approach, Leo Nelson had smiled wanly, but

refused any help. Jack was pleased to see, though, that on the urging of the ambulance crew, the man had clambered into the vehicle and was accompanying his unconscious colleague to the hospital. If Nelson was suffering from shock, and he showed every sign of it, the nursing staff would take care of him. Jack could relax, his only job now to walk Flora home to Cleve College.

'I don't understand it,' were her first words as they opened the front door of their apartment. 'One minute the man was standing at the front of the float, playing at being a ferocious bandit, and the next he was in the gutter and bleeding.'

'That's putting it graphically.'

'Well, it was graphic. Horribly so.'

He took her gently by the arm. 'You should put it out of your mind, Flora. Forget what you saw. Now, let me scrub these hands and I'll make some tea unless—'

'No, no brandy!' she interrupted him. 'We're driving to Abbeymead this evening and I want to arrive safely.'

Jack came to a halt at the door. 'Are we? Driving to the cottage still?'

Thursday evenings, once he'd seen his last student of the day, was their usual time to return to Abbeymead, but this week they had stayed in town to be part of Bonfire Night, deciding to drive back to the village early tomorrow morning in time for Flora to open the All's Well.

Friday was a day she savoured, he knew. It was the day she took charge of her treasured bookshop again. Rose Lawson had proved an able assistant while they had been living part of the week in Lewes, but the All's Well was far too precious for Flora to relinquish entirely.

'We can go, can't we?' There was a pleading note in her voice.

'If it's important to you, of course we can. We'll be late home but at least you'll be sleeping under the roof you love.'

The cottage, bequeathed by her aunt Violet, was only a little less precious to Flora than the All's Well. She had never really settled at Cleve, and he couldn't blame her. Despite the homely touches she had tried to bring to the flat, it remained a dreary and less than comfortable bolthole. She had never really settled in Lewes either, he thought wryly, though she'd tried her best. Its numerous bookshops had been an attraction, at least initially, and she'd found a role for herself that she enjoyed – volunteering as a classroom helper at Riverdale, a local school.

But Thursday evenings, when they packed their travel bags and left for the village, was always going to be the high point of her week. Then four whole days lay ahead, to be spent at the bookshop or pottering in her garden or catching up with the friends she'd known for most of her life.

'What do you imagine actually happened?' She followed him into the small kitchen area, where he was busy at the sink. 'You muttered something about a stabbing.'

'It's all I could think of at the time. The man was bleeding profusely – you saw my hands. It's unlikely the fall caused all that blood. It had to be from a wound we couldn't see.'

'If he was stabbed, it must have been by someone on the float. Someone standing behind him maybe.'

'That's a leap ahead! One of your specials?' he teased. Flora's flights of imagination had become a running joke between them. 'But in this case, I'm not sure the leap works. I'm not absolutely certain he *was* stabbed, or where for that matter. And there were at least a dozen people on that float. Why would any one of them carry a knife to a celebration? If someone wanted to attack the man, there must be plenty of better places to do it.'

'That will be for Alan Ridley to discover, I imagine.' Fetching the milk from the marble slab that functioned as the flat's only cool spot, Flora sounded tired. 'He'll be in charge of the case?'

Alan Ridley, a detective inspector with the Brighton police, was an old acquaintance.

'I guess so. Although if the chap recovers well, he might hand it on to a junior officer.'

Jack warmed the small brown china teapot, swirling the hot water into the sink. Turning, he found himself gazing into a pair of hazel eyes. Questioning eyes. 'You're not to worry, Flora. It's not our problem,' he said firmly.

'I have a feeling that it could be.' And, for once, she sounded unenthusiastic at the thought of another adventure.

Fitting the solid brass key into the All's Well's lock, Flora opened the wide front door of her bookshop. Her short ride on Betty this Friday morning had been invigorating. A trundle in the sharp chill of November – her ancient bicycle had only one chosen speed – along a mist-covered lane and past hedges swollen with rose hips, had blown away the cobwebs and brought new colour to her cheeks. She felt ready for the day ahead.

First, though, an inspection of the premises. It was something she felt compelled to do. Always. And found it impossible to stop herself. Had shelves been thoroughly dusted and the floor swept? Were book spines neatly aligned and the latest bestselling publications displayed attractively on the front table? Were the window seat cushions plumped ready for browsing customers to enjoy? It seemed they were. Once more, Rose had done a good job.

Today, though, it was Flora's turn to tackle the chores: a light dusting before her first customers arrived, a flick through the accounts perhaps, and a brief descent to the cellar to check for any parcels that needed unpacking. But once she'd divested herself of coat and gloves and tucked away her packed lunch, she felt curiously reluctant to begin.

The earlier energy she'd felt in riding to the All's Well had dissipated and, instead of wielding a feather duster as she should, she retreated behind her desk, annoyed with herself for her listlessness. Why this sudden slump of energy? She was home again and should be in the best of spirits. Was the dull nag she couldn't quite rid herself of connected in some way to those last few hours in Lewes? Was today being tainted by what she'd witnessed yesterday – a riotous performance that had turned to blood?

The bonfire celebrations had been extraordinary and, for an hour or so, she'd been completely absorbed. But then, that sudden and frightening halt to the procession when the man, what was the name she'd overheard? – Trevor French, that was it – had tumbled from the float. Was it Trevor's fate that was bothering her? Flora didn't think so. She didn't know the man, had never even met him, and he would be well cared for in the hospital, she was sure.

It was a feeling that went deeper, an uneasiness that this might be the beginning of something new. A disruption to their lives for which she'd no wish. Not now. Not when Jack was about to finish work at Cleve College and, in a few weeks, she would return home for good – back in Abbeymead, back at her cottage and back in her bookshop. Her time in Lewes hadn't been all bad, she conceded, but somehow it had never seemed real, a fleeting interval, something to push through before she could return to a settled life. And, more than anything, settled was what she had begun to want.

Feeling decidedly *un*settled, she finally began the morning's chores. This man's accident, she mused... Jack would be involved... she was certain. Why, how, she didn't know, but yesterday's disaster wouldn't be the last they'd hear of

November the fifth. Jack would be involved, whether he liked it or not. Whether she liked it or not.

Jack was involved. He'd been working at his desk in the spare room for around an hour when a loud knock at the cottage door had him stop typing and listen.

Could he ignore it? He was halfway through a vital chapter and needed to press on. The knock came again, this time, if anything, louder. Whoever was at the door wasn't going away. Thrusting back his writing chair, he made for the stairs, jumping them two at a time. Get rid of his unwanted caller, he told himself, get back to the book, devise a way of rescuing his hero from the precipitous ledge to which he'd left him clinging.

But it was Alan Ridley at the door, and Jack knew his hero would have to wait to learn his fate.

'Morning, old chap. Good to see you.'

'And you,' he said tepidly. 'Would you like to come in?' His voice held an element of hope that the inspector might be too busy.

'Thanks, I will. It's a trifle nippy out here. Could do with a cuppa as well if you've got the kettle on.'

Jack resigned himself to the inevitable, peeling off to the kitchen and telling Ridley to make himself at home. Which the inspector did. By the time Jack returned to the sitting room with a tray of tea, his visitor was half asleep, draped horizontally across the sofa.

'Nice cushions,' he observed, opening an eye and pulling himself upright. 'Too tempting, though. If you hadn't come in just then, I'd have been away. Up half the night,' he explained.

'The bonfire celebrations?' Jack guessed.

'Right first time. But then you would be, you were on the spot and saw what happened for yourself. The chap who fell – Trevor French – I need to know more. All I've got so far is that he was chairman of one of the bonfire societies.' The inspector consulted the notebook he'd taken from his coat pocket. 'The Grove society,' he confirmed, 'and that Mr French ended up in a bit of a mess.'

'You could have sent Norris to question me and gone home for some sleep.'

'I could, but all my officers, including my sergeant, are busy. They've a monumental task on their hands, interviewing everyone who was on that float, plus any bystanders who saw the fall. But you're the one I chose to have a chat with.'

'I'm flattered, but I don't think there's very much I can tell you.'

'You didn't know French?'

Jack shook his head. 'I didn't even know the man's name for sure, until now.' He poured the tea, then made a dash back to the kitchen for the ginger biscuits that were Ridley's favourites.

'Did you know anyone on that float?' the inspector asked when he reappeared.

'Leo Nelson. I knew Leo. He's taken over the tenancy of Overlay House and I've met him several times. He seems a nice chap.'

'Nice chaps can sometimes turn out differently.' Ridley began to dunk a biscuit.

Jack put down his cup, suddenly alert. 'Meaning?'

'French is dead. Died during the night. The doctors did what they could, but... We have a murderer on our hands, Jack. According to initial findings, someone who's happy with a knife.' He paused for another bite of his biscuit. 'As far as I can make out, your Mr Nelson was standing right by the victim's side before he keeled over.'

Jack was about to repudiate his ownership of Leo Nelson but instead turned his mind to retrieving the scene from last evening, trying to picture it clearly in his mind. It was difficult.

There had been so many people, so much noise, so much smoke, that his view of the float had been hazy and now, in memory, hazier still. Where had Nelson been standing exactly? But then he wouldn't really know, would he? He hadn't known for sure that the man was definitely on the float, not until Nelson had torn off his mask. He could well have been standing on one side of the dead man, as Ridley claimed. But carrying a knife?

'It was definitely a stabbing?'

The inspector nodded, helping himself to a second biscuit. 'In the side, looks like, but the post-mortem will tell us more. Died from internal bleeding, according to the hospital. The thing is, Jack, what did you see?'

Jack sat back in his chair and closed his eyes. The image was becoming clearer now and he did his best to paint it accurately.

'It was the float that caught my attention. For a start, it was being towed by a tractor and that seemed unusual. Every other float had been on a simple trolley and pulled by members of their society. But this one was on an elevated platform and had people on it, too. The main effigy was of Fidel Castro and I remember thinking how well he'd been made. He was at the centre of the tableau – people all around it were dressed as South American peasants, or bandits. They were wearing masks, every one, I think. But there were Tudors as well! In some amazingly elaborate costumes. The effect was strange, to say the least. Quite bizarre.'

'Most of the Tudors would have been marching behind the float, I reckon, and rushed forward when they saw what had happened. But the whole damn business is bizarre,' the inspector grumbled. 'Every year, there's trouble and this is the worst we've had for a long time.' He took a noisy slurp of his tea. 'So... if Leo Nelson was on one side of the victim, do you remember anything of the man on the other? It was a man, I take it?'

'Yes, it would be a man.' Jack screwed up his eyes in concentration. 'All the figures at the front were men and all wearing masks, so I've no idea of their faces. Now that I know one was Leo Nelson, he was probably the chap on the left of the victim. The man on the other side, I think, was much stockier, muscular in a kind of brawny way. That would be the chap who told me his name was Brooks or something like that – he was dressed as a Mexican or Cuban, like the others, but he had a bandolier strung across his chest. I remember thinking it looked heavy.'

'Dummy ammunition, I hope, or we might have had even more fatalities. Edwin Brooker,' the inspector confirmed. 'That was the chap's name. But what were either of them doing prior to French's fall?'

'Doing? Nothing. Just standing there. Waving to the crowd. Blowing a kiss to people on their balconies, that kind of thing. All pretty innocuous. I can't see how either of them could have wielded a knife without being spotted.'

'If that's so, the blow would have come from behind. The pathologist's report will tell me more. Anything else catch your eye?'

'There was a jumble of people crowding round the Castro. I couldn't see anyone very clearly.'

'That's my problem – my chaps' problem, too – working out exactly who was on that float and who might have had the opportunity to attack French. So, what happened when you tried to help the victim?'

'I bent down... I think I checked his pulse... it was there, but very slow. I tried to move him onto the pavement. He was half on and half off. A lady was dabbing his face with water, and Nelson and another Cuban looked as though they were just about to lump him onto the pavement before I stopped them. I was worried he might have a head injury. That was until I bent down to move him myself. Then it became clear that whatever he'd done to his head, he'd suffered a far worse injury elsewhere.'

The inspector sighed. 'Thanks, but not a great deal of help, my friend.'

'I did warn you.'

'It was worth a shot, I guess, and the tea was good! You never know – in time, you might remember more. Get in touch if you do.' Ridley heaved himself off the sofa and walked to the front door with Jack following. 'It's always possible I'll need to come back,' he said, giving his host a cheerful wave.

Jack hoped not. He was fairly certain that he could add little more to the account he'd given. He'd seen nothing to suggest that skulduggery was likely. Until he was looking at the blood on his hands, he had thought the man had simply lost his balance and fallen. Yet, when he thought about it more carefully, Trevor French – and he was beginning to see that front row more clearly – hadn't appeared in the least unstable. Jack's impression had been of a man standing straight and tall at the front of the float, waving and smiling, perfectly secure. That should have given him pause.

And now, it seemed, both Leo Nelson and Edwin Brooker would be in the inspector's sights. Again, he hoped not. He hadn't liked what he'd seen of Brooker but Nelson was a decent man and, if he was in trouble, Jack felt a compulsion to help. He barely knew the chap, it was true, but in Nelson he sensed a fellow traveller, a man who had deliberately chosen to hide away. People who walked through life alone – and Nelson had made it plain that he wanted to – had most often a reason. Jack's had been the shock of betrayal on the eve of his first wedding. What had Leo's been? he wondered. There would be something, he was sure, and felt a natural sympathy.

It wouldn't please Flora. She was counting the days before their move back to the village, eager to leave Lewes and its endeavours well behind. Anything that got in the way, she'd want to brush aside. More than brush aside, Jack thought wryly. She'd wield the broom herself – and fiercely.

3

Alan Ridley's visit had given Jack plenty to think about. Leo Nelson was clearly in the inspector's sights as a potential murderer, a possibility that Jack was reluctant to believe. He had to admit, however, that Nelson would inevitably be a suspect. It seemed the man had been standing side by side with Trevor French seconds before the latter had been stabbed and Ridley would be negligent if he failed to investigate Nelson's relationship with the dead man. But the inspector was a fair officer – he'd realise soon enough that Leo was an unlikely killer.

But if he didn't? Flora would be averse, he knew, to them taking any interest in Nelson's likely fate. The murder had occurred in Lewes, at an event for which the town was famous, and it was Lewes she was longing to leave behind. Any investigation on Jack's part, any enquiries, would necessarily prolong his involvement with the town and its business, when in Flora's mind she had already escaped.

Still, he felt he should make at least a small push to prevent Nelson being unfairly embroiled in a murder case. But what exactly could he do? A friendly chat, perhaps, to discover just how involved with the victim Nelson had been? Information he could pass on to Alan Ridley which might deflect him? A chat wouldn't hurt. Surely, neither Flora nor the police could object if he were to drop into Overlay House, take his customary walk around the garden, and ask a few casual questions...

So it was that on Monday morning, once he had seen Flora leave for the bookshop, waving her and Betty off down the lane, Jack shrugged himself into his old Crombie overcoat, rammed the fedora on his head and, feeling somewhat guilty, took a walk along Greenway Lane to Overlay House. At the very least, he could check if Leo Nelson had recovered from his bonfire ordeal.

It was another chilly day, lacking in sun but dry and crisp, and the familiar walk to the house, which in some way Jack still thought of as 'home', was refreshing. Striding up the front path – the flower beds on either side were again thick with weeds, he noticed frowningly – he realised that the curtains were still drawn in the rooms facing onto the lane. Taking the knocker in his hand, he rapped hard, but received no response. He knocked again, if anything a little louder this time, but was once more met with silence. Perhaps Nelson had been detained by the hospital, given a bed for several nights. Jack wouldn't be surprised. The man had looked exceedingly unwell when he'd last seen him.

While he was here, though, he could take a look at his beloved garden. It was easy enough to stroll around the house and through the side gate which, as long as Jack could remember, had remained unlocked.

His first glance at the once pristine garden was a shock. The lawn had not received its autumn cut, and the grass was already ankle deep and invaded by creeping buttercup and white clover. The roses he and young Charlie Teague had planted remained unpruned, the autumn flowering not cut back and, as for the vegetable patch, Jack averted his eyes. A physical pain struck him as he viewed the morass this once charming place had become. Where was the gardener he'd found for Nelson? The man could not have come near Overlay for weeks.

He had turned to go, not wanting to stay another minute, when he heard the French doors being tugged back and, blinking, Leo Nelson stepped out into daylight.

'Hello there!' he called out, his voice shaky as he shuffled down the path towards Jack. 'Sorry I didn't get to the door. I wasn't expecting visitors.'

That was obvious. The man's face was as grey as the sky above and the deep wells beneath his eyes spoke of sleeplessness and fatigue. Clothes seemed to have been thrown on by guess, one of his trouser legs hitched to his knee and his shirt only half buttoned.

'I'm sorry to have disturbed you,' Jack said. 'Look, I'll go. You shouldn't be out here in just a shirt. Not in this weather.'

'No, don't go, not yet. I've been trying to sleep, that's all, but I can't. Up half the night, too. Come into the kitchen and I'll put the kettle on.'

Jack was surprised. It was the first time he'd been invited into the house, but he followed Nelson through the French doors into a sitting room he knew well – it still hadn't been repainted – and through to a kitchen he knew even better. How many ham sandwiches had he made at that counter? he thought. They'd been the perfect aid to help him through the trickiest of writing problems.

Leo's movements as he took the kettle to the sink were slow and cumbersome, as though he were walking through a fog and Jack had forcibly to restrain himself from leaping up and making the tea himself. Eventually, two full mugs appeared on the kitchen table along with a box of biscuits that looked seriously stale. He wouldn't be putting them to the test, he decided.

'I can't believe it happened,' Leo said into his mug. 'Trevor... I mean... gone. And not just gone. All that blood. He was attacked, wasn't he? Someone did that to him.'

'It looks like it,' Jack said carefully. 'You were good friends with Trevor?'

'He was the best. A decent man, a good man. The first chap I really spoke to when I came back.' He shook his head like a wounded creature. 'Why? I mean, why would anyone do that to him?'

Jack thought it best to avoid a direct answer. Best, perhaps, to change the subject. 'You've been living in Australia, I think you told me.'

'Been there for years, many years, but I'm Sussex born and bred.'

'Is that why you came back?' Jack hazarded.

'Sussex means home for me,' he said simply. 'And six months ago, I decided that this is where I needed to be.'

'Any particular reason to come back now?'

'Getting old, mate. That's all I can think. Getting homesick for my country, my town – it does that to you.'

'And you met Trevor where?'

Leo frowned and Jack realised their conversation was beginning to resemble an interrogation. 'I'm just interested,' he said mildly, 'that you were part of the bonfire celebrations when you've been out of the country, out of Lewes, for so long.'

'I wasn't going to join a bonfire society – hadn't even thought of it. It was Trevor who said I should. I met him on the train coming back from the football, you know, and we got talking. I told him I was newly back in Lewes – I was renting a flat in the town at the time – and he invited me out for a drink.'

That didn't tally with what Jack knew of the man. But perhaps village gossip had exaggerated Nelson's reclusiveness.

They were the kind of stories Alice might have jumped on to explain the stranger in their midst.

'The truth was,' Nelson went on, 'I wasn't keen on seeing anyone and a drink in a pub was the last thing I wanted. I suppose I needed time to adjust. Life here's very different from what I've been used to. But Trevor wasn't having any of it. "You be at the Mason's Arms," he said, "or I'll come knocking on your door." The long and the short of it was that I went and I enjoyed the evening. He was good company and I liked his mates.'

'And it was Trevor, you said, who suggested you join the Grove society?'

'That's right. He's their chairman... was their chairman.' He stopped speaking for a moment, staring at the wooden table and swallowing hard. 'I was dubious,' he continued after a while, 'not really my kind of thing, but he promised I'd like it and the society always needed new members, so he'd sponsor me.'

'You have to be sponsored to join a bonfire society?'

'I think so. Actually, it's not that difficult and I can see why. There's a whole lot of work to be done every year, just for those few hours on one day, and the more people there are to do it the better, I guess.'

'How have you found being a member?'

'It's been OK. Loads of meetings, of course. Big discussions on the theme they've chosen and how to bring it to life – who their main effigy will be, what it will look like, who'll make it, what everyone will wear in the procession. And then there's the fundraising to pay for new costumes and what's always a huge amount of fireworks.'

'But you've enjoyed it?'

Leo shrugged. 'It's been OK,' he repeated. 'Some of the people there have been friendly. Some haven't. It was really for Trevor that I kept going to meetings. Bonfire was important to him and he always made sure I was included. He was a top chap. I can't believe... I can't believe he's gone.'

Nelson jumped up and walked to the door, then walked back again, looking confused. He picked up the two empty mugs. 'I don't know what to do, Jack.' His voice had begun to crack.

'In what way?'

'I should be trying to find out what happened, shouldn't I? Who did that to him. But I've no idea where to start.'

'Which is just as well. That's the job of the police.'

Leo Nelson bent over him, his chin thrust forward. 'I don't trust them.'

'Why ever not?'

'I just don't,' he said, taking the cups to the sink without volunteering any more information.

Sloppily, he slooshed the mugs in cold water and then turned to face Jack. 'They'll try to pin it on someone, you'll see. It's what they do. Pin it on whoever's the easiest target.' Jack began to murmur a disagreement, but his host stopped him. 'The inspector that's in charge, he called here yesterday, did you know?' Jack shook his head. Ridley had been busy, it seemed. 'And I got the very strong impression that it's me that will be the target. That's what they've decided.'

'From my experience of Inspector Ridley, he's a fair man,' Jack objected. 'He won't do that.'

Leo looked unconvinced. 'If you say so, but... I did hear – on the grapevine, you know – that you're a pretty dab hand at discovering killers, as well as writing about them. Would you—'

'I think it's better we leave the investigation to Alan Ridley,' Jack said firmly, 'but thanks for the tea. I must go, but if you really can't sleep, Leo, you should see Dr Hanson. He'll help you get back on your feet. Help you get over it.'

Nelson shook his head. 'He can't. No one can. It's too dreadful. There'll be no getting over it.' Suddenly, he shot out a hand and grabbed his visitor's arm. 'You don't understand. It's almost the worst thing that's ever happened to me, Jack. Losing a really good friend in that dreadful way and likely to be blamed for his murder.'

Walking back to the cottage along Greenway Lane, Jack was left wondering. If French's death had been almost the worst thing to happen in Nelson's life, what had actually been the worst?

4

Leo Nelson had appeared desperate. If French had been the very good friend he'd described, he was bound to feel deeply upset. But, for Jack, the man's reaction had been extreme – begging him for help, clinging to his arm, as though Jack's involvement in the murder were a life and death matter. It was disturbing. And Nelson's refusal to believe the police would give him a fair hearing, to dismiss them out of hand as untrustworthy, felt uncomfortable, too. For society at large, there was a presumption that the police could be trusted, that they wouldn't do what Leo was suggesting. Why, then, had he been so adamant? Alan Ridley had included the man in his list of likely suspects, but only along with a host of others, unless... in the interview with Nelson, the inspector had made it plain that Leo was his number one choice.

Walking slowly back to the cottage, Jack pondered what he should do. If, in fact, he should do anything. Perhaps if he talked again to Alan, he'd have a better idea of how the case was shaping up, whether indeed Leo Nelson had anything to worry about. It was still only late morning and, rather than telephone, he could drive the twelve or so miles to Brighton and hope to find the inspector in his office. Clear the air, as it were. It would be his only chance to do so before he returned to Lewes and Cleve College for most of the week.

Nearing the cottage, a sudden angry rustling in the bushes had him look up. The hedgerow's few remaining leaves had come to life, it seemed, and, for the moment, he'd been startled. A bird or a frightened animal perhaps.

It took only minutes to collect the Austin's keys from the kitchen counter and drive out of the village, taking the road to Brighton. Traffic was surprisingly light and in less than an hour he was parking in Bartholomews, a few yards from the neo-classical façade of the town hall, its once honey-coloured stone faded to an indeterminate grey. Brighton police station was housed in the building's cellar.

At the bottom of the steps leading down to the police headquarters, Jack stopped. The atmosphere felt changed in some way – an unusual quiet, an unusual tidiness? He couldn't put his finger on the difference. The institutional cream paint and green tiles hadn't changed, nor the stiff-backed wooden chairs supplied for visitors or the huge oak desk straddling the entrance.

He walked towards the desk. 'Would it be possible to speak to Inspector Ridley?' he asked the sergeant on duty.

The officer looked up from his writing and gave a slow shake of his head. He should have telephoned, Jack thought crossly, made an official appointment. But he hadn't wanted to pre-empt the meeting, reasoning that if he caught Ridley unawares, the inspector might be more willing to listen to what he had to say. What amounted, Jack thought, to a defence of Leo Nelson. Not that he could say much, he admitted to himself, but perhaps enough to convince the inspector, if necessary, that he should look more widely for a suspect.

'I can always wait,' he offered. It would mean abandoning the current novel for another entire day, but this was important.

'Inspector Ridley's not here, sir. He's not on duty. You can mebbe see Inspector Brownlow.'

'Brownlow? Where is Inspector Ridley? He's not unwell, I hope.'

'Not Ridley. His mother,' a voice came from behind.

Jack turned to see the speaker. A short, stubby man, tow-haired and with eyes the palest blue Jack had ever seen. Almost transparent, he thought, recoiling slightly.

'Mrs Ridley has taken ill,' the sergeant added, leaning across his desk. 'Quite bad, too, I believe, and the inspector's had to take compassionate leave.'

'That's enough, Sergeant,' the tow-haired man said sharply, his tufted eyebrows almost meeting across his forehead and giving him the appearance of being permanently annoyed. 'I'll deal with this.'

He placed himself in front of his visitor and had to stare upwards, Jack's lanky figure hardly improving his mood. 'I'm Inspector Brownlow. Who exactly are you?' he demanded.

Jack was taken aback by the tone but said as amiably as he could, 'My name is Jack Carrington. I'm an author, a crime novelist, and Inspector Ridley has helped me a good deal in the past. Made sure I got things right.'

He had seen immediately that it would be unwise to say anything of their true relationship. No mention of their meetings at the Cross Keys or of the information that passed between them, or the investigations with which he and Flora had assisted. Any or all of these would be anathema to this man.

'Well, Mr Carrington. Allow me to tell you that it won't be happening on my watch. And should never have happened. The police are far too busy to waste time helping out the odd scribbler. In fact, should you be here at all? If you're not a member of the public with a question for the desk sergeant here, then you shouldn't. We can't have every Tom, Dick and Harry bothering the police force. We're professional people.'

'I, too, am a professional person, Inspector Brownlow,' he said, attempting to keep his voice even. 'But thank you for the advice.'

Without another word, Jack swung around and walked back up the stairs into the cold grey of the November day. He walked rapidly towards the Austin, fury consuming him, his heart thumping in time with his steps, and it was a minute or so before he realised he was being hailed from the other side of the street. Turning his head, he saw Sergeant Norris waving at him, the officer evidently on his way back to police headquarters.

'You were in a daydream, Mr Carrington,' Norris said jovially, when he'd crossed to Jack's side of the road. 'Called you three times.'

'I'm sorry, I—'

'Have you been to the office?' He jerked his head towards the town hall behind them.

'I've just emerged from your cellar – with a drubbing,' he confessed.

'Don't tell me. You met Brownlow?'

'I did and not a happy meeting, I fear. But I'm sorry to hear the inspector has trouble at home.'

'The poor old girl's pretty bad, I'm told. Had a fall over the weekend, but then followed it with a stroke. The boss wouldn't sign out for anything that wasn't serious.' Norris fidgeted from one leg to another. 'We've got a right one there,' he said at length. Again, he jerked his head towards his headquarters.

'Rude,' Jack said succinctly.

'Bloody stupid,' was Norris's response. 'How he ever got to be an inspector... but stay clear, Mr Carrington, that's my advice.'

'I'm sorry that *you* can't.'

'Not sorrier than I am! Look – I know you were there when

that chap – French, wasn't it? – got himself killed, but don't get involved. Stick to just giving a statement when you're asked. Let Brownchops mess it up, all on his own. He's already decided whodunnit, even before the post-mortem.'

'Who?' An icicle had lodged in Jack's chest. Brownlow, he suspected, was the kind of officer who would be desperate to wind up an investigation in double-quick time and bask in the glory.

'One of the chaps on the float. A drifter, according to Brownlow. Therefore, an obvious killer! Horatio something – was that his name? It rings a bell.'

'Nelson?'

'That's the chap. Mind you, he looks pretty dodgy. No job, no fixed abode. Australia, Lewes, and now your neck of the woods. Do you know him?'

'A little,' Jack admitted. 'Sergeant Norris, can I stay in touch?' If he had Norris on his side, it could only be good. Alan Ridley trusted the man implicitly.

The sergeant looked quizzical. 'If you need to, Mr Carrington. I'm always available. But the boss could be back sooner than we expect.'

Jack could only hope.

5

He was putting his old Remington to bed for the night, cover in hand, when Flora arrived in the doorway.

'You're early,' he said. She'd surprised him. 'I was hoping to have started supper before you got home.'

'Betty was in a good mood. She fancied a race along Greenway. And I was worried.' She walked up to the desk and bent to stroke his hair. 'You didn't answer when I telephoned. I wondered if you were unwell.'

'It must have been when I was out and about,' he said breezily.

Idly, she flicked through the finished pages of the novel he was working on. '*Another Way to Die* seems to be going well.' Then in less than a breath, 'Where were you?'

The sudden question left Jack faltering and, when he answered, it was to mumble, 'I walked up to Overlay House.'

Flora sat down on the bedroom's only other chair and fixed him with an accusing eye. 'You went to see Leo Nelson, didn't you?'

'What if I did? He's not a proscribed person, is he?'

'No, he's a suspect in a murder case that doesn't concern us.'

Jack swung the office chair full circle and took hold of her hands. 'But it does, Flora. Me, at least. I was the one who went to help the dead man – and I'm the one who knows Nelson.'

'Although not very well.' She tucked the stray strands of copper hair behind her ears and straightened her shoulders. 'In fact, minimally, I'd say. You walk around your old garden from time to time and maybe exchange a few words with the new tenant, if he's at home.'

'He's treated me pretty decently,' Jack said, sounding a trifle limp.

'Leo Nelson has given you free rein of a garden that he's totally uninterested in. I can't see that means you should put yourself in danger for him. Particularly now, when we're leaving Lewes and starting our life back in Abbeymead. I want to say goodbye to the town, Jack, and all its troubles – including Bonfire Night. A permanent goodbye.'

'It won't be dangerous,' he tried to argue. 'Why would it be?'

'It's always dangerous. And weren't you the one who said we should rethink the sleuthing we've been doing?'

'That was in Venice,' he objected. 'After we landed ourselves in a huge mess.'

'Exactly.' She jumped up from the chair. 'That's exactly what I mean. Why should Lewes be any different? How do you know what you'll be involved in? Nelson was standing within an inch of the man who died. Who better to slide a knife into his ribs?'

'No matter how bad things look, I don't believe the man is a killer.' Jack dug in his heels.

There was a tense pause before Flora walked towards the door. 'I'll get supper started,' she said, unwilling to argue more.

Bounding across the room, he caught up with her on the landing, wrapping his arms around her and nestling his face against her hair. 'Try to understand, sweetheart. Think about what happened in Venice. I was reluctant to get involved, but whenever *you* sense an injustice, you don't let go, and I feel the same about this case. I have a strong suspicion that Nelson will be unfairly targeted. The circumstantial evidence isn't good, I agree, but I don't believe the man is capable of murder.'

Flora pulled back. 'Because he lets you walk around his garden?'

'No, because of the man I sense he is.'

She reached up and kissed him gently. 'OK, *I'll* try to do the understanding this time. But if it gets hairy, please drop the questions. And *I'm* not involved. Agreed?'

'Agreed. Now what's for supper?'

At the bottom of the staircase, Flora paused before going into the kitchen. 'There's a photograph in the local paper that might interest you. It was delivered to the shop today and I brought it home. A photograph of the Fidel Castro float and a fair number of those who were on it. I reckon it was taken just before Trevor French plunged to the ground.'

Jack gave a small laugh. 'Didn't I just hear that you weren't to be involved?'

'I'm not,' she said airily. 'It's simply that Rose – she called into the shop to collect her umbrella, rain is forecast tomorrow – said that she knew the woman. The woman in the Tudor costume who was chafing Trevor's hands after he fell. You remember? Rose and I were looking at the newspaper together and she pointed her out. She's a dressmaker and Rose seems to know her well. Goes to her when she can afford it – you know how super smart Rose dresses.'

'Show me.' On the surface, it didn't seem much of a help, but you never really knew. He was willing to be convinced. But...

'After supper,' she said firmly.

. . .

The washing-up was done, the dishes stacked, and the uneaten half of an enormous steak and kidney pie stored on the cool shelf of the pantry. Jack made tea for them both and brought it into the sitting room where Flora was flicking through a magazine her good friend, Kate, had lent her.

'Katie is a splendid source of magazines,' she said, as he came in with the tray. 'They can be too expensive to buy, but she doesn't need to. She simply picks them up from the table after her customers have left!'

Kate Farraday, a girl Flora had known most of her life, ran the Nook, the village café, along with her husband, Tony.

'And the newspaper?' he asked, manoeuvring the tray between the clutter of magazines on the table.

'Oh, here.' She pulled a crumped wodge of newsprint from behind the cushions. 'There.' She jabbed a finger at a blurred figure hovering behind the men lined up at the front of the float. 'That's the woman Rose knows.'

Pulling black-rimmed glasses from his pocket—he hadn't yet succumbed to a pair of tortoiseshells—Jack could barely make out the image. 'The photograph is pretty hazy, but she is in Tudor costume,' he said slowly. 'I suppose she was the woman.'

'Her name is Thomasina Bell. Perhaps you could get the inspector to have a word with her. See, she's standing just behind Trevor. Maybe she saw something.'

'I would, except that Alan Ridley is no longer on the case,' he said heavily.

'Really? Why not? And how do you know that?'

'Last question first – I went to Brighton after I saw Leo. To the police station, hoping to see Ridley.' He refused to meet Flora's eyes, ignoring the frown he knew would be gathering. 'But he's on compassionate leave. His mother fell extremely ill over the weekend and he's more or less living at the hospital. As to why I drove over there, I had the strong impression talking to

Leo today, and to the inspector on Friday, that Nelson is police suspect number one.'

'And you were going to change Alan Ridley's mind? Insist he accept your word that Nelson is completely innocent?'

'You know that wouldn't happen, Flora.'

'Then why?'

'I suppose I went there hoping to get Alan to think beyond Leo. There were a lot more people on that float other than him. Another man was standing beside French, in fact – Edwin Brooker.'

'And you don't think the police will look at Brooker?'

'They certainly should, but I'm fearful that they won't.'

'If the inspector is away, is Sergeant Norris in charge?'

Jack pulled a face. 'I think he wishes he was. He seemed decidedly unimpressed with the new man he has to work with. An Inspector Brownlow has been drafted in, goodness knows from where, and, from what I can see, he's a man with an inflex-ible mind.'

'And he's fixed on Leo Nelson as his villain?'

'I'm guessing. He didn't say as much. He wasn't going to tell me anything – almost ordered me off police property.'

Flora's eyes widened.

'Brownlow isn't exactly amiable. The thing is' – Jack put down the teacup he'd been holding and plumped down on the sofa beside her – 'I reckon the truth won't be too difficult to discover, if this new inspector could only be bothered. There's long-standing rivalry between all four bonfire societies and Martin Winter at the college, my source of all Lewes history, tells me that in the last year or so rivalry has spilled over into outright enmity. There's sure to be plenty of people ready to talk about it, if Brownlow were willing to listen – but that will be the rub, I think.'

'But you are – willing to listen?'

'You don't need to ask, do you?' He sat silently for a while, looking into space. 'Flora,' he began... 'I know you're keen to stay uninvolved, but if you *were* mildly interested, Thomasina could be an ideal starting point.'

'Because she's a woman?' Flora pursed her lips.

'Because she's a seamstress and you like clothes. Because she knows Rose and you like Rose.'

'And?'

'And because she's a woman,' he admitted finally, laughing out loud as she grabbed him around the waist and tickled unmercifully.

The next morning, a few minutes before leaving for their weekly stay in Lewes, Flora telephoned her assistant at her lodgings. It was still very early and she apologised for the hour, but once she was back at Cleve College, telephoning was almost impossible. Flora had a request. On the pretext of ordering a winter dress for herself, she asked Rose if the next time her assistant saw Thomasina Bell, she would ask the dressmaker to call at the All's Well. Or, if this wasn't convenient, arrange a meeting elsewhere.

It *was* a pretext, since Flora was unlikely ever to order the fictitious dress. She was nervous at putting herself in the hands of a dressmaker – how much would the garment end up costing and what if she didn't like the finished product? On the rare occasions she treated herself to new clothes, she preferred to buy from a shop. As for alterations and repairs, Aunt Violet had always maintained that any woman could and should do her own mending and Flora had instinctively agreed. She might not be particularly skilful, but she'd been left a sewing machine by Violet, a pre-war Singer, beautifully made with an oak stand and pearl inlay, and that sufficed for any small jobs that appeared.

. . .

It wasn't until the end of her week in Lewes, much of it spent as a volunteer at Riverdale school, that Flora's request bore fruit. Late on Thursday afternoon, a telephone message arrived from Rose, brought round to the apartment by the college porter, that Thomasina would call at the All's Well tomorrow. The note made no mention of any specific time, but it hardly mattered. Flora would be in her bookshop all day.

She had been in the middle of packing their bags for the drive back to Abbeymead when the porter knocked and now, walking back to the bedroom, she paused to look around the college flat and felt more grateful than ever. In just a handful of days, they would be leaving this cheerless apartment for good – back to the village and back to the cottage she loved.

Though for how long, Flora wasn't sure. On their return from honeymoon, there had been talk of a move to a larger house – the old School House that Ambrose Finch, its current owner, had hinted he would soon be selling. Jack had been keen, though he'd tried to disguise his eagerness, hoping, she realised, that in time she might come round to the idea. She had to admit there was sense in what he was thinking.

The cottage her aunt Violet had left her, along with the All's Well bookshop, had been her home since she was six years old. It was where she felt safe and at peace. But for Jack, without that history, it felt uncomfortably cramped. And, if they were ever to have a family – and Flora remained as unsure as ever – it would feel decidedly overcrowded. The School House, on the other hand, was spacious and airy with every modern convenience anyone could wish for and with a stunning rear garden to complete the picture. Perfect for young children.

A move there would be saying goodbye to a draughty chimney, a leaking gutter, and windows that frosted so badly that on winter mornings their breath painted spirals in the air. Perhaps worth the heartache of leaving her childhood home? Since that first suggestion, though, Jack had said nothing more and recently Flora had learned from Alice Jenner, a lady rarely wrong on village gossip, that Mr Finch might be having second thoughts.

For the moment, then, it was a problem she could banish to the back of her mind and, meanwhile, there was Thomasina Bell to question. No, to talk to, she corrected herself, crossly. That was as far as her involvement would reach.

6

It was a few minutes after Flora had finished her lunchtime sandwich of corned beef and tomato that she spied a small pink van parked outside the All's Well, an unusual motif stencilled on its side. Quickly, she squirrelled away her lunch box and wiped her lips clean, already feeling at a disadvantage. She hadn't been entirely sure that the dress-maker would actually call, but here she was walking through the door and dressed, Flora imagined, in one of her own creations. A button-through pencil-skirted dress in sage wool, worn with a jaunty dark-green beret and green court shoes. A neat leather pouch was tucked under one arm and, despite the chilly weather, there was no coat to mar the effect.

'Flora Steele?' the woman asked brightly, allowing the shop door to clang shut behind her.

'Yes. Miss Bell?' Flora walked forward to greet her frighteningly smart visitor. 'How good of you to call.'

'Thomasina, my dear. Call me Thomasina. I had to drive through Abbeymead in any case – I have a client in the next village.'

'I'm sure you must be very busy. Rose tells me how brilliant a seamstress you are.'

Thomasina looked unimpressed. 'Rose Lawson is a good client,' she acknowledged, 'but then she has the perfect figure to dress. And I *should* be good at my work.' Her tone was dismissive. 'I left college as the best student in my year.'

'Congratulations. Was that in London?'

Flora had little interest in where Miss Bell had studied, but if she were to discover anything useful from this fearsomely rigid woman, she needed to break through her reserve.

'No, in fact. I studied locally,' the woman answered her airily. 'And it turned out to be the best thing I could have done.' Then recovering her curt tone, added, 'London fashion colleges are highly overrated, you know.'

'Really? But won't you sit down?' Flora led the way to a cushioned window seat.

'So,' Thomasina began, 'a winter dress, Rose tells me. Do you have a pattern in mind? And a material – wool, bouclé, corduroy, velvet?'

'I... I haven't really thought that deeply,' Flora stammered. This was going to be more difficult than she'd anticipated.

'You need to have some idea.' The tone now verged on impatient, but Flora's nervous expression had her visitor say, 'Why don't you come to my studio when you're in Lewes again? I can make suggestions, but you're the one who needs to decide. You won't be short of choice, I promise. I've plenty of pattern books you can browse and shelf after shelf of materials.'

'Thank you.' Flora grasped the lifeline. 'That would be sensible and I'm sorry that you've had an unnecessary call.'

'It doesn't matter, my dear. I had to be out and about, as I said, and I'm always happy to meet new clients. Come and see me... when would be suitable?'

'Wednesday.' She made a stab at a date. 'Yes Wednesday. I finish early at school that day.'

'Two o'clock then,' Thomasina said briskly, getting up to leave.

'Wonderful!'

Then suddenly remembering why she'd asked the woman to call, Flora began on the small speech she'd prepared in a wakeful hour last night. 'You might not remember seeing me, but I was in Lewes on Bonfire Night and witnessed that terrible accident. I do remember seeing you, though. You jumped down from the float and tried to comfort the man who'd fallen.'

Thomasina frowned, seeming taken aback. 'I *didn't* see you.'

'I'm not surprised. I was part of a large crowd. My husband, too. He tried to help Mr French.'

'That was your husband?' Flora nodded. 'He was kind to try.'

'Did you know Trevor French?' she asked innocently, knowing full well that the woman must.

'We both belonged to the Grove society, so yes, of course.'

'How sad for you to lose a friend in such a dreadful way.'

'I wouldn't say Trevor was a friend. He only joined Grove a year ago. But we've worked together these last few months. There's a huge amount to do for that one night, you know. People who aren't in Bonfire don't understand. It's a job that goes on all year round, and a lot of work for everyone.'

'I'm sure it must be,' Flora said soothingly. 'It was a magnificent spectacle. Your Tudor costume was fabulous.'

'Thank you.' Thomasina preened a little. 'I use my skills to create beauty wherever I can. Much of the time, unfortunately, my work goes unacknowledged – but isn't that the case with all artists?'

'In what way unacknowledged?'

'People can take it for granted that new costumes will appear – just like that! There's no thought of the hours one must spend planning, cutting, sewing, quilting, pleating. For them, the dresses simply arrive – conjured out of the air.'

'But the Grove society... your members must have a huge appreciation for your work.'

'You think so? I have my doubts, Mrs Carrington.'

'Flora, please.'

'Our chairman... sorry, our former chairman... didn't share your certainty.'

'You mean Trevor French?'

'Yes, Mr French. Last year's costume competition made that clear. The societies compete every year for the best costume in the parade,' she explained, seeing Flora's puzzled expression. 'I've found it to be grossly unfair.'

'The best costume, as in, the most authentic?' Flora asked, ignoring the harsh judgement.

'Exactly!' Thomasina appeared pleased. 'Authentic is the word. The Tudor costumes I made this year are true to the original down to the last button on the linen shifts. The competition, of course, has been abandoned – because of Trevor's unfortunate demise – but last year...'

'You didn't win,' Flora guessed.

'Clearly not. Our float was themed on a Turkish harem – so much possibility!' Thomasina paused, seeming to retreat into a world of dream. 'My costumes for both the men and women were brilliant, I have to say.' Abruptly, she came out of the dream. 'Everyone did say it. I made a particularly special gown for Edwin, an Ottoman sultan's robe. It took an absolute age to sew – so many hours, all of them after I'd finished the day's work for my own clients. It was by far the most exquisite costume in the parade, but of course, there was no way it would win. The judging was patently crooked.'

'What makes you think that?'

'Think? My dear girl, I *know*. The judges had been bribed. It was when Trevor was with the Harland society – before he changed his loyalties. He was the one who chose the judges. It was plain that at least two out of the three were beholden to him

– one for her job and the other for the money he'd lent him. That was something I discovered later. But is it any wonder the judges chose the Harland costume? A Cleopatra outfit that was plainly shop-bought. Shop-bought!' She almost spat out the words.

'There is something I don't understand,' Flora said tentatively. 'Why did Trevor French switch his allegiance to Grove? I thought that once you were part of a bonfire society, you stayed in it for ever.'

Thomasina gave a dismissive sniff. 'I never knew. Nobody did, not really. There was a rumour that he'd fallen out with someone at Harland – badly. I expect it involved a woman, it usually does. Then suddenly French is with us. And just as suddenly, he's the chairman.'

'And Leo Nelson? He joined when?'

'Nelson?' For a moment, Thomasina looked uncomfortable. 'I don't know when, exactly. Sometime during the year. As far as I could see, he contributed very little.'

'Trevor sponsored him, I understand, even though he was a newcomer to the area. But I guess they must have been friends in the past.'

'Maybe. I've no idea. If you're interested, I'd be inclined to ask Lilian French.'

Flora wondered whether to pursue this avenue, then decided that a different question might be more useful. 'It's unusual, isn't it? To become the chairman after such a short time with a society? It must have put a few noses out of joint.'

Her visitor gave a sardonic laugh. 'You could say that. Edwin was our chairman for ten whole years, then suddenly he wasn't. Displaced in a coup, you could say.'

'You're talking of Edwin Brooker?'

Thomasina nodded. 'Edwin Brooker,' she confirmed. 'A man who is definitely not happy.'

. . .

'As far as I can see,' Flora said, over a supper of lamb chops that evening, 'if you're still interested in defending Leo Nelson from the dreadful inspector, you should talk to Edwin Brooker. According to Thomasina Bell, who appears to know him well, he's a very unhappy man. And he would be, wouldn't he? He lost out to Trevor French in the Grove society, deposed from his position as chairman. And that's after ten years at the helm.'

Jack said nothing, finishing the last inch of mashed potato, but his expression was sceptical.

'Brooker was at the front of the Castro float, you said, and as far as you can tell, standing right next to French,' she pursued.

Jack put down his cutlery with a little puff that could have been a sigh. 'That was delicious. You grew some sterling potatoes this year and Mr Preece, for all his faults, knows how to do a lamb chop.' He slumped back in his chair. 'You're probably right about Brooker. I'll try in the next day or so, though he'll be a difficult character to persuade into talking. I met him only briefly on Bonfire Night, but I'd make a guess the man is never happy.'

'But losing his position. Thomasina called it a coup. These societies seem extremely hierarchical and to be deposed like that must feel quite shameful.'

'Shameful enough to take a knife to the big occasion with the deliberate intention of sticking it into your rival?'

'Maybe.'

'And how do you actually manage a coup in a bonfire society?'

'If you talk to Edwin, you might find out,' she said mischievously. 'Also... there was a strange comment that Thomasina made. At least, I thought it a little strange. About Lilian French, Trevor's wife. She's another person you could talk to.'

'Unless... you...?'

'I've done all my talking – to Miss Bell – who, incidentally, has her own grudge against Trevor. She reckons he corrupted the judging process in last year's costume competition, but that could just be sour grapes. Although her costumes *are* pretty magnificent.'

'I don't know whether Miss Bell will prove important or not, though I shouldn't forget her. But Lilian French? I don't think... she's a widow now and... maybe a woman talking to her would fare better.'

'There it is again! Only women can talk to women.' Flora got to her feet to clear their plates.

'It might help. Please?'

She turned round from the sink. 'On one condition, Jack. Not until after the funeral. I'm not calling on her until the poor woman has buried her husband.'

'It's a deal. By the way,' he said casually, taking the tea towel from its hook and beginning to dry the dishes, 'I saw Ambrose Finch today at the bakery. I thought a walk would do me good and collected the loaf you ordered. Finch isn't selling, after all.'

Alice had been right, she thought, but then she had never doubted her old friend would be the one to know.

'Did he say why he'd decided not to?'

'Some story about a lost son. You may know more than me.'

Flora shook her head. This was one piece of Abbeymead gossip that had passed her by. 'I didn't even know he had a son.'

'From what I can gather, the boy slammed out of the door after a huge row with his father – that would be the door of the previous home. It was several years ago, but Ambrose has never seen or heard from him since.'

Flora wiped her hands on the tea towel he was holding. 'What has that to do with selling the School House?'

'Finch said he bought the place, hoping his son would come back and they'd make a life together in the countryside, but it didn't work out. He's hung on there, waiting for the boy to return, though his preference would have been to be back in the city. Back at work. When he decided to sell, he must have given up any hope of seeing his lad again.'

'Which means that things have changed. That he expects to see him soon?'

'I don't think it's that definite, but there's a chance, Finch believes. He's had a private detective looking for him ever since the lad left – and recently the chap has dug up a lead that suggests the son might be in Italy. So, for the time being at least, Finch has decided to stay at the School House.'

Flora took hold of his hand and pulled him close. 'Are you disappointed?' she asked quietly.

'I'm not.' And the grey eyes when she looked into them held honesty. 'I was never sure he'd sell at a price we could afford. But I *was* sure that you'd hate leaving this cottage. So...'

'We stay where we are.'

'And so does Ambrose. I hope for his sake he gets good news very soon.'

_____

7

A possible move from the cottage had been shelved and Jack had been quick to dismiss any disappointment he felt. Despite his calm assurance, though, Flora was uncertain the situation would be resolved quite so neatly. She felt relief, of course, that now she would be spared the decision – a huge decision – to uproot herself again, this time permanently, from the house she'd known all her life. But unexpectedly, she felt sad, as well.

Sadness for Jack? Most likely. No matter how unconcerned he appeared on the surface, she knew the School House had caught his imagination and possibly his heart. Not just the house itself, but what it represented, what it might say of their future. Of the family they might one day have, a subject altogether more weighty and, to Flora, more worrying. Yet, she felt sad for herself as well, she realised with a start – that the possibility of a different kind of future had, for the moment, retreated.

It wasn't a thought Flora wished to dwell on and, over the weekend, she pushed the School House forcibly from her mind and made no attempt to continue their earlier conversation. Jack, too, seemed content to let Ambrose Finch's change of plan pass by, spending most of his weekend in a flurry of writing. Occasionally, when needing a break from the demands of the Remington, he'd joined Flora in the cottage's small garden, where she was busy clearing the mass of debris the autumn storms had brought. And so the hours had slipped by virtually unnoticed before they were once more on their way to Lewes and to Cleve College.

On his first day back, Jack made a point of going to the staffroom for the mid-morning break. Having spent his last hour in confused conversation with a student who couldn't decide whether her play should be couched in iambic pentameters – the rhythm of the human heart, she'd breathed to Jack – or simple prose, a cup of tea would certainly be welcome. But it was Martin Winter he was hoping to see.

The room given over to the staff was an eclectic mix of styles, constructed from a former classroom – replete with shiny tiles and shiny paint – that had been awkwardly joined to what had once been the original owner's study, the mansion's ancient oak panelling still exuding an aristocratic stateliness.

Martin was at the hot water urn, a permanent feature on the rickety table bunched against one wall.

'Morning, Jack,' was his cheerful greeting. 'Back for another week, eh? Can I pour you a cuppa?'

'Thanks, yes. I could do with one.'

'Can't we all. Days to go until the next weekend. How's village life, then?'

'Good, thanks – actually, it was the town I was hoping to talk to you about.'

Martin Winter raised an eyebrow. 'Fire away, squire.'

'Specifically Bonfire. Do you know much about the Grove society?'

Winter chewed at his lips. 'Let's sit,' he suggested, leading the way to a grubby chenille-covered sofa, part of the motley collection of seats provided for college staff.

'Grove,' he said thoughtfully, settling back into cushions that had seen better days. 'It used to be one of the best. One of the most innovative.'

'And now?'

'Now, I don't know. A new chap took over as chairman – around a year ago, I think. He wouldn't have had a lot of time to bring about change, and... wasn't he the man who...'

'He was.'

Martin shook his head. 'That was a bad business.'

'He made the move from another society, I believe. Do you know why?'

'Not for certain. There was gossip, but then there always is. Talk that Trevor French – that was the chap – wasn't always straightforward.'

'Dishonest, you mean? About money?'

'Not sure about the money, but there are other ways of being dishonest. Whenever I've talked to anyone from Harland – he was the society's chairman previously – I had the impression of a stand-off. A long-running battle, with French involved in several things that left a bad taste in members' mouths. I guess he stuck it out until it got too hot for him.'

'But to bounce into Grove. Would that be normal?'

'I reckon he'd be seen as worth taking on. He'd won prizes for Harland and Grove must have felt they could do with some. Lately, the society'd become a trifle lacklustre.'

'Do you think that's why they made him chairman over Edwin Brooker?'

Martin took a long sip of his tea before answering. 'French was one of those men who can be all things to all people,' he said carefully. 'Do you know what I mean? He would have made friends quickly. Got people on side. He was chatty, amenable, happy to agree with whoever.'

'And Brooker as chairman wasn't?' From Jack's own experience, that rang true.

'Edwin was a man of tradition, born and bred in Lewes. He was the town through and through and the Brooker family have been members of Grove since its inception. Bonfire is in their blood. But he was also a man who could be abrasive, bossy, easy to fall out with. Maybe he fell out with just one too many.'

Jack nodded, thinking that sounded all too likely. 'Would you have any idea where Brooker lives?'

Martin Winter looked slightly startled. 'I don't. Know where he works, though. He's an electrician, owns the family firm. Apprenticed as a lad, I believe. He has a small shop in Foundry Lane. Do you know the road?'

'I can find it,' Jack said smiling. 'Thanks.'

Once he'd closed his afternoon workshop dealing with misdirection in crime novels – it was a particular favourite among students – it took Jack half an hour to walk from the college to Foundry Lane. Brooker Electricals was halfway down the small street on the left-hand side and luckily, or perhaps not so luckily, Jack reflected later, Edwin Brooker was packing up to leave for the day.

'Mr Brooker,' he greeted the man as he walked through the door. 'Could you spare me a minute?'

'Depends what you're bringing me. I've a week of appointments in the diary already.'

'Nothing electrical,' he said, hoping that was the right response. 'Just a brief chat – about Trevor French.'

'What about French?'

It was a simple question, but he made it sound intimidating. Brooker was a large man, tall and broad, a little overweight around the middle, but with big shoulders and hefty arms. Jack eyed them with respect. Even though he must be approaching sixty, the electrician boasted a physically impressive figure.

'I was in the crowd when Mr French fell from the Grove float.'

'Yes?'

'I tried to help him, you might remember. You spoke to me at the time.'

'Yes?'

'I understand you used to be chairman of the Grove society.' In face of the man's obduracy, it was all Jack could think to say.

'What's that got to do with French?'

'He took over from you.'

'Took over!' Brooker picked up a loaded haversack and slung it effortlessly over his shoulder, striding directly towards Jack so that he had hastily to back out of the shop. 'Took over! Is that what you call it?'

'I don't call it anything. I don't really know what happened.'

He was facing Jack now, a stone pillar less than a foot away. Poking his finger into Jack's chest, he said, 'Let me tell you then. That man was a serpent. A sly underdog who got chucked out of one society and came sniffing round mine. Mine! I've been a bonfire boye all my life, joined as a five-year-old and moved up the ranks till I was crowned chairman. Then what happens? I go into hospital, small operation on my foot, and when I get back from the convalescent home, who's in charge? None other than that snake, French.'

'Difficult,' Jack said lightly, trying to disentangle the varied images. 'But didn't your members protest at the change?'

'Weak, that's what they are. Weak in the head. "Oh, we didn't know how you'd be when you got home, Edwin," he went on in a mincing voice. "We thought as there was so much to organise we better appoint another chairman and Trevor is so good with people."'

Brooker had motive and a half for this killing, Jack thought. Plainly, he was eaten up by jealousy.

'Do you have any idea how... how Trevor might have fallen?'

Brooker shrugged two solid shoulders. 'Not a clue.'

'Could he have been pushed – accidentally?' He chose his words carefully.

'I don't know and I don't care. Good riddance, I say. French'll be six feet under very soon and where will I be? Back where I belong. There'll be plenty who'll support me. Plenty who've known my family all their lives, angry that I've been cheated. They've done their best to show it and now they'll get their reward.'

'How *did* they show their support?'

'They were naysayers.' Brooker gave a low chuckle from somewhere deep inside. 'Our friend Trevor never had any of his ideas adopted. Whatever he suggested was voted down. Whatever *I* suggested got the green light. Like the tractor.' Brooker beamed widely. 'An idea of genius, I reckon.'

The tractor had appeared an oddity in the procession, but why this should count as genius was beyond Jack.

Seeing him look bewildered, Brooker was sharp. 'It got us noticed, made Grove special. We were up there for everyone to see.'

When Jack continued to look puzzled, he said angrily, 'Fidel Castro fought the Cuban Revolution, didn't he? What could be better than mounting him on a tractor? *Viva* the peasants!'

Before Jack could respond, he'd slammed the shop door behind him them both and, without another word, marched off down the lane and into the lower end of the high street.

Jack was left blinking. A tractor? Perhaps these days South American peasants regularly owned tractors. It was something he'd never considered before. It was certainly something that pleased Edwin Brooker, a man undoubtedly difficult to please.

Turning back to the high street himself, he almost bumped into a figure hurrying towards him down the lane. He stepped back to allow the man to pass. It was Inspector Brownlow.

The inspector screeched to a halt. 'What are *you* doing here?' were his first words.

Quickly, Jack searched for inspiration. 'I had a broken bedside lamp,' he said. 'Brooker's said they could mend it for me.'

The policeman's face filled with suspicion. Craning his neck to look ahead, he muttered, 'The shop's closed.'

'It is now,' Jack said sweetly, 'but not when I arrived. Mr Brooker has just left.'

Brownlow scowled, his eyebrows seeming to twitch, Jack noticed, until they touched each other. It was a fascinating sight. 'I hope that's the only reason you're here, Mr Carrington.'

At least this time he'd been given his name.

'What else would I come to an electrician for?' he asked, pleased with how puzzled he sounded.

'I dunno, but if you've got any idea of doing what I've learned you're in the habit of doing – you and that woman – banish the thought from your mind.'

'You wouldn't by any chance be referring to my wife?' he asked, his mouth set. 'Her name is Flora Carrington. Please use it.'

He strode off, leaving the inspector to stare after him. Really, the man was an oaf. The sooner Alan returned, the better. But interesting that Brownlow had been about to call on the electrician. An indicator that he harboured suspicions beyond Leo Nelson? If so, it was all to the good. Jack harboured suspicions, too, and after his encounter with Brooker this afternoon, they'd grown even stronger.

8

————

After supper that evening, Jack left Flora deep in a book to take a stroll around the college grounds. He needed to clear his head and a brisk walk on a cold, dry evening should do the trick. He'd gone only a few yards, however, before deciding otherwise: he would telephone Sergeant Norris and hope he might still be at work. The sergeant might have news when Alan Ridley was likely to return to duty, a return that now seemed even more pressing.

The grace-and-favour apartment they occupied at the college lacked a telephone, and it meant retracing his steps to the Queen Anne mansion that accommodated most of the class-rooms and asking the evening porter if he could use the college phone, available to staff for emergencies.

Reg Easton was behind the desk, a man with whom Jack was on friendly terms, and he was straight away waved to the telephone booth along the passage. 'Take your time, Mr Carrington. Long as you want – and don't worry about chalking it up.'

Members of staff were rarely allowed to use the college

phone and, when they did, had religiously to time themselves and pay the fee they'd incurred.

Jack was lucky to have his call answered immediately and to find that Norris hadn't yet left the station.

'The inspector won't be back for several weeks, I reckon,' the sergeant said in response to Jack's first question. Norris sounded depressed. 'His ma is right poorly. He might drop in to see us from time to time, but casual like.'

Jack sighed. It wasn't what he'd wanted to hear. 'So... in his absence, how's the French case going?' he asked, hoping for some enlightenment.

There was a loud sigh at the end of the line. 'I shouldn't say this, Mr Carrington, not of a senior officer, but Brownlow is an idiot.' His words were almost whispered into the receiver and Jack wondered who else might be close by.

'I saw him this afternoon,' Jack confessed, 'when I went to Edwin Brooker's shop. I thought Brooker was worth talking to – he was one of the men at the front of the Grove float, and standing right beside Trevor French. I imagine your inspector was there on the same mission.'

'Probably,' Norris said gloomily. 'He's going through the motions, but that's all.' He paused. 'A word of warning, Mr Carrington. This is likely to end up in a pile of—' He didn't go on to specify. 'I'd keep well clear, if I were you.'

'When you say the inspector is going through the motions,' Jack repeated, ignoring the sergeant's advice, 'what exactly does that involve?'

'Pretending. Pretending he's actually investigating when he's already made up his mind. He is in a bit of bind now, though.' There was an unexpected chuckle. 'The post-mortem,' Norris explained. 'The pathologist couldn't be clearer. The stab wound couldn't have come from behind. It had to have been administered from the side. The knife – though the chap couldn't be sure of the weapon – had a thin blade and was slid between the rib bones sideways, but – to the centre of the *left* breast. It didn't hit the heart bang on, but the aorta.' There was a shuffle of papers. 'The descending aorta,' he read out. 'The blade was held low and the blow struck upwards. Then the bleeding out did the rest.'

Jack thought for a moment. 'And Leo Nelson was standing on the *right* side of French,' he said, trying to focus his mind to see a clear image of the Castro float.

'Exactly. You have to do a bit of mind jiggling to make him guilty of stabbing the chap from the left.'

'And Brownlow, I guess, is keen on the mind jiggling.'

'Seems second nature to him, though this is giving him a bit of a problem. But he'll get there. "There was a big kerfuffle," he's already said, "people everywhere. Nelson could have slipped from his place, inched his way round, and attacked from the left."'

'There was no kerfuffle, not until the moment French tumbled out of the float,' Jack objected. 'A lot of noise – chanting, singing, fireworks, drumming – but the people on the float hardly moved, except to wave their hands.'

'Brownlow won't have it. "The crowd were going mad," he says. "I reckon Nelson took his chance, whipped to the other side of the float and stabbed French." That's his argument. I knew he was going to see Brooker today and reckoned he was hoping to get the chap's confirmation that, at some point in the procession, Nelson moved his position. Squeezed himself in to stand to the left of French, with the electrician shuffled along the line.'

'Will he have got the confirmation, do you think?'

'What's your guess? When Brownlow tells Edwin Brooker the results of the post-mortem, which he will, though he shouldn't, the man's going to swear that he saw Nelson move. Otherwise, it's Brooker nearest the dead man. Brooker who's in the frame for murder.'

'Does the inspector have a reason for discounting Brooker as a suspect?'

'Not that I know. I don't reckon he's ever met him before. He just seems fixed on making Nelson the villain.'

'But why?'

'I've no real idea, Mr Carrington. Maybe because Nelson is a bloke with money and Brownlow isn't. Nelson doesn't work so where has he got his cash from? He's travelled halfway round the world but pops up in Sussex for no apparent reason. He's a drifter. A bit of a vagabond. All Brownlow's prejudices rolled into one, I guess.'

When Jack had mentioned on Tuesday evening that he'd seen Edwin Brooker but, disappointingly, the meeting had got him no further, Flora was unsure whether to believe it was the whole truth. She suspected her husband was keeping information to himself, temporarily stymied but still trying to feel his way into the investigation he'd taken on.

It was frustrating. True, she hadn't wanted to be involved, but it was clear that Jack wasn't giving up and, though Flora had serious doubts about Leo Nelson – she certainly wasn't as convinced as her husband of the man's innocence – she appreciated Jack's desire to get to the truth. Truth mattered to them both. Justice mattered. If an innocent man were likely to face the death penalty, Jack would do whatever he could to rescue him, and would tell her, she was sure, when he had something concrete to show for his sleuthing. Perhaps, she mused, she could add her own small mite after next week, when she'd promised to speak to Lilian French.

Meanwhile, they were back in Abbeymead for four days and had the weekend to look forward to and, with it, an exciting treat. A special Saturday evening. Sally Jenner, the owner of Abbeymead's prestigious hotel, the Priory, had offered them a table at one of the twelve-course gala dinners she had begun to run at the hotel. It was a thank you for the help they'd given in Venice to a friend of hers and – though it was never openly stated – for putting themselves in danger to do so.

For days, they had been looking forward to the evening, both keen to find some distraction from the wretchedness of Bonfire Night which, despite their best efforts, continued to linger. It would be a small way, too, of celebrating their return home to Abbeymead.

It was fortunate that Saturday meant early closing for the All's Well, giving Flora as many hours as she wanted to make ready for what would be a fabulous evening, their best since the dinners they'd enjoyed in Venice.

Over a modest lunch of soup and toast, Jack mentioned his phone call to the Priory that morning. 'Just to check they know we're coming! You won't be too tired?'

'Definitely not! I may have been run off my feet this morning, but I've been thinking about the meal every few minutes – what is it, twelve courses and specialist wines? I shall wear my red dress.'

The red dress had become something of a totem, first worn on their honeymoon where it had met a savage fate, but since then cleaned, pressed and mended, and brought out of the wardrobe occasionally although only for Flora to admire – her life had few opportunities for 'dressing up' and tonight was one of those rare occasions.

'You'll need to wear a cardigan,' he warned. The daring red satin was an off-the-shoulder style. 'It's not exactly Venice weather.'

'Not a cardigan, Jack!' She sounded shocked. 'A stole maybe – except I don't have one. It will have to be a large scarf and I'll hope the Priory's boiler is going full blast.'

. . .

In the event, the scarf went unneeded, the hotel's heating proving more than adequate. Amid a sea of starched white tablecloths and sparkling glassware, Sally had given them a table for two, tucked quietly into an alcove of the Priory's elegantly refurbished restaurant: crystal lights, pale grey walls, and thick blue carpet.

'This is like our own private dining room,' Flora said, her face sunny with pleasure. 'Clever Sally!'

Looking around, Jack agreed. The restaurant was virtually full and the majority of tables hosted large and, in some cases, noisy parties.

'She's certainly hit on an idea that works. Who could have guessed a gala evening in Abbeymead would be so popular?' He pulled a face. 'There must be a lot of greedy people around!'

'I'm not sure how *I'll* manage twelve courses,' she confessed, taking a sip of the cocktail Jack had ordered. A negroni, something Flora had first tried in Venice, and which, after an initial dislike, she'd come to enjoy.

Luckily for her appetite, the courses were small, some of them mere tasters, and even at the halfway point of the menu, she felt able to manage more. It was at this juncture that Sally appeared at their table, carrying a bottle of champagne in a wicker carrier.

'This is to take home,' she said. 'I imagine the wine we're serving will be enough for this evening.' She gave a small giggle, tight blonde curls bouncing in tune.

Having already sipped her way through several glasses of wine since the negroni, Flora silently agreed. It felt more than enough.

'It's to say thank you. Again.' Sally beamed at them and before they had a chance to wave away her thanks, she went on, 'I have to tell you that Charlie has helped to cook this evening's meal. Alice was a little nervous at letting him loose tonight, but he's done so well. Really, with my sous-chef teaching him, he's come on leaps and bounds.'

'We should congratulate him,' Jack said, after Sally had disappeared. 'Maybe go backstage after the meal if the kitchen staff don't object.'

'We should! Who would have thought that young Charlie Teague would turn out to be an amazing chef? Your very own protégé, Jack!'

'He was always the best when it came to eating, and a dab hand in the garden, but cooking – who could have guessed?'

It was when they had consumed so much that neither of them felt they would ever get to their feet again, that Sally reappeared, coffee pot in hand.

'So, how was it?'

'You've well and truly spoilt us,' Flora said.

'You deserve it, both of you. It was the least I could offer after what happened in Italy. Now, about Charlie. He's feeling very proud of himself and I was wondering – would you like a word? Auntie is supervising, but it's Charlie who's the hero of the evening. Go now, if you like, and I'll bring fresh coffee when you're back.'

When they walked into the kitchen, Alice was giving the waiters their last orders as they hurried to serve the final few desserts to any table that had lagged behind.

'Well, what did you think?' Alice asked, her cheeks almost scarlet in the steam-laden atmosphere.

'It was a very special meal.' Flora gave her a hug. 'You surpassed yourself! And we hear you had some help.'

'The lad's just finishin' up. Charlie's done well tonight. It wasn't easy for him, not with Hector absent.' Hector was Alice's sous-chef. 'But the man has to have some time off, I suppose, now he's married.' The thought produced a noisy sniff. Hector's marriage to Rose, following so soon after his abandonment of her niece, was never going to meet with Alice's approval.

'Charlie,' Flora called out to him. 'The meal was delicious.'

'You've done brilliantly,' Jack agreed, 'and looking every inch the chef, too.'

Charlie Teague, now a strapping sixteen-year-old, appeared the most professional Jack had ever seen him, his once-white apron and battered chef's hat bearing witness to the last frantic few hours of cooking.

Charlie walked up to them, a ladle still in his hand, but with a smile that spread between his ears. 'I did good, didn't I, Mr C?'

'You certainly did. We enjoyed every single course.'

'What about the trout cevish?'

Jack took that to mean that the trout ceviche was Charlie's particular contribution. 'Excellent,' he said. 'Really excellent.'

If it was possible, Charlie's smile spread wider. 'Mrs Jenner said I done well.'

'That's the highest accolade you can receive! And you deserve it. Cooking professionally is a tough job. Tougher even than helping me in the garden,' he joked.

Jack's initial lack of gardening knowledge had, at times, made Charlie despair.

'I liked workin' at Overlay, though,' he said decidedly. 'We grew some smashin' stuff, didn't we? That man, the one who lives there now...'

'Leo Nelson.'

'Yeah, him. I don't like 'im.'

'You said that before. I had to find him another gardener when you turned the job down. Not that you'd have the time to work there now.'

'I did call at the house. Mum wanted me to. Said I could

earn a bit of pocket money, but I knew the bloke wouldn't pay proper, not like you, Mr C.'

'Not even a glass of lemonade, if I remember rightly.' Jack had to suppress a smile.

Charlie's expression was dark. 'No lemonade was nothin'. He's worse than that. Much worse. When my mate, Tig, knocked at Overlay in the summer – he was collectin' for the Boys' Brigade – the bloke yelled at 'im, chased him down the path with his fists up.'

Jack frowned. 'Are you sure?'

'Course I'm sure. There's somethin' wrong with 'im. I tell you. Last week, when Hector tried to speak to 'im at the green-grocer's, he told Hector to— wouldn't speak to him,' Charlie amended quickly. 'Just ignored him and walked away.'

'Why would Hector want to speak to Nelson?'

'The bike.' Charlie seemed at his most cryptic. When Jack looked bewildered, he said casually, 'There's a bike in the shed. Didn't you know?'

'I lived there for five, six years, and you're telling me there was a bike in the shed all that time?'

'Behind the spades and ladders,' the boy said helpfully. 'And...'

'And I told Hector about it. He's just married and he's got no money. It's 'spensive gettin' married, Mr C.'

'Then you'd better not do it too soon.'

'Don't worry, I won't. Got enough with Ma and Mrs Jenner naggin' me.'

'The bike? Tell me more.'

'It's not much of a bike, but it still works and I said to Hector that he should go and arsk the man, what's 'is name—'

'Leo Nelson.'

'Yeah, go and arsk 'im. He isn't usin' it, is he, so Hector could have it to get to work.'

'But Mr Nelson didn't think so.'

'He told him not to come near the house. Left Hector standin' there like a lemon. He's weird, honest injun. Mrs Jenner reckons he's a spy.'

'I know she does, but I shouldn't take that too much to heart.'

'What are you two gossiping about?' Flora had left Alice to take off her pinafore and sit down for a much-needed cup of tea.

'A bike,' Jack said quickly, not wanting to mention Nelson or his oddities.

'Yeah, a bike,' Charlie said, looking hard at Jack and divining, it seemed, that his old employer wished him to say nothing of the strange tenant at Overlay House. Charlie was growing up.

9

Tuesday afternoon saw Flora once more back at Riverdale and packing away dog-eared copies of *The Story of Babar* after her last reading session of the day – it had been with the five-year-olds, the babies as she thought of them. She'd made a decision. Today, she would grasp the nettle. Delay no more. Today, she would pay the visit to Lilian French. She still felt awkward, fearing she was imposing on a newly widowed woman in asking questions about her husband but, if she left it any longer, her condolences would sound hollow and the visit would feel even more awkward.

Collecting her overcoat from the cloakroom, she pulled the woollen bobble hat over her ears and prepared to walk to the western edge of the town where she'd learned the French family had lived for most of their married life.

The house in Glebe Avenue turned out to be an unremarkable 1930s semi-detached, pebble-dashed walls and leaded-glass bay windows still in place. From the multitude of plants that filled the flower beds on either side of the front path, it seemed the garden had once been well cared for. Now, however, those same beds had been colonised by a particularly rampant weed, while the climbing rose that framed a downstairs window had been left unpruned and the dainty square of grass to one side had missed its autumn cut.

Somewhat nervously she knocked on the door, almost hoping that Mrs French would not be at home. But Lilian was, and answered Flora's knock wearing a none too clean full-length pinafore and carpet slippers, her hair uncombed and her face almost waxen. Flora's heart sank. Did she really have the determination for this?

'Mrs French?' she asked quietly.

The woman nodded.

'My name is Flora Carrington. I run a bookshop in Abbeymead, the—'

'The All's Well,' the woman finished for her.

'You know it?' She was astonished.

'It's become one of my favourites,' Lilian replied, the glimmer of a smile lighting a face that Flora saw had once been extremely pretty. 'Lewes has plenty of bookshops, of course, and I spend a fair amount of time in them, but the All's Well is special.'

'I think so, too,' she answered warmly, wondering why she hadn't recognised Lilian. But these days she was in the shop for only half the week and it could have been Rose who had served her.

There was a slight pause while the two women took stock of each other before Lilian said, 'Won't you come in?'

'That's kind of you, thank you.'

She was shown into a sitting room which, though the same size and shape as every other sitting room in the road, was a testament to its owner's taste. A sophisticated taste. Light carpet and walls, a pale sofa, and a pair of chairs in periwinkle blue that sat either side of a circular ebony table. Above a white sculpted mantelpiece hung a golden sunburst mirror and, from the ceiling, a glass chandelier. A classically elegant space but with just enough colour, Flora thought, for it to feel warm and inviting.

'What a handsome room,' she said, and meant it.

Again, there was the same glimmer of a smile. 'Thank you. Can I offer you tea?'

'No,' she said hurriedly. 'I really didn't want to disturb you, but I felt... I felt I had to come and pass on my condolences. My husband's, too. I could have written, but somehow...' Flora trailed off, struggling, unusually, to find the words.

'That's all right, my dear. I understand how difficult these things are. You were there, weren't you, on Bonfire Night, when Trevor died?'

For a moment, Flora was taken aback. She hadn't expected such an easy way into the subject she was keen to raise. 'The police gave you our names?' she suggested.

'Yes, they did. A very nice inspector. Ridgeway?'

'Ridley,' she amended.

'That was him. A nice man,' Lilian repeated. 'He told me everything he could of what happened that evening. I wasn't there, of course. I did go to Bonfire once, it must have been the year after Trevor and I married, but I never went again. He was always hugely enthusiastic, of course, but it left me cold.'

She waved a hand at one of the periwinkle chairs. 'Take the weight off your feet, Mrs Carrington. Have you walked far?'

Flora sat down while her hostess took the chair opposite. 'Only from Riverdale school, so not too far.'

'Maybe it's because I'm not from Lewes myself.' Lilian was continuing with her earlier thought. 'Being interested in Bonfire, that is.'

'But you are from Sussex?'

'I am, my dear. From Chichester, though I met Trevor in London on an evening out. He worked in the city all his life.'

Flora nodded politely.

'Ran a department store, you know. He was General

Manager.' She said it proudly. 'Creaseys, it's called. In Kensington – do you know it?'

'I don't. I'm afraid my knowledge of London is fairly limited.'

'Ah well, the city's not for everyone. Not for me now, though when I was a girl, it was exciting. I met Trevor at a dance at Chelsea Town Hall, and the first thing he did was offer me afternoon tea at Creaseys!'

'And did you go?' Flora asked, amused.

'Of course I did. A free tea was heaven for an art student with no money! I remember...' Her eyes misted slightly. 'I remember he helped me choose a perfume that day, for my mother's birthday, and told the girl behind the counter to chalk it up to the store. I thought then that he was a keeper.'

'Did Trevor travel to London daily after you moved here?'

'He commuted for more years than I can count. He only retired last summer. We had all kinds of plans...' She broke off, unable for the moment to continue.

'I am so sorry.' Flora had never felt so inadequate.

'I do have friends,' Lilian said wistfully, 'but it's not the same, is it? Have you been married long?'

'A little over a year now. There's just the two of us.'

Flora felt cross with herself. Why had she felt compelled to say that? Almost as though she were excusing herself for having no children or any sign of them. But the guilty feeling, though suppressed, was always there – that at nearly thirty years old, she had failed to conform to social expectations.

'There were three of us,' her hostess offered. 'We have a daughter, Sheila, but she's married with a little girl. My granddaughter, Maisie.' Her voice softened. 'They live way up north in Newcastle – for my son-in-law's job – and I don't see a lot of them. Sheila comes down when she can. She was here for the funeral, naturally, and stayed a while but obviously her own family need her.'

'The friends you mentioned...' Flora prompted. She'd discovered nothing that was likely to help Jack, but hoped she could end this uncomfortable half hour on an upbeat note.

'My friends have been marvellous. Rallied round to make sure I wasn't alone too much. And Leo has been a huge support as well, which I wasn't expecting.'

Flora's hearing switched to alert. 'You know Leo Nelson?' She supposed Trevor must have introduced them. And was that a blush on Lilian's cheek? Surely not.

'I've known... Leo... for a long time. Longer than I knew Trevor, actually.' She said nothing for a few minutes. 'We were courting when I met Trevor.'

Flora felt dazed. That was certainly a stunner. 'I didn't know. I assumed that Leo was Trevor's friend.'

'He was. They palled up when Leo came back from Australia. They'd never met before, but they got on like a house on fire.'

Had Trevor known of his wife's earlier friendship with the man? It was a possibility that Lilian appeared to have skimmed over. But it was a question that needed answering.

'It was strange, really,' her hostess went on. 'Leo turning up after all those years and becoming such good friends with my husband. He and I had been going out for a year or so when I met Trevor at the dance. And that was it. Trevor was such a different man. To me, he seemed so glamorous. He was in charge of this huge department store – I was able to buy some wonderfully smart clothes and all at a discount – and he lived in this lovely flat close by. After I'd been going out with him a few months, I moved to Kensington to be nearer – some grotty bedsit behind the Albert Hall, but I was young and these things don't bother you, do they?'

'And Leo?'

'Well, he wasn't happy.' That must be an understatement, Flora thought, if ever there was. 'And we never got to say a proper goodbye. It wasn't until I went home to Chichester one weekend to see my parents that I heard he'd gone. Upped sticks and moved to Australia. He had a brother there, I knew. I'd never met the brother, but I think Leo was quite close to him.'

'Did you have any idea why he moved so suddenly? And such a long way from home?'

'Not really, though there wasn't much to keep him in this country. His parents were dead and he had no other family, and before we split up he told me the shop he managed wasn't doing particularly well.'

'What kind of business was that?'

'I'm not sure. Hardware, I think. To be honest, he never really talked about his work.'

'Was the shop in Lewes?'

'I don't know that either, but it might have been. He was always driving. Most times, he would pick me up from home in his van.'

For someone who had courted Leo Nelson for over a year, Lilian seemed exceptionally uninformed. Unless she was pretending not to know. But why would she?

'I did wonder,' Lilian continued, 'whether it was breaking up with me that made him leave, but probably not. At the time, Australia was being advertised as the land of opportunity. The Ten Pound Poms scheme – you remember? Maybe he thought he'd have a better life there.'

'And did he?'

'He never got in touch. I never spoke to him again, not until Trevor brought him home that day. They met at a football match – Brighton and Hove Albion, another interest I didn't share! – and, as I say, they got on really well. But talking to him now,' she said thoughtfully, 'he seems to have enjoyed himself in Australia. And been very successful.'

'So, the bonfire society... your husband took him along to the meetings?'

'Trevor was really keen that he joined Grove. He said it would help Leo settle into his new home and perhaps he was right. Trevor had just been made chairman of the society a few months previously, and he was happy to act as a sponsor.'

'It's good that you and Leo have met again,' Flora said, her tone neutral, 'even though the circumstances aren't the best.'

'They're not, but Ne— Leo has been a great comfort these last few weeks. He's persuaded me to keep living here, not that I ever really wanted to move. Trevor was keen to sell up after he retired. Let's get a place in the countryside, he said. It will be nice and peaceful and, if we buy a small cottage, we can save some money. I couldn't see that we needed money and it was quiet enough here. Why would I want it any more peaceful?'

Flora sensed the loneliness in the woman. 'It's as well that you stayed put. You need your friends close by.'

'I do.' Lilian's face cleared, and the beauty she had once been shone through. 'I'm not selling, Mrs Carrington, that's certain. I love this house. It was me who persuaded Trevor to buy it ten years ago, although he said it was too big and too expensive! But this is where I belong and I couldn't contemplate moving to a cottage in the middle of nowhere.'

Had the disputed move created conflict between husband and wife? Flora wondered. And what of the possibility of an even greater conflict if Trevor had discovered his wife's previous friendship with Leo? In their conversation today there had been no suggestion that Trevor knew anything of his wife's past. But if he *had* found out... then what? Bitter feelings? Acrimony? Which could well have a bearing on Trevor's death, except that Flora baulked at asking the obvious question. It would be too unkind. Lilian was a woman whose grief at losing her husband seemed painfully genuine and if she wished to skate over any quarrel, that was her right. She was hardly a suspect, after all – she had been nowhere near her husband when he died.

'I have quite a few friends nearby,' her companion continued, 'and my neighbours are kind. Mr Dauntry, two doors along, will do the garden for me and, like I said, Leo pops in most days. I'm luckier than most.'

'And Bonfire – you still won't join?'

'No interest, my dear. Trevor was always trying to persuade me when I was a young woman, but he never succeeded.' She gave a small gurgle that Flora imagined was the nearest to a laugh she could manage, but it quickly turned into a sigh. 'I used to ask him why he kept doing it when he was so tired from all the travelling. Endless meetings, the fundraising, then organising the big event. Let someone else do the volunteering, I said to him, but he was the chairman of Harland and felt the responsibility. Then, when he left Harland, he was chairman again! – with Grove this time. There was no way he was giving it up.'

Here was another question Flora felt unable to ask. Why *had* Trevor left the Harland society when he was so obviously dedicated?

Lilian was quiet for a moment. 'I did hear that Edwin has taken over again at Grove,' she said, breaking the silence. 'Do you know Edwin Brooker?'

Flora had inched her way to the edge of her chair and was ready to leave, but her hostess seemed keen to keep chatting. 'I don't, but I've heard the same, that Mr Brooker is the Grove chairman again.'

'I'm not surprised. From what Trev told me, he never accepted he had to stand down. Caused all kinds of fuss. Trevor dealt with him as best he could, tried to placate him whenever possible. Edwin was the one who suggested they should use a tractor to pull the float, you know. Daft idea, I thought, and so did Trev but, for the sake of peace, he agreed to it. And look what happened. My poor husband falling and...' She couldn't finish the sentence.

Flora searched for something distracting to say. 'Do you

think Leo will stay in the Grove society now that his sponsor, his best friend, is no longer there?'

'I don't really know, my dear, and that's a fact. Lately, he's been talking of going back to Australia.'

'Really?'

'I'm not sure life in England is quite what he expected and he has his brother still there. He'd be happy to put Leo up until he was settled again. It's only an idea at the moment, I think, but if he ever does go, he's invited me to visit!'

'And would you?'

'I don't know,' she said again. 'I suppose I might. Now I'm on my own.'

Was that why Leo was talking of returning to Australia? Flora wondered. So that he could take his former girlfriend with him? What exactly were the man's feelings for Lilian?

'Of course, he could always invite Thomasina instead,' her hostess added unexpectedly. 'She seems very... very interested. Do you know *her*? Brilliant seamstress. She's made all the costumes for Grove for years.'

'I've met Thomasina,' Flora confirmed, feeling that caution might be needed here. Picking up her handbag, she rose from her chair, Lilian following suit.

'I think Leo is a bit soft on her,' she confided, when they'd walked to the door. 'Though it might be the other way round!'

'Perhaps in the end Leo will decide against going – if it means leaving you here,' Flora suggested.

'Perhaps he will,' the woman agreed softly.

10

Tonight's dinner had not been a success. Flora's struggle with the flat's outdated cooker was nearing an end but, in a mad moment, a final flurry perhaps, she had tried to cook a recipe Alice had passed on for a twice-baked soufflé. *It's delicious and not that difficult*, her friend had said. *Just catch it right and you'll be fine.* Evidently Flora hadn't caught it right. Even twice-baked, the meal had fallen flat and they'd been reduced to scrabbling through the larder for cheese and biscuits to fill the gap. It was fortunate there was still a half-eaten jar of Kate's chutney on the cold shelf. Between serving customers at the Nook and caring for her small daughter, Kate was an expert cook of chutneys. The apricot and walnut had saved the evening.

'Only a few more meals on this apology for a cooker,' Jack said soothingly, hanging the tea towel to dry after they'd washed up in silence. 'And then a return to civilisation!'

'I'm not sure how civilised it will be,' she said a little glumly, still smarting from the culinary disaster.

Jack looked perplexed. 'It was a rubbish soufflé, so what?'

'It's not the soufflé. It's...' She struggled to say what exactly it was. A general unease? The sense that a shadow had darkened their return to Abbeymead?

'I went to see Lilian French today,' she said, when they'd slumped cosily onto the sofa, the rest of the evening before them. Until this moment, it was news she had kept to herself.

'Why didn't you say? Is that what's worrying you? Tell me!'

Sitting by his side, her head on Jack's shoulder, Flora tried to articulate the ill-defined fear she'd been carrying ever since her conversation with Lilian.

'Leo Nelson,' she began. 'I know you're convinced he's an honest man, but I'm scared that you're being led up the garden path. And not just Overlay's!' The small attempt at a joke fell by the wayside.

But that was it, wasn't it? The reason for her uneasiness, the darkness she felt hovering. A fear that Jack's good nature was being exploited, that in some way he was being duped. A fear he would become involved in something he couldn't control, something dangerous, and without even Inspector Ridley shielding his back. Instead, by the sound of it, his wretched stand-in, Brownlow, wouldn't lift a finger to help if Jack should fall into trouble.

He stroked her hair back from her face. 'Tell me,' he said again.

'You'll listen with an open mind – you won't be prejudiced?'

'I'll try.' He curled a long strand of hair around his little finger.

'Lilian was Leo Nelson's girlfriend before she married Trevor.'

Jack sat upright, the curl forgotten. 'Nelson's girlfriend?' He sounded astonished, as well he might.

'She seems to have gone out with him for quite some time

before she met Trevor French at a dance in London. And, suddenly, Leo was no longer her boyfriend. Reading between the lines, I think she was dazzled by Trevor: his job – he managed a London department store, Creaseys – and he had a smart flat in Kensington, while Leo lived at home and was the manager of a local hardware store. There was no way he could compete.'

'Where was the hardware shop?'

'That's another thing. Nelson told you he came back to Lewes from Australia because he was getting old. He missed his country, he said, and missed his town. But I don't believe he ever came from Lewes. He might have rented there for a few months when he first came back to England – before he took on Overlay House – but it looks as though as a young man he lived and worked in Chichester. Lilian, too.'

'Chichester is in the same county,' Jack said mildly.

'The point is that he lied. Blatantly. If he's lying about where he came from, what other truth isn't he telling? And why never mention that he knew Trevor's wife? Not just knew her either, but was courting her. Lilian actually blushed when I mentioned Leo. It's made me wonder what exactly is going on there.'

Jack relaxed back into the sofa. 'She seems to have been quite open to you about their friendship, so probably nothing.'

'*She's* been open, but he hasn't. What if he still likes her? What if Lilian is why he came back from Australia? Perhaps he hoped that by now she was single again, but when he got here found Trevor was still very much alive. Her husband was in the way and had to be got rid of.'

'Trevor has been in the way for many years – how long had Lilian been married? And why would Leo suddenly decide that he wanted his old girlfriend back? And that maybe he'd have to murder to get her. It's a crazy notion.'

'Yet, out of all the people Leo Nelson could have made

friends with when he returned, it was Trevor who became his best pal. Is that one of your famous coincidences?'

'Why not? Nelson met Trevor on a train carrying a load of football supporters and it would be easy enough to fall into conversation with any of them. It's just that the one he had with Trevor stuck.'

'Nelson still lied,' Flora said stubbornly. 'At least, by omission. *And* there's something else. I'm wondering if he really is Leo Nelson.'

'What!'

'At one point – it was when we'd been talking for a while and Lilian was relaxed and perhaps not thinking – she stumbled over his name when she mentioned him. She corrected herself pretty quickly, but there was a definite stumble. Was that because she knew him as someone else?'

'And, after her husband's murder, is deliberately keeping quiet about Nelson's mysterious background,' he teased.

Flora sat up, stretching tall to straighten her back. 'I'm not saying she's deliberately covering anything up. I liked her and I think she's a truthful woman, but she might feel under pressure to pretend. Or, with her husband dying so suddenly and so horribly, she might simply be confused.'

'As I am,' Jack said ruefully.

'And me, too.' Flora yawned. Another early morning beckoned tomorrow. 'The only definite fact we have is that Trevor French was murdered. Everything else is fuzzy. And I don't like fuzzy.'

'No? Really? I hadn't noticed!' He pulled her down beside him.

'Jack,' she said, cuddling up, 'you should talk to the man, try to pin him down on why exactly he came back to England. Not wishy-washy reasons like feeling homesick. He's lived in Australia for most of his adult life. Why come back now? That's

what we need to know. And see if you can discover how he feels
about Lilian French.'

'Flora!' he protested.

'You can do it. Gently, unobtrusively.'

'How unobtrusive is asking the man if he's still in love with
a woman he knew forty years ago and who's just lost her
husband?'

'Well, if you can't, I'll do it.'

'No, definitely not! If there's anything smoky about Leo –
and I'm fairly certain this will be one of your flights of fancy – I
don't want you anywhere near a possible danger. I'll call at
Overlay House once we're back in Abbeymead. It's a promise.'

Jack had enjoyed a few calm days in which to think how best to
approach Leo Nelson. It was far better that he was the one who
asked the questions. Gentle unobtrusiveness was not exactly
Flora's style and he was worried that she could run into trouble.
He understood her concerns, though – that Nelson wasn't the
open, honest chap he'd taken him for – and it seemed right to
include him in any list of suspects for Trevor French's killing.
Particularly if you added a possible relationship with French's
wife.

He was doubtful, though. In his opinion, Flora was placing
far too much weight on that suggestion. If the pair had been boy
and girlfriend once and parted reasonably amicably, it was
inevitable they would be friendly all these years later. But to
suggest that Nelson had returned from Australia specifically to
reclaim his old flame verged on the risible.

He had information himself, news that he hadn't passed on
to Flora – not that he'd deliberately kept it from her. It was more
that there'd not seemed sufficient time to talk over his conversation with Sergeant Norris. If the stab wound had come from the
left, as the post-mortem made plain, then how had Nelson

delivered it, when from every photograph Jack had seen since the murder and from his own memory – though admittedly unclear – the man was standing on the right?

Yet it was Nelson that Inspector Brownlow appeared to be targeting. Fishing, Jack suspected, Brownlow hoping he might come across evidence to support what he'd already decided. More damagingly, according to Norris, he was prepared to dangle in front of Edwin Brooker the possibility that just maybe, at some point in the procession, Nelson had shifted his position to the other side of the float and when the victim fell, he'd been the one standing closest.

He imagined the net might be closing fast on Nelson and, whether the man had lied about his origins and been reticent about his relationship with Lilian, Jack felt strongly he deserved a fair hearing. What Nelson didn't deserve was to be dished by an angry electrician, still smarting from having lost his position as chairman of the Grove society.

Unable to concentrate fully on the scene he'd begun to create – his hero was about to suffer another life-or-death moment – Jack covered his typewriter, finishing early for lunch and, after a ham sandwich and several cups of tea, donned overcoat and fedora and made his way along the lane to Overlay House.

The curtains were once more closed and there seemed little sign of life. A small hope that Nelson might be out and about flickered into being, but was firmly repressed. He owed it to his wife to try to talk to the man. Flora had doubts about Nelson and Flora could be right. In so many cases, she had been. When he met her from the All's Well this evening, it couldn't be with some limp excuse that, after all, he hadn't been able to ask the questions they needed answering.

Striding up Overlay's front path and trying not to look too closely at the bedraggled garden, Jack lifted his hand to the knocker, but found a doorbell instead. A new doorbell! Where had the old lion-head knocker gone? Was it possible that at last the landlord had actually spent money on his property?

He pressed the bell, and instantly jerked back. An enormous wave of fire had swept through his veins, spasming muscles and forcing him to his knees. As Jack slumped to the ground, his head hit the solid wood of the front door. A blinding light behind his eyes – and then darkness.

11

A hazy shape, a dark shadow bending over him. The figure of a man, Jack gradually discerned.

'That's right, old chap. Eyes open. You're back with us again.' The figure gradually metamorphosed into Leo Nelson, his face etched with concern. 'Do you think if I help, you can stand?'

Jack tried to nod his head, but the pain shooting across his forehead was so severe, he lay mute.

Seeming to take this as assent, Nelson bent lower and tucked his hands beneath Jack's arms, gradually heaving him into a sitting position. It took several more minutes and several more heaves before Jack was on his feet, leaning heavily on his rescuer.

Nelson guided his visitor through the front door and very slowly manoeuvred him along the black and white tiled hall and into the sitting room. The lumpy sofa, so detested by Flora, was his final destination. Still here, was Jack's only clear thought. Leaning back against the battered cushions, he closed his eyes, his head swimming, and only came to again when he sensed his host bending over him.

'Whisky?' Nelson said. 'Sorry, it's all I've got in the cupboard, but it will probably do the trick.'

'Thank you,' he murmured. Even if it didn't, he thought groggily, it would taste good.

The whisky, however, worked its magic and, a few sips later, he was able to string half a dozen words together and do so in a sensible order.

'Your doorbell,' he croaked. 'Don't touch it.'

Not that Nelson would need to. He would use his key, but others...

'Don't let anyone else touch it,' he amended.

Leo looked bewildered. His visitor's knock on the head appeared to have affected his mind, Jack could see him thinking.

'It was a shock,' he tried to explain. 'When I rang your bell, I suffered a huge electric shock and buckled under it. I must have smacked my head on the way down.'

'The doorbell?' Nelson sounded incredulous. 'It's only just been fitted and, as far as I know, the current is too low to cause a shock. The transformer reduces the voltage – tenfold.'

'Then the transformer can't be working. I suffered the full voltage, believe me. Who fitted the bell?'

'Some business the landlord sent round. The old knock-er... it more or less fell to pieces.'

Jack leaned back into the cushions again, exhausted. That was a pity, he thought dreamily. I liked the lion.

He shook himself awake. 'You didn't know the man who did the job?'

'It was a Steyning firm, I believe. That's what I saw on the side of the chap's van. Why? You don't think he deliberately messed with the bell? I mean, why would he?'

'I've no idea, but someone has messed with it, that's for sure. You're right about the low-voltage wiring – it's highly unlikely you'd suffer shock from a doorbell. But yours seems to have been rewired to electrocute anyone who rings it.'

Nelson was grappling with the enormity of Jack's suggestion, making small, hardly audible noises of protest. 'No one could have done that, Jack. The wiring is in the house. It's not accessible from outside.'

'Who's visited you recently, apart from the Steyning electrician?'

'No one – only you today. And the front door is kept locked... except...'

'Except?'

'If I go out for a walk, a short stroll down the lane, I don't bother with the key.'

'And anyone could walk in?'

'I guess so, but who would do that? I'm only gone half an hour or so. Who would take the chance that I wasn't in?'

Jack closed his eyes again. The whisky was lulling him to sleep. Struggling to stay awake, he said, 'Someone who was watching you maybe?'

'But why?'

'I can't tell you why, only that the bell has been tampered with and you should make sure that no one else touches it. It needs dismantling and quickly. Anyone with a weaker heart could have died from that shock.'

'I'm sorry, mate, really I am. And yes, I'll get the Steyning chap back and he can take the bell down. I'll get a knocker fitted instead and pay for it myself. A knocker shouldn't cause problems.' There was a worried look on Nelson's face.

Jack finished his whisky with one large swallow. 'That was good. Thank you, Leo. It's breathed new life into me,' he lied. Wriggling to the edge of the sofa, he hoped he could get to his feet.

'You're going already?'

'I was just taking a walk, one of your strolls down the lane, and dropped in on the off chance of a chat.'

'Don't suppose you fancy one now.' Nelson grimaced. 'But just in case – how's the book going?'

'It's coming along.' He forced himself to smile. 'I did a few hours' writing this morning and I'll be back at the typewriter as soon as I'm home.' Would he, he wondered, with a head still throbbing this badly?

Shuffling even closer to the edge of the sofa, he was on the point of leaving when through the fog closeting his mind he remembered why he'd called at Overlay House.

'To be honest,' he said, trying to gather his wits, 'my attention isn't all it should be – leaving Cleve College is on my mind.'

It wasn't at all, but he had to find something to talk about, something that might, if he were lucky, lead to the questions he needed to ask. 'I've a lot of ends to tie up,' he continued, 'students to see, work to critique. And the days are dwindling – I can count what's left on two hands.'

'But once you walk out of the place, your life is your own. Something to celebrate, surely!'

'It should be. I guess work isn't a worry for you—I imagine you're fully retired now.' He tried to sound casual, hoping to encourage Leo Nelson to talk, but somehow his remark felt glaringly awkward.

'Absolutely retired. A life of leisure for me, I'm glad to say. I give the *Evening Argus* a glance sometimes, the situations vacant, you know, but, really, do I want any of the jobs? No, is the short answer!'

'You're in a fortunate position, Leo. What did you do in Australia?'

'I ran a business, owned it with my brother, Norman. We bought a hardware store together – turned out to be the most successful move we could have made. We were living in a small town, you see, and our store was the only place you could buy hammers, screwdrivers, power tools, gardening equipment... a whole range of stuff.'

'Have you always worked in hardware?'

'Mostly,' Nelson said, but gave no further information. 'It's a trade I know well. But there can be a lot of heavy lifting, and you don't want that at my age.'

'I can well understand. So, did you sell the business before you came back?' Jack was guessing.

Nelson nodded. 'It was a mutual decision. My brother's a bit older than me, mid-sixties. He'd had enough, didn't want to go solo, so we sold the store. And got a very good price. Here, I've got a picture somewhere. The local rag got hold of the story and featured us. The brothers Nelson! Hang on a minute and I'll find it. You'll get some idea of the town, too. We called it a town but...' Trailing off, he made for the stairs.

Jack had no real interest in hardware stores or, for that matter, small Australian towns, but his host was enthusiastic. More so than he'd ever seen him. And if the words Leo and Norman Nelson appeared on the store front, it would put an end to Flora's suspicion of a name change. Leo's brother would surely have refused to become someone he wasn't.

While Leo was upstairs – he could hear his footsteps overhead – Jack decided to test his legs. That had been one almighty shock and his limbs felt uncomfortably weak. Holding on to his much-loved sofa for support, he gradually got to his feet. All well. He walked over to the window and then quickly turned away. The sight was too sorrowful. The garden that he and Charlie had brought to life had retreated into a deathlike slumber.

Treading a cautious path back to the sofa, he inadvertently brushed against a small stack of papers sitting on the occasional table he'd once used for his own correspondence, and scattered several of the sheets across the threadbare carpet.

One, in particular, caught his attention. A sheet of thick, cream parchment. It lay face up, but the marks of where the folds had been made were clearly visible, along with a first line of large black lettering. It was a will, he realised. Perhaps waiting to be witnessed. Quickly, he bent to retrieve it, meaning to replace it on the pile. Investigating Nelson shouldn't mean prying into his most confidential affairs.

Jack stopped, the sheet of parchment in his hand. Prying or not, his eyes were riveted. For a moment, he was sure they were playing him false. Neil Leonard. This was the will of a Neil Leonard, not Leo Nelson. A friend maybe for whom he was doing the witnessing? Really? Jack didn't think so. Flora's fancy, as so often in the past, hadn't lied. Leo Nelson – rearrange a few letters and you had Neil Leonard. One and the same person.

Hearing a stair creak, he moved away from the table as quickly as he felt able.

'On your feet then. That's good.' Nelson gave a genuine smile. 'Took a while to find, but here it is. The picture the newspaper took. What do you think?'

Jack took his time in studying the photograph. Leo's hardware store was one of a line of small shops, a continuous wooden veranda running along their front entrances. It could have been a still from an American cowboy film – the dusty main road, the pick-up trucks – but it was Australia, for sure: the advertising boards priced in Australian pounds, the men wearing khaki bush hats. The hardware store was called The Handy Hub.

'You were obviously an important part of the community,' he said, for want of anything better. 'You must have made plenty of friends over the years. Sad for you to leave them behind. Sad to leave your brother behind.'

'Norm will be fine. Got a wife and kids to look after him! And I still had a few friends here, believe it or not – it's been good to meet up with them again.'

'Friends like Lilian French?'

Leo looked a trifle startled.

'Mrs French mentioned she knew you many years ago.'

'It was many years ago,' he said reminiscently. 'But Lilian hasn't changed – she's still the lovely woman I used to know.'

Something of what Flora suspected could be true, Jack decided. But only something. To make the move back from Australia, uproot a life you'd led for twenty years, because suddenly you had a yen to see your old girlfriend again? That was a notion that Jack dismissed out of hand.

Leo walked with him to the sitting room door. Stumbled, more like, he thought derisively. His limbs were moving as though they belonged to quite another person and he suddenly felt incredibly tired.

His host looked at him with concern. 'Will you be OK to walk home, old chap? I could maybe find some transport.'

'No, really, I'll be fine. I'll do it slowly.'

'Well, if you're sure...' Leo turned to lead the way into the hall.

It was difficult now to think of him as Leo, but that's what he must do, Jack told himself firmly. A growing consciousness of how this new knowledge could play out was telling him to focus on the name he knew, avoid any slip which might give away what he'd just learned. And what he'd just learned was only the beginning, Jack felt certain.

Opening the front door, Leo stood back to allow him to pass, but instead of walking out, Jack was brought to a sharp halt by a figure on the doorstep: a woman he'd never met, fashionably dressed, and with face and hair immaculately presented. She was reaching up as though to knock but, seeing Jack in the doorway, her hand dropped.

'Thomasina! Hello.' Leo had appeared from behind and was welcoming his new visitor. For a supposed recluse, the man seemed to have an unusually lively social life.

'Let me introduce you. This is Jack Carrington, a neighbour of mine who happens to be an amazing crime writer!' He paused, an uncertain smile on his face. 'And Jack, this is

Thomasina Bell. She's a founder member of the Grove society and a dab hand with the sewing machine.'

'It's good to meet you, Mrs Bell.' Jack held out his hand.

'Miss Bell,' she said a little snappily, and offered him a reluctant handshake. 'I'm here on society business,' she added, adopting an official tone. 'A few things I need to check with you, Leo.'

'Oh, right.' Nelson seemed unsure what things they could be.

And so was Jack. Leo Nelson had been a member of the Grove society for a matter of months only. It was true that he'd been sponsored by its chairman, but otherwise in terms of the society's hierarchy, he was a nobody. What possible checks could he be involved in? Miss Bell's words had all the hallmarks of an excuse, Jack decided, a ploy to explain why she'd come to Overlay House.

Why had she come, he wondered, and why – the thought came suddenly – had she not reached for the doorbell?

12

Flora took one look at her husband as he limped into the kitchen and dropped the potato she was peeling to guide him into a chair.

'Whatever's happened?' She was alarmed, her hands grasping the edge of the kitchen table.

'A small accident, nothing more. But I could do with a cup of sweet tea.'

'Jack! What?'

'Tea?' he said quietly.

Trying hard to suppress her fear, she filled the kettle and lit the gas.

'Now, tell me, please. An accident?' She sat down in the seat opposite.

'There was a problem with the doorbell at Overlay House.'

For a moment she thought he was joking but then noticed his pallor and the way his shoulders had slumped. A deep frown creased her forehead.

'You're being cryptic again, Jack. What do you mean? The house doesn't have a doorbell.'

'It does now. A new one. The old lion knocker has gone – I wish I knew where, I would have liked to keep it. As a souvenir.'

Flora was beginning to lose patience. 'If you don't tell me in the next few seconds what's happened to you, I shall wrap the kettle round your neck.'

'I was electrocuted. That's what's happened. But I'm OK,' he added quickly. 'Just a little weak in the arms and legs.'

For a moment, she was bewildered, trying to make sense of what he'd said. But then scolded herself – do something useful, she thought – and jumped up to make the tea, ensuring she added several spoons of sugar to Jack's cup.

'I still don't understand. Electrocuted?' She bent to kiss him on the cheek and gave a suspicious sniff. 'Have you been drinking?'

'It's whisky. Leo Nelson came up trumps. The bell had been wrongly wired and it knocked me out for a while, but the whisky got me on my feet again.'

'Only just, by the look of it. Nelson is all right, presumably? He didn't know his doorbell was dangerous?'

'Not a clue, but he does now. He's getting it removed.'

Flora sat down again, her hands spread across the table, her mouth pursed. 'But how, Jack? How do you wire a bell so badly it electrocutes your visitors? Who fitted it?'

He took a long drink from the tea she'd made. 'This is good, thank you. It was a firm from Steyning, a perfectly reputable business, it seems. There must be someone else taking an interest in the house.' When he saw her still puzzled expression, he added, 'After the Steyning chaps left, someone must have deliberately rewired it.'

Flora thought about this for a few minutes. 'If so, it would have to be someone with electrical knowledge. It wouldn't be for an amateur.'

'I reckon so.'

'Edwin Brooker!'

'He comes to mind. But why on earth would he do such a thing?'

'Because he doesn't like Leo Nelson? Because Leo was a friend of his arch enemy? Because Brooker is a psychopath? I really don't know, but he's the only person we're aware of who would have the knowledge and who, in some way, is connected to Nelson.'

'So... Brooker sets out to hurt any visitors to Overlay House, even possibly kill them if they have heart trouble? Unless he *is* a psychopath, that doesn't make much sense.'

Flora jumped up, a bundle of activity – emptying the kettle, covering the potatoes with water, shuffling a shopping list to one side – but all the time thinking hard.

'He could be hoping to hurt Leo.'

Jack pushed his teacup to one side. 'That doesn't make sense either. Leo wouldn't use his own doorbell, would he? And why would Brooker want to hurt him? Trevor French was his rival and Trevor is dead. What possible threat is Leo? He's a new member, a nobody in the Grove society, whereas Edwin Brooker is chairman again. In charge once more.'

'But he's the only electrician we know,' she insisted, 'and he was standing next to Trevor on the Grove float. *And* he was the one who suggested a tractor was used to pull the float.'

Jack frowned. 'So?'

'It made it easier to kill Trevor French. They were standing side by side on a slow-moving vehicle, rather than walking in the procession and mixed up with torches and tar barrels. From that position, he couldn't miss with a knife, could he? And from that height, Trevor could be badly injured from the fall. If the stab wound itself wasn't sufficient, it would make sure the man died.'

'Even if all that were true, it's Trevor French you're talking about. What has that to do with Leo?'

'Simple. Now Trevor is dead, Brooker has moved on to his

best friend. Perhaps Brooker is worried that Leo knows something, that he saw something on Bonfire Night that he shouldn't have.'

'But we've just said that Leo is unlikely to use the doorbell himself, so how would tampering with its wiring hurt him?'

Flora ran a hand through a tangle of waves, seeming temporarily at a loss. 'Really, I don't know. We're going round in circles. Unless... he's hoping to hurt others and so discredit Leo. Someone calling at Overlay House gets badly hurt and it's all Leo Nelson's fault. He could be arrested, charged with negligence if there is such a charge.'

'That takes some complicated thinking and I don't get the impression that Edwin Brooker has a mind that does complicated. There *is* something else I should tell you,' he began tentatively.

'Here, let me pour you another cup. Your face is looking a better colour now.'

She got up to go to the counter.

'Nelson isn't Nelson,' he announced. 'At least, I don't believe so.'

Flora whirled around, teapot in hand, spilling half its contents over the kitchen tiles.

'What!'

'Sorry, I should have mentioned it earlier, but we got hung up on electrics.'

'And now we're onto false identity?'

'Pretty much. I think you were right when you doubted his name.'

She handed him a fresh cup of tea. 'What on earth have we got involved in? And how do you know – about the name?'

'I saw a will on the table – Nelson's will, it seemed. Maybe it was waiting for a signature – except that it wasn't Leo Nelson's last will and testament. It was Neil Leonard's.'

'A friend's then?'

'That was my initial thought, but—'

'But the letters are too alike,' Flora finished for him, her eyes suddenly bright. 'I told you! The man's a rascal. I always said so. Or why would he be hiding his true identity?'

'He could be a dyed-in-the-wool villain for all I know,' Jack said glumly, 'but one thing's for sure, he didn't tamper with his own doorbell.'

They sat in silence for a while, Jack slowly drinking his second cup, until she asked, 'Did you get any answers to the questions we had? Anything that might explain what Nelson is doing in Abbeymead and why he's living under a false name?'

Jack shook his head. 'All I learned was that he ran a hardware store in Australia. Owned it with his brother – but that won't get us far.'

'Lilian French mentioned he had a brother.'

'At least that seems true. He told me that hardware was a trade he knew well, and it would be reasonable to assume he ran a similar store in Sussex before he left for Australia. If I could discover what it was called or where it was, it might throw some light on what Nelson or Leonard or whatever his name is, is up to. *Was* up to, perhaps, when he set sail all those years ago.'

'Nelson said that he originally came from Lewes, didn't he?' Jack nodded. 'I don't remember a hardware store in the town when I was growing up, though as a child I hardly ever visited. I certainly don't remember one in the village.'

'It's unlikely you would have noticed. It's not something a child would be interested in – and we're talking twenty years ago, O youthful one!'

'I'll ask Alice,' she said decidedly. 'She'll know for sure and I'm seeing her tonight.'

'Of course, I'd forgotten. The Friday meal.'

Friday evening was the time the friends – Alice, Kate and Flora, and occasionally Alice's niece, Sally – had set aside to meet over supper. A chance to catch up with each other's news and, even better, chew over whatever delicious tidbit of gossip was circulating the village that week.

'I was in the middle of making you a cottage pie when you limped in,' she said, half smiling. 'You'll be OK on your own?'

'With a cottage pie to keep me company, what more could I want?'

'I'd best get a move on then.'

She got to her feet and Jack followed suit, putting his arms around her and hugging her close. 'I'll enjoy my supper,' he said, 'and make sure I keep clear of doorbells for the evening.'

It was Kate's turn to host the Friday meal and when Flora arrived at the terraced cottage tucked behind the grey stone bulk of the village church – a cottage that Kate had inherited from her father, Cyril – the small kitchen already seemed full to bursting. Sally had taken the evening off from managing the Priory, a rare event, and was busy helping Kate assemble plates and cutlery.

'I'm making myself useful,' she joked. 'I think. Auntie, where did you put the soup spoons?'

Alice's reply was lost in the cheese scone she'd taken a nibble from. 'These are good, Katie. Not for this evening?'

'Not really,' Kate said apologetically. 'Tony cooked a whole batch at the Nook this morning. He thought they'd do for our lunch next week. In fact, he's cooked most of this evening's meal.'

'Keeps him in practice,' Alice said briskly. 'I'll take the soup in. Pumpkin, isn't it? I love a drop of pumpkin.'

As soon as they were seated round the dining room table and the pumpkin soup was disappearing fast, Flora dropped hardware stores into the conversation but was careful to steer clear of any mention of doorbells.

'Jack went to Overlay House today. You know how he likes to stroll around his old garden – it's a source of inspiration, he says – and he saw Leo Nelson. Actually spent time talking to the man. Apparently, the chap once ran a hardware store in this area, but I don't remember ever seeing one. Perhaps it closed when he left to go abroad.'

'I'm a relative newcomer,' Sally said, laying her soup spoon to one side, 'but I can't recall seeing one locally.'

'I don't remember one either,' Kate murmured, jumping up to clear the table.

'There wasn't one,' Alice said flatly. 'Not in Abbeymead and I'm pretty sure not in Lewes either. We always went to Worthing for any goods we needed.'

She disappeared into the kitchen, returning with a dish of vegetables in each hand, destined to accompany the fat chicken pie that Kate had just rescued from the oven.

'I told you there was something suspicious about that man.' Alice plumped herself down. 'Pretendin' he was here for the peace and quiet, and now pretendin' he ran a store locally. Is he lyin' about Australia, do you think?'

'I'm fairly sure he's been living in Australia for years,' Flora said, 'but it's odd that no one knows of a hardware store.'

'No one knows of him.' Alice snorted. 'Not one person I've spoken to recognises the man.' She ladled carrots onto each plate with a firm hand.

'If he lived in Lewes, it's unlikely people here would know him,' Kate suggested gently.

'I reckon they wouldn't know him in Lewes either.' She passed the ladle to Sally, who was sitting nearest to a tempting dish of sauteed potatoes. 'There's somethin' wrong about him. He doesn't talk to anyone, stays holed up in that house.'

'It's clear he's your spy, Auntie.' Sally waved the ladle in the air.

'He could well be, my girl. You wait and see. Somethin' will happen here and then we'll say, remember that man who moved to the village for no good reason.'

'What I don't understand,' Sally said, taking a large mouthful of chicken pie, 'is why, if he's such a recluse, he was keen to be part of the bonfire celebrations. He was there that night, wasn't he, Flora?' she appealed. 'I mean, would you do that, if you didn't want to mix with people, didn't want to talk to them?'

'Maybe he was fed up with being a recluse and needed to spread his wings. And on Bonfire Night he'd be in fancy dress,' Kate said, smiling. 'It's a kind of protection, I suppose.'

'He's certainly a conundrum,' Flora agreed. 'He says he lived in Lewes for years before going to Australia and missed his hometown, but when he came back, he was only there a few months before moving to Abbeymead.'

'And why he moved here, we'll never know.' Alice put down her knife and fork. 'Whatever you say about fancy dress, Kate, he's a strange one. A man who doesn't want to be with people, standin' at the front of the Grove float on Bonfire Night for all to see.'

And he's also a man with a doorbell that electrocutes people, Flora added to herself.

'I don't know. Maybe Kate is right,' she said aloud. 'On Bonfire Night Leo Nelson was just another Mexican or Cuban. The costumes were extraordinary and made a very good disguise.'

'Does the Bell woman still do them?' Sally began stacking empty plates to one side of the table.

'She does. Do you know her?' Flora was surprised.

'She made some curtains for the Priory when we first opened. The floor-length blue chenille in the main lounge.

They're lovely material and beautifully sewn. I found her a little sharp to deal with, but she's very skilful. Efficient, too. I had hoped to order new bedroom drapes from her, but...'

'But?' Alice asked, as she carried a large rhubarb tart in from the kitchen, Kate following with a jug of custard.

'She came on to Benedict,' Sally said reluctantly. 'I had to find someone else.'

Three pairs of eyes fixed on her.

'Well, you know what he was like.'

Three heads nodded in unison. They all knew what Sally's former partner was like.

'I don't think Miss Bell would need much encouragement,' Flora said, remembering what her husband had told her earlier. 'When Jack went to leave Overlay today, Thomasina was on the doorstep. He thought it likely that she was there quite often.'

There was a buzz of interest around the table. 'I'll be seeing her soon,' she went on, surprising them again. 'I'm going to her studio for a fitting.'

'Won't she be expensive?' That was Kate.

'She certainly was for the curtains.' Sally pulled a small face.

'I'll ask for an estimate and if it's too high, I won't go ahead. It's just... I thought I'd like something special...' Flora searched for a reason that would sound plausible to her audience. 'Rose always looks so smart when she comes to the shop, and I know she uses Thomasina quite often.'

'It's a wonder how she finds the money.' Sally was sounding tart. 'She's a part-time shop assistant. I'm sure you pay her well, Flora, but...'

It was clear that Rose's marriage to Hector, Sally's former beau, still stung. How long would that last? Flora wondered.

'She ought to be saving the pennies.' Tony, Kate's husband, had made himself scarce for most of the evening but now appeared with a tray of tea in his hands.

'Tea up,' he said, 'and leave the dishes. I'll deal with them later.'

'Sarah?' Kate asked anxiously. Their small daughter had for months been prone to colic.

'Sarah is sleeping – soundly,' her husband reassured her.

'You're a darling,' Kate said, handing him the empty dessert bowls.

'You've earned Brownie points, Tony.' Sally's curls were on the bounce. 'But you're right – about the money. Those two need to save hard. Hector has stayed in his room at the Priory and I imagine Rose still rents from Mrs Waterford. It's not exactly the best way to begin married life.'

'I met Hector last week,' Tony said, 'coming out of the post office. He looked pretty woeful – as though he'd taken his harp to the party and no one asked him to play!'

'Where did that come from?' Kate was laughing.

'My ma. Always one with a pithy saying.'

Loading the empty pudding bowls onto his tray, he smiled around the table and disappeared into the kitchen.

'Jack had the idea that if we ever did think of buying the School House, we could rent our cottage to Hector and Rose – at a reasonable price.'

'What a splendid idea!' Kate exclaimed.

'I thought it was clever,' Flora responded – and hated the thought of it, she said to herself. 'Except that now Mr Finch is no longer selling. In any case, the house would probably have been too expensive for us.'

'Flora's right,' Alice chimed in. 'About Ambrose Finch. He's stayin' put. It's cos he thinks he's found his son – I expect he's hopin' the lad will come and live with him there.'

'When did the boy go missing, Alice?'

'I dunno ezactly. Ambrose wasn't livin' in Abbeymead then. But it was years ago and the man's been searchin' for him ever since. Employed a private detective, so I heard.' She sounded awed.

'And where is this long-lost child now?' Sally looked amused.

'*That* I haven't managed to find out,' Alice admitted.

'You're losing your touch, Auntie,' she teased.

'What I do know,' Alice said with deliberation, ignoring her niece, 'is that old Finch is thinkin' of throwin' one great big party when the lad arrives. And I bet none of you knew that!'

13

Jack was tucked beneath the blankets when Flora arrived home.

'I'm not asleep,' he murmured, switching on the bedside lamp as she crept into the bedroom. 'Just shattered.'

'Tomorrow, you must see Dr Hanson,' she said severely, walking over to sit beside him on the bed, 'and ask him to check you over – just in case. And don't say there's no need.'

'There is no need!' He reached for her hand. 'But... if I feel close to collapse, I'll make an appointment.'

'Promise?'

'Promise. What news on the village grapevine?'

'I asked about a hardware store,' she said, starting to undress. 'Alice is certain there was never a shop in Lewes – Worthing was the nearest – and there was certainly never one in Abbeymead. Sally hasn't lived in the area long enough but neither Kate nor I can remember anything when we were children.'

He pulled a face.

'And Jack?' She came back to the bed and sat down again. 'No one seems ever to have met or even heard of Leo Nelson before he left for Australia. I haven't mentioned the name of

Neil Leonard but if I had, I'm fairly sure the answer would be the same.'

'A mystery man indeed. But there must be some mention of him somewhere.'

'If you're still keen to keep looking,' Flora said diffidently, plucking at the bedspread, 'you could ask Ross Sadler to search for you.'

Ross was a good friend and former colleague of Jack's, still working as a journalist on the *Daily Mercury*.

Jack was hesitant. 'I don't like to bother him, not unless it's really urgent. You know how busy he is.'

'Then ask him to help when or if he has the time. He could take a look maybe at some of the old local newspapers. Otherwise, it will be you that has to go to London to start searching the archives – if you're still concerned.'

Jack sighed. 'I'm not sure I am. Not any longer. When I thought Nelson was an innocent man in danger of being treated unjustly, I felt compelled to help. To do something. But now – I'm sure what the man is or who he is.' He reached up to stroke the nape of her neck. 'Come to bed. It's getting late. I'll give Ross a ring in the morning.'

'If you do, be sure to mention Chichester. Lilian French definitely lived in the city and she told me that Leo used to pick her up from her house.' She got up to go to the bathroom, but turned at the door. 'Phone Ross and then forget about it. We have another treat tomorrow. Have you remembered?'

'Of course, *North by Northwest* at the Dome! I'd forgotten. We should go out for tea as well.'

'An early Christmas present?'

'Why not? It's time we had another treat. It feels as though it's been work, work and more work since we came back from Venice – for both of us.'

Flora yawned. 'I'll be five minutes,' she murmured, and disappeared into the bathroom.

When she walked out those five minutes later, Jack was lying on his back, quite still, and staring at the ceiling. He seemed unaware that Flora had returned and was standing at the bedside, looking down at him.

'You're thinking!' she accused him.

Jack half sat up. 'It came to me just now. Something strange. It was your mention of Chichester and Lilian French. You said when you spoke to her that she stumbled over Nelson's name and it's obvious, isn't it, that she has to know his real name? Know that he's living under a false identity in Abbeymead – unless he's been masquerading all his life – but she's said nothing. She's gone along with the pretence and we've never mentioned how odd that is.'

'I assumed she must know but decided to stay silent. I never asked why, though.'

'It seems an important question,' he said, turning out the light. 'Why *is* she keeping silent?'

Before he sat down to a morning of writing, Jack made a phone call to the *Daily Mercury* and was fortunate to find Ross at his desk.

'I'm following the most extraordinary story,' his friend said. 'You won't believe your ears. In fact, I don't think I believe mine. I'm beginning to think it's a bag of moonshine. Have you heard?'

'Hardly, Ross. I'm sitting in deepest Sussex.'

'Prince Charles,' he said succinctly. 'There's been an attempt to kidnap him from his boarding school.'

'Let me guess – you're off to Berkshire to investigate.'

'Taking the train tomorrow. Hopefully, there's a story at the end of what's likely to be a tedious day. But did you need me for something?'

'You're busy, I can see.'

'Always busy, Jack, but how can I help – spit it out!'

'I'm trying to trace a man who was in Sussex around twenty years ago. His name is either Leo Nelson or Neil Leonard.'

'An anagram – almost. Living in Sussex, you say.'

'Possibly Chichester, and possibly running a hardware store in the town. Or somewhere else in Sussex,' he finished, a trifle desperately.

'That's a lot of possibles, but I'll give it a go once I've returned from the rural wastes.'

Mindful of Ross's heavy workload, Jack was lavish in his thanks and happy with his friend's promise to investigate Nelson as soon as he had the time. He felt a lingering guilt at burdening Ross with a search that was likely to prove pointless, but in the past the journalist had proved a useful source of information, at times extremely useful, and, if there was anything to find in the newspaper archives, Jack knew he would find it.

Wrenching his mind from dangerous doorbells and mystifying anagrams, he settled down for a full morning's work and was pleased that, by the time Flora returned from the All's Well for a late lunch, he had racked up another thousand words. The current work-in-progress had been the idea of his agent, Arthur Bellaby, who held a fascination for the Second World War and was eager for a mystery with Italian politics in the background.

Another Way to Die would dramatise any likely connections, any dubious links, between the establishment in Rome and the Sicilian mafia during the years of war. In Venice, Jack had managed a few hours of research in the university library at Ca' Foscari and returned with several possible plots in mind. Now, he was well into his chosen narrative and Arthur had given the detailed synopsis his blessing. For once, the novel appeared a smooth ride – what lucky authors, rarely Jack, referred to as 'the book writing itself'.

Although the day remained chilly, a sun low in the sky was

attempting to shine, and he suggested to Flora, as they donned hats and coats for their trip to Worthing that afternoon, that they take a walk on the seafront before tea and scones at the Quiet Kettle. They would have plenty of time, their chosen performance of *North by Northwest* not showing until six o'clock.

By the time they had parked the car on Worthing seafront, however, the sun had almost vanished and only a slight sliver of gold across the surface of the waves suggested it had ever shone. Their walk turned into a brisk and mercifully short trot, the Quiet Kettle and its home-made scones proving irresistible.

A blast of warmth greeted them as they stepped across the café threshold, a cosiness that was echoed in deep pink walls and olive tablecloths. The café's main talking point, though, was the ceiling. From it hung line after line of fringed, floral lamp-shades, a quirky decoration that Flora loved. She walked through the mismatched furniture to one of the few tables that was still free, where a waitress in traditional black dress and white-frilled pinafore was waiting for them.

'Still keen on sultana scones?' Jack asked, gesturing towards a counter crammed with chocolate cake, a fudge slice, several Victoria sponges and a dozen different small cakes.

'Yes, please,' she said to the waitress. 'With cream and strawberry jam.'

'Me too,' Jack agreed, waiting for their server to leave before he said, 'I wanted to ask... we didn't have time to speak much last night, but was there any other news from your evening of gossip?'

'Gossip you want to hear,' she pointed out.

'I do. Otherwise I've no idea what's happening in the village. And we were both too tired to talk much.'

'I was fine,' she said pointedly.

'And today *I'm* perfectly restored. No Dr Hanson necessary. Now, last night?'

'Ambrose Finch was mentioned.' She sounded cautious.

Jack's idea that they might buy the School House and move from the cottage had been something they'd found difficult to discuss. That was her doing, Flora acknowledged. The fault of very strong feelings for her cottage – and for a past she couldn't quite leave behind. For a future she couldn't quite contemplate.

'The fact that Finch isn't selling up?'

She nodded. 'The village is interested but no one seems to know very much, even Alice. Only that Mr Finch believes he's found his son at last and is hoping to welcome him to the School House. Oh, and when that happens, there'll be a massive party to celebrate.'

A large floral teapot with matching cups arrived at the table, a second waitress coming behind with a plate of sultana scones and small bowls of strawberry jam and clotted cream.

Jack took some time spreading his scone with jam and cream.

'The Cornish way,' Flora observed.

'After our adventures there, always loyal to Cornwall. But spreading a scone?'

'If you'd spread cream first, then jam, that would have been the Devon way.'

'I had no idea.' He went on spreading, then with what Flora thought a studied casualness, said, 'Now that the School House is off the market, you can stop worrying.'

'I wasn't worrying. At least, not much. But it did start me thinking – about extra space. I thought that maybe we could extend the cottage.'

Jack looked blank. 'Extend the cottage? How on earth would we do that?'

'It might be possible to knock down the kitchen wall and build into the garden.'

'You're not serious, Flora? The cottage is two hundred years old – if you start knocking it to pieces, it's likely to collapse in a heap of brick and plaster and goodness knows what else.'

'It might be stronger than you think. And it would give you more space.'

'But only if it didn't fall down in the process. It's not sensible, and I have space enough.'

'That's not what you've said before.'

'It's what I'll stick with. Space for writing. Space for sleeping and space for eating. What else do I need, in all honesty?'

Flora was silent. He wasn't being completely truthful, she knew, but as always she shied away from talking of their future and wasn't about to challenge him. She'd begun to understand that though Jack, now in his late thirties, enjoyed being godfather to Kate and Tony's small daughter, the future for him meant children of his own. For Flora, however, having lost parents and an unborn sibling at far too young an age, the idea of creating a family remained discomfiting.

Quick to change the topic, she said, 'After yesterday, after the doorbell, you won't go visiting Nelson again, will you?'

'Why not? The doorbell will be mended – and there'll be no problem.'

'The bell might not be a problem, but something else could. You were in real danger yesterday and you could be again. Please don't go back.'

'Anyone could have rung that bell. There's no reason to think I'm being targeted.'

'But Leo Nelson is. If it was Edwin Brooker who tampered with the wiring, he won't stop there. Whatever his reason, he's out to get Leo – or Neil – and I don't want you in his way.'

'I wish Alan Ridley was back at his desk,' Jack said suddenly, pouring them both second cups of tea. 'I could hand over what little we've discovered and know it would be put to good use. Anyway, about Brooker – maybe he just wanted to give Leo a shock, a reprisal for daring to join the Grove society under Trevor's auspices. Now he's done it, he'll leave him alone. Brooker is the chairman again, he'll have plenty to keep him busy. And talking of being busy.' He looked at his watch. 'We should be going soon. Cary Grant won't wait.'

'He'll have to,' she said flatly. 'I've a second scone to finish and this jam is delicious.'

14

Thomasina Bell, it turned out, lived in a sprawling, semi-detached house to the north of the town, with a sewing room that took up half of the rear garden. The studio, as Thomasina had called it, was a chalet-style construction – certainly far superior to the shed that Flora had imagined – and built of cedarwood, with a short flight of steps to a wrap-around veranda. A metal picnic table and chairs had been pushed to one end – it was hardly picnic weather – and ornamented wooden flower boxes, now empty, sat neatly on either side of the sliding door. The whole was as perfectly fitted as Thomasina herself.

The seamstress was bent over an enormous square table and slicing through a length of cloth with a pair of sharp scissors. She looked up as she heard Flora's footsteps at the door.

'Come in, Mrs Carrington. I'll be finished very soon.'

She waved her visitor into a sweet-smelling interior: woody and warm with subtle hints of spice. That was the cedarwood, Flora imagined, breathing in the aroma of rich, deep forest.

Thomasina's scissors slid through the material with ease

and, with a few expert flicks, she'd folded the two halves into uniform squares and laid them to one side.

'Have you decided what you want?' she asked, in a tone that suggested it would be well for Flora if she had. Thomasina's time was evidently precious.

'I thought a woollen tea dress,' she replied.

'A little vague, Mrs Carrington. Colour?'

'Blue, maybe.'

Thomasina pursed a pair of cherry red lips and shook her head. 'With your colouring, you should go for green. A deep green, I think. Conifer.'

'I'll take your advice,' she accepted meekly.

'And wool? What weight should it be? How warm do you want to feel?'

'The dress will be for Christmas.' It was a credible reason for this sudden order.

The seamstress tutted. 'You'll be lucky to have it by Christmas,' she warned. 'We're already in early December and my order book is full.'

'New Year, then,' Flora said a trifle feverishly.

In truth, she doubted she would ever go ahead with the wretched dress. It was likely to prove far too costly and, once this fitting was over, she could telephone to cancel. By the sound of it, Thomasina had more than enough orders and a cancellation would hardly be a disaster.

'Go behind the screen and undress to your petticoat,' she ordered, and Flora did as she was asked.

'You have a good figure,' Thomasina admitted, expertly girdling Flora with a tape measure. 'Really, you should make more of it.'

What that meant, Flora had no idea, but she was happy to pounce on the suggestion. 'Perhaps I need one of those Tudor costumes,' she joked, hoping it would take her where she wanted to go. 'All those tight bodices and low necklines.'

'You would have to join Bonfire to wear one.'

'I've thought about it,' she lied. 'Since we've been living in Lewes. How many people join every year?'

'A few,' Thomasina said offhandedly.

'It must be fun to be part of the procession,' she gabbled. 'To be right in the middle of such a huge event – and this year, from a tractor! Were you able to see much of what was going on? I don't remember seeing you at the front of the float.'

'I could have been,' she said tersely, 'but I chose not to.'

'Don't say you let the men have all the glory! Mr Brooker and Trevor French – I saw *them* that night. It must have been so scary when Mr French fell. You were very swift to react.'

'Someone had to. The rest of the group were standing around like dummies.'

'Did none of them come to help? I don't remember.'

'Eventually,' she said, clearly bored with the subject.

'Mr Brooker and Leo Nelson – they were standing on either side of Trevor French, weren't they? Mr Brooker on the left and Leo on the right.' Their positions on the float were crucial and Thomasina, standing some rows behind the men, might be a witness with whom Inspector Brownlow couldn't quarrel.

Thomasina frowned. 'Why are you so interested?'

'It was such an upsetting evening. I keep replaying it in my head. I can't seem to stop.'

'You should. Much better to forget what you saw,' she advised. 'Right, I have all the measurements I need and you can get dressed now. I'll leave you to choose your material. There's a very nice bolt of dark green merino on my top shelf that might suit.'

A few minutes later, emerging fully clothed from behind the screen, Flora took in for the first time the range of materials Thomasina stocked. Shelves had been fitted to all four of the studio's walls and were filled with fabrics of every kind: serge and worsted for winter, cottons and linen for summer, and beautiful silks for every season. But despite the profusion, each bolt of cloth sat trim and tidy, stacked in a geometry of neat columns.

The dark green merino that Thomasina had mentioned was a gorgeous colour and, holding a swathe of it to her face, Flora saw immediately that the woman had been right – the green was the perfect shade to set off the copper of her hair and bring it alive.

'This would be perfect,' she said, earning an approving look from the seamstress.

'Now, the pattern,' Thomasina said briskly. 'A nipped-in waist, I think, and a big skirt. Yes, I can see that working well. Here.' She pushed a pattern book towards Flora. 'You'll find something suitable in there.'

She had just begun to flick through a bewildering variety of tea dresses – most of them, it seemed, sporting nipped-in waists and big skirts which wasn't exactly helpful – when a telephone rang. Flora hadn't noticed it before, tucked away on a small ledge that sat between two walls, but its presence made sense. The studio was a business premises and a businesswoman needed to communicate with her clients.

Leaving the pattern book open at a dress she thought might flatter, if she were to change her mind and go ahead with the order, she waited for the conversation to end. Had her visit here been worthwhile? she pondered, her eyes on Thomasina. She had learned very little and might end up paying a hefty bill for that little. Despite her best efforts, she'd been unable to persuade Thomasina to talk of anything beyond her trade. But she refused to fret; she doubted anyone could have done better.

While the seamstress continued to talk on the telephone – her voice had undergone a subtle change, softer, more emollient – Flora walked over to the chair set aside for clients. An enormous bouquet of flowers adorned the nearby coffee table and a card was propped against the hand-painted glass vase. Still keeping her eye on Thomasina, she bent to read it. The flowers had come from a florist in Steyning, Beautiful Bunches. She remembered the name from Aunt Violet's yearly bouquets, sent by an unknown admirer, and from the first investigation that she and Jack had undertaken. They had been at odds most of that time, she recalled, smiling to herself, yet both of them had known in their hearts, even then, that they were destined to be together.

The message was typed and easily legible. *I hope you enjoy these few flowers*, it read. Few? The vase contained a veritable greenhouse. *They come with my very best wishes and with hope.* It was signed – *Edwin*. What! Flora had quickly to wipe the astonished expression from her face, but the questions came thick and fast. Edwin was hardly a common name. The card must have come from Edwin Brooker but what was Brooker doing sending flowers to Miss Bell? And what was the hope he had?

Thomasina had finished her call and was looking pleased. 'That was Mr Nelson,' she announced. 'He's a darling!'

Flora blinked. The surprises kept coming and she was feeling unnerved. 'You're...?' she began tentatively.

'Such a gentleman,' Thomasina gushed. 'The kind of man a girl needs, don't you think?'

Putting aside the fact that Thomasina had said goodbye to girlhood some years previously, the announcement left Flora struggling to respond. All she could do was simper inanely and retrieve her handbag, ready to leave. Any idea of requesting an estimate had taken flight.

'I'll telephone the All's Well,' Thomasina promised, seeing her to the door. 'When I have something for you to try. You'll be at the Abbeymead shop?'

'Yes,' she murmured. 'I'm there every day very shortly.' But how did Thomasina know she was moving back to Abbeymead?

It wasn't Flora's only question as she walked down the hill and back to their college apartment, her mind badly unsettled. Why was Edwin Brooker sending the seamstress flowers? And that phone call from Leo Nelson. Was *he* courting her, too? Were the two men rivals and that was the meaning of the dangerous doorbell? It sounded a convincing motive.

If so, what about Lilian French? Nelson had been *her* boyfriend all those years ago and since her husband died, he'd visited Glebe Avenue daily. According to Lilian, he'd even suggested she go to Australia with him. So, what *were* his true feelings?

Such a tangle, Flora mused, half walking, half running, down the steep hill that led to Cleve College, and with no evident path ahead. Brooker's flowers – maybe they were the next step; but when Jack had mentioned casually that he might go looking for Brooker once more, she had asked him not to. After his injury at Overlay House, she hadn't wanted him near a man who could be dangerous.

But Brooker was the one to talk to, Flora could see. Perhaps *she* could do it instead. She might have more luck in getting the man to talk. At this, she pulled a face. She hadn't been exactly successful with Thomasina. But Brooker might not see her as a threat, whereas Jack...

∾

Unbeknown to Flora, Jack had pre-empted her. The more he'd thought about Edwin Brooker and the likelihood that under police questioning he would lie to protect himself, the more he'd realised he needed to get to him first, before he signed any witness statement. Hopefully, there was still time. Inspector

Brownlow hadn't struck Jack as a particularly active officer. If Brooker *had* been the one to mess with Leo's wiring, then it was something that Jack could hold over him: tell the police the truth, he could say – that you stood to the left of Trevor French on that float and stayed there – or I'll be telling them what I suspect.

Just before four that afternoon, his last student of the day packed away her notes and left him free for the next few hours. Instead of making his way to the staffroom for the obligatory cup of tea, Jack donned his overcoat and walked through the college grounds to the ornamental gates and, from there, up the hill that led to the high street. Following the road until it dwindled to a narrow thoroughfare, he arrived at Foundry Lane once more.

Brooker was already closing up. Evidently, in the winter months he kept limited hours. Jack retreated to the shelter of a nearby building, watching as the man locked the shop door, top and bottom. He had hoped to discover just what Brooker had told the police and maybe what, if anything, he'd had to do with the damaged wiring. Not that he expected to get a straight answer, let alone an honest one, but seeing the way the man responded might offer a clue.

Watching Brooker as he turned his key in the bottom lock, Jack had second thoughts. Rather than confront him at his place of business, it might be sensible to follow him. It was too early for the pubs to be open and it was likely that he'd be going home. Knowing where exactly Brooker lived might be useful.

His house, Jack soon discovered, was just a short walk away, one of a terrace of cottages built by the riverside. It would be prone to regular flooding, he reckoned, but nevertheless an attractive setting, the river and its assorted wildlife – swans, ducks, the occasional kingfisher – providing a moving picture from the cottage windows.

Brooker disappeared through his front door but Jack remained where he was, invisible in the darkening light, and thinking what best to do. Challenge the man immediately or take a look around? There was a gate to the side of the cottage that was tempting him. He tiptoed over and carefully felt the latch. Unlocked. Edging the gate half open, he slid through the gap into what was a fair-sized rear garden. A wooden shed stood at the end of a short path and, still walking as quietly as he could, he reached its safety within seconds. From behind the shed, he was certain he could not be seen from the house.

Peering through its filmy windows, Jack made out a jumble of old furniture, damaged pictures and half-used pots of paint – but tools, too. Brooker, he recalled, had been in prime position if he'd wanted to kill Trevor French, and had a strong motive to do so. As far as Jack knew, the murder weapon had not yet been discovered, so could there be a knife in the midst of that jumble? He had to find out. And that meant finding a way in.

Gently, he tried the door to the shed which proved similarly unlocked and, thanking his good fortune, Jack whisked himself inside. Surrounded by so much debris, he could see that he'd find it difficult to move, let alone search. But was that a bag of tools a few paces away? An open bag at that. Edging towards his prize, Jack leaned across and lifted the bag, staggering beneath its sudden weight. Somehow, he managed to empty its contents across what little space existed and began systematically to sort through every item. How lucky that he'd worn gloves! But nothing resembling a knife came to hand and, with a sigh, he replaced hammers, screwdrivers and wrenches.

Standing back, his eyes roved around the space. There was another bag, he saw, smaller this time, lying on the floor some yards away and lodged between copies of *The Stag at Bay* and *When Did You Last See Your Father*, two pictures you would never want on your wall. Wriggling his way around and over assorted broken chairs, he found the bag tightly zipped. A padlock winked mockingly at him. Why was this bag locked, if not for security? It had to be worth investigating – it was a hammer he needed.

Inching himself back through the melee of broken wood to the original bag, he retrieved the strongest-looking tool he could find and had begun hammering at the padlock when a voice spoke from the doorway.

'Mr Carrington? What on earth are you doing?'

Jack swung around. Inspector Brownlow was framed in the doorway.

'You're on private property,' the inspector said, his tone officious. 'And causing damage.'

'Private property,' Brooker echoed, appearing at the policeman's shoulder. 'Breaking and entering, that's what you're guilty of.'

'I'm guilty of entering,' Jack agreed placidly, 'but not breaking. The door was unlocked.'

'You're guilty of trespass, Mr Carrington.' The inspector's expression was thunderous.

'And damaging private property,' the electrician added.

'A few dents in a padlock,' Jack countered.

'You've no right to be here.' Brooker seemed to have grown to twice his size. 'And it looks like you were planning to steal.'

'Steal? From this jumble?'

'Steal!' Brooker repeated angrily. He pointed to the hammer. 'That's evidence.'

The inspector elbowed his companion aside. 'You're to come with me,' he said, trying to get a foot through the door, but faced with a mountain of rubbish. 'Down to the station.'

'What!'

Jack was shocked. Until this moment, he had been playing along, thinking how ridiculous this charade was. True, he'd been caught red-handed, but embarrassment had been his overriding emotion, nothing more serious. Edwin Brooker would seek to punish him, Jack was sure, but that was for the future. Now, though, the situation wore a far more threatening face.

'To the station, Mr Carrington,' Brownlow repeated. 'You have questions to answer.'

'If the police don't prosecute you, I will,' the electrician stormed. 'I'll take you to court.'

'And our friend here would have every right,' the inspector muttered, taking Jack by the arm and marching him to the waiting police car.

15

Flora looked up at the kitchen clock, a wartime utility model of cream Bakelite and bold figures that the college had not yet decided to replace. Whatever the model, it told her that Jack was late. Very late. He'd had several appointments this afternoon, she knew, but could one of his students be so eager they were still discussing their work with him? It seemed unlikely. Perhaps she should walk over to the elegant Queen Anne mansion that housed the majority of the college rooms and check, but she shrank from appearing an anxious wife.

Shovelling the tray of pork chops back into the temperamental oven – for once it had cooked the meat to perfection – she sat down at the kitchen table and waited. It was another half an hour, however, before she heard his key in the lock. The chops would be almost inedible, she mourned silently, but at least he was safely home.

Shrugging off his overcoat, Jack threw his fedora onto the hatstand, straddling the curly hook at his first attempt, a skill that Flora had never managed to emulate.

'I'm sorry,' were his first words.

She jumped up, walking over to give him a hug. 'Is there a

reason you're so late?' Then standing back, she looked closely at him. 'Something's happened, I can see by your face. What's happened?'

He gave her a wry smile. 'I was arrested.'

'Jack!'

'But not charged,' he reassured her. 'Unless, in future, Brooker decides to take me to court.'

'Brooker? You've been to see him? Sit down and tell me everything. I'll make tea.'

He slumped down into a kitchen chair. 'But dinner?'

'The chops must be ruined so you might as well have a drink first.'

'Sorry,' he said again and, while Flora made tea for them both, he recounted his adventures of that afternoon.

What Jack told her left Flora deeply worried and, joining him at the table, she reached for his hands, needing to feel their strength. 'You were taken to Brighton police station?'

He nodded.

'What does that mean? What will happen to you?'

He stroked her hands, trying again to reassure. 'Hopefully, not a lot. Trespass is a civil not a criminal offence, and the police can't prosecute. As for criminal damage? A few dents in an old padlock. Brooker can sue, of course, but it takes money to start legal proceedings. My feeling is that he'll try to punish me in some other way.'

'That's even more scary.'

'I get the feeling that he's a man who uses his muscle to intimidate, but keeps clear of direct confrontation. If it was Brooker who tampered with the wiring – and, I agree, he's the likely culprit – it was damage done at a distance. And if he killed, I reckon it would be slyly.'

'But that could prove worse. Something cowardly,' she prophesied, 'like the weapon that was slid into Trevor French. Do you think there was a knife in that zipped bag?'

'Who knows? There could have been. I wasn't given the opportunity to search.'

'And Inspector Brownlow certainly won't,' she said crossly. 'Why was he at Brooker's house, anyway?'

'The inspector was a model of discretion and I learned nothing! I'm assuming, and it is only an assumption, that he was there to get Brooker's witness statement, which I'm sure will claim that, at some point in the procession, Leo Nelson moved his position on the float to stand to the left of Trevor French.'

'Which means we haven't progressed an inch, and to make matters worse, you have a police record now! Jack, I wish you hadn't gone to that house this afternoon.'

'I wish I hadn't, but it's too late to be sorry, sweetheart – water under the bridge, I'm afraid.'

'I was planning to speak to Edwin Brooker myself,' she said, getting up to peer into the oven, 'but I'm thinking that after today it's wiser to keep my distance.' She pulled the tray of chops towards her. 'They don't look too bad – will you try them? I've cooked a few roasties and a really nice cauliflower.'

'I'm starving. I'll eat anything.' Then, seeming to realise that wasn't the most diplomatic response, he added hastily, 'I'm sure dinner will be fine. Why were you intending to talk to Brooker? I'm glad you're not, by the way.'

'I went for my fitting with Thomasina Bell this afternoon and learned a few things. Guess who's sending her bouquets?'

'Not Brooker?'

'The very same.' Flora closed her eyes to the plight of the wizened chops and ladled them, along with vegetables and gravy, onto two plates. 'There's something going on between those two.'

'He wants her as a girlfriend? I can't see that working out. But this looks good,' he lied, picking up his knife and fork to do valiant battle.

'If Brooker wants her for himself, then so does Leo Nelson, I think. He telephoned her while I was there and Thomasina literally gushed. And *that* relationship doesn't make any sense.'

Jack's eyebrows formed a question mark.

'Lilian,' she said. 'Lilian French. She told me that Leo calls in to see her every day and that he's asked her to go to Australia with him. I had the impression it was a holiday trip she was talking about, but still...'

Jack's knife remained suspended. 'If Leo *is* courting this dressmaker, it puts to bed your suggestion that he came back from Australia in order to kill Trevor French and purloin his wife. Not that I ever thought that likely. When we're back in Abbeymead, I'll talk to Leo again. Maybe discover what he's really up to with these women. This is actually OK, by the way.' He pointed to his plate, now a little emptier.

'I don't think you should go to Overlay House. You could land in trouble – there could be another Edwin Brooker moment.'

She saw a stubborn expression settle on his face and added, 'If you must go, wait until Ross Sadler rings with any information he's found.'

'What if he finds nothing?'

'Then we stop being super sleuths and leave it to Inspector Brownlow.'

'Really?'

'Yes, really. The only reason you started the investigation was because you thought Leo Nelson innocent and in danger of being wrongly accused. Yet ever since, the man has looked murkier and murkier.'

Jack laid his cutlery aside. 'OK,' he agreed. 'I'll wait for Ross to ring.'

∽

It was Sunday morning before the call came from Ross Sadler. Jack was looking for a pair of wellingtons he was sure he'd stored in the understairs cupboard when the telephone shrilled from the hall. A light dusting of snow early this morning had encouraged Flora to suggest a walk and he'd been persuaded to take a stroll before lunch through Church Spinney and up Fern Hill to the golf club.

'Sorry for ringing on a Sunday morning, Jack, but it's been a trifle hectic here,' his friend began.

'It's good to hear from you any day. Did you get to Berkshire? Did you get your story?'

'And how! A real blockbuster. Went out yesterday, the second article on the front page.' Jack made approving noises. 'But despite all the hoo-hah, I managed a few minutes in the archives. I was lucky – a colleague here was driving to north London and I bagged a lift.'

'And? Was there anything worth finding?' In his heart, Jack hadn't believed there would be. Leo Nelson had been out of the country for years and, before then, had led what appeared to be a blameless life.

'The name of Neil Leonard, manager of a Chichester hardware store, came up in just one report,' Ross said briefly. 'In the *Chichester Herald*. It was a report of an accident.'

'What kind of accident? How was Neil Leonard involved?' Jack had come alive.

'One thing at a time, old chap. It was a road accident in the south of Chichester and Leonard was the car driver. The date was June 1938.'

Just before he left for Australia? Jack's mind queried. 'And?'

'And he hit two people, a mother and young daughter.'

He felt a sickening lurch in his stomach. Ross had certainly come up with information, but it was difficult to hear. 'They both died?'

'To be honest, I'm not sure. One of them, at least, judging

by the charge. It was a single report and focused primarily on the court case that followed. Leonard stood trial for causing death by dangerous driving, but the jury acquitted him and he walked free.'

'On what grounds was he acquitted?'

'A witness testified to the fact that the child ran out into the road after a ball she'd dropped and her mother followed, rushing to rescue her. As far as the witness could judge, Nelson was driving at a legal speed but, at the time, coming out of a bend. He had no chance of seeing the pair before he hit them.'

'I see... thanks, Ross.'

'Helpful?'

'It probably will be,' he hedged, 'and thanks again for giving up precious time to research it.'

'For an old chum, my pleasure. So, when are you coming up to London again? Let's make it soon!'

Jack murmured something suitable and rang off. Ross's information had landed like a bombshell, but was it in any way helpful? His mind tried to make sense of it. Nelson, or rather Leonard, if this was his name, had been involved in a terrible accident, an accident that had happened out of the blue but, with very bad luck, could have happened to any driver. He'd killed someone and then stood trial, the possibility of a long prison sentence hanging over him. Huge life events.

Harrowing events which, it was possible, had been responsible for sending the man into exile, travelling thousands of miles to a new life in Australia, yet Nelson had never once referred to this traumatic episode. Never mentioned it in conversation. But then why would he? Would he, Jack, tell a chance acquaintance of a calamity that had rocked his world, as it must have done Nelson's?

Nevertheless, there was a lack of openness that Jack couldn't like. It had only been through a string of accidental revelations that he now knew what he did. If he'd not brushed against that table and seen Nelson's will, he would never have known the man was masquerading under a false name. If he hadn't been shown a picture of a hardware store – Nelson's pride getting the better of his discretion? – Jack wouldn't have known his trade and been able to pass on the information to Ross. And if Lilian hadn't confided in Flora that Nelson had once been her boyfriend, they wouldn't have known even to search the Chichester newspapers for a mention.

Lilian, he thought. Perhaps talking to her might throw more light on what Nelson was up to. The man himself had been resolute in revealing nothing of his earlier life and was unlikely to be persuaded into confiding now.

Pulling his boots from their hiding place at the very back of the cupboard, Jack wondered if his wife could once more use her charm – on Lilian French.

16

It had been a peaceful weekend. Apart from their brisk walk in the snow, now no more than slush, Flora had spent much of her time making chutney with the apples she'd been storing since autumn. Kate's recipe had proved complicated, demanding her full attention, so it was as well that for most of his weekend Jack had squirrelled himself away in the spare room, the typewriter his sole companion. By Sunday evening, amazingly, he had written his way to the denouement of *Another Way to Die*.

Unlocking the wide front door of the All's Well just before nine on Monday morning, Flora was feeling happy. Tomorrow, they would drive back to Lewes for what would be their last but one week in the cheerless college apartment. A moment then of undiluted pleasure. Half in and half out of the door, she was surprised to hear cycle wheels pulling up at the kerb. Betty had been safely parked in the cobbled courtyard adjacent to the shop and it was her assistant that Flora saw, as she turned to greet the newcomer.

'Rose! How lovely to see you! These days, it feels as though we're ships that pass in the night. I was going to leave you a note about the new Agatha Christie. I had a few ideas of how we might display *Cat Among the Pigeons*. But... are you feeling OK?'

Rose's face had largely been hidden by the wide brim of her cloche hat but, as she pulled it off, Flora noticed how pale she looked, her cheeks chalk white.

'I'm not ill,' she reassured Flora. 'It's just this wretched pain in my back. I tried to carry a box down to the cellar – on Thursday, it was – and felt this really sharp spasm. It's been hurting ever since.'

'Why didn't you ring me? You can't work when you're in pain.' Flora thought rapidly. Could she pull out of her reading classes at Riverdale this week at such short notice?

'I'll be fine in the shop. Honestly,' she added, when Flora looked doubtful. 'As long as I don't carry anything. I'm working at the post office this morning, so I have to be OK. But it's the deliveries. Perhaps I shouldn't have, but I promised several customers that I'd deliver their books this week. I was going to leave you a note about it, but now I don't think I can manage Betty *and* the books.'

'Don't even think of it. I had no idea you intended to start a delivery round again.'

'I didn't, but then some of the more elderly villagers came to the shop – or rather hobbled to the shop,' she said, a slight smile on her face, 'especially to ask if I could. And I felt obliged. But you're not to worry. I think I've sorted it out – Charlie has agreed to help. I came by this morning to warn you that he'd be here on Friday.'

'Charlie? But surely he'll be working. He must be full-time at the Priory.'

'Not quite, I believe. Officially, he's still training but he no longer goes to the Nook on a Friday afternoon, so he's free for a few hours. He's promised me he'll come back to do the deliveries, for a while at least, until Sally asks him to work Friday evenings.'

'It will be a walk back to the past having Charlie delivering again. I'm not sure Betty will be too pleased, though.' Charlie's treatment of the ancient bicycle had been cavalier, to say the least. 'But Rose, should you be working at all, if you're in such pain?'

'I've taken aspirin and... really, I can't afford not to. I'll be here tomorrow, Flora, don't worry. Only a few more weeks and you'll be back yourself.'

There was anxiety in her voice and Flora realised that they had never properly discussed how she and Rose would manage sharing the shop once she was back in Abbeymead full time.

'When I get back from Lewes this week, we must talk,' she murmured. 'Set up a timetable between us.'

But, with a wave of her hand, Rose had already mounted her bicycle and was heading in the direction of the post office. Flora hoped that Dilys, their acerbic postmistress, might discover a hidden well of kindness today.

Mechanically, she began the daily chores: dusting shelves, tidying books, checking orders and, deciding as she did, that she would leave *Cat Among the Pigeons* until the end of the week. Perhaps Jack could come in for an hour to help carry up the several large boxes she'd seen in the cellar. In the middle of imagining a new display for the books, the shop bell rang. She looked up, ready to greet her first customer of the day, and her eyes widened. Inspector Ridley, of all people!

'Mrs Carrington.' Courteously, he raised his trilby. 'Or I should say, Flora.' He cleared his throat. 'I'm glad to see you looking so well.'

'And you,' she responded, though the skin around his eyes bore dark circles. His moustache, she noticed, had grown since their last meeting, though still lacking in flamboyance. 'But your mother?'

'Better, thank you, much better. She's out of hospital now and staying with me for the time being.'

'And you're back to work?' she hazarded.

'Not quite. I still need to be at home for much of the day and I'm working part-time. Working my way back into the job, as it were, gradually taking over from my replacement.'

'Inspector Brownlow.' She hoped her face was expressionless.

'Yes, Brownlow,' he said thoughtfully. 'I hear from my colleagues at the station that Jack has run into a spot of bother with the inspector.'

Ridley knew of the Brooker incident then. It must have become the talk of Brighton police and Flora was unsure how best to reply.

Alan Ridley rescued her. 'Sounds like a storm in a teacup to me, but I wouldn't want your husband landing himself in serious trouble.'

'Can you lose the report that mentions him?' she asked boldly.

'Mrs Carrington!' He looked slightly shocked, but then relaxed. 'Lose it, I can't, but I can add a rider. A paragraph or two that might soften the effect of the official account. Lessen any idea of deliberate trespass and intent to steal.'

'Thank you, Inspector. I'd be grateful.' And for the first time in their somewhat fractious acquaintance, Flora *was* truly grateful.

'Is Jack anywhere around?' he enquired, his gaze roaming across the rows of bookshelves, as though expecting her husband to emerge from his hiding place.

'He's at the cottage – preparing for a lecture he's giving tomorrow.'

The inspector nodded and was silent for a moment. 'Would he mind if I interrupted him, do you think?' he asked at last.

'I don't think he'd mind at all. You should pay him a visit,' she said warmly.

He would be delighted, Flora knew. Anyone else, perhaps,

might receive a less than enthusiastic greeting, but Jack had been desperate to talk to Alan Ridley for days.

Raising his hat again, he said, 'I'll be off then. I'll tootle along to the cottage. It's been good to say hello, Mrs Carr— Flora.'

'Send my best wishes to Mrs Ridley,' she called out, as he disappeared into the high street.

Flora wished she was going with him. Wished that she could have her ear to the sitting room door – it was a conversation she would have liked very much to hear.

The sound of the knocker had Jack pause mid-thought. Cursing, he took a while before he inched himself from his writing chair and walked down the stairs to discover who was his annoying caller.

'Good grief!' he exclaimed, when he opened the door to a smiling Ridley.

'Unexpected visitor, eh? I won't stop if it's a difficult time.'

'No, come in, come in.' He almost dragged the policeman over the threshold. 'Let me take your coat. And a drink? Tea, coffee, something stronger?'

'It's cold enough. Bitterly cold today. And I'm not strictly on duty. A snifter would be good,' he admitted.

'Whisky it is, then.'

Jack led the way into the sitting room and, delving into the cupboard of shabby glasses that had accompanied him from Overlay House, brought out two odd tumblers. He poured a hefty slug of whisky into each – this was a visit to celebrate.

'And how is Mrs Ridley?'

'Much better,' the inspector repeated. 'Still finding her way, but improving slowly. Which is more than I can say for you. What the hell have you been doing, Jack?'

'You mean the Brooker incident?'

'There are more?'

He grinned. 'Just the one arrest. Not really an arrest since Brownlow couldn't charge me with anything.'

'But this Edwin Brooker can. He can bring a civil case against you for trespass.'

'He can, but he won't,' Jack said confidently. 'It would be far too costly and I caused no damage.'

'Brownlow's report suggests you were there to steal. That's a serious business.'

'Poppycock. I stole nothing. What was there to steal? All I was doing was looking through the rubbish Brooker keeps in his shed.'

Alan Ridley took a first sip of his whisky. 'You'd better tell me the whole story.'

And for the next half hour, Jack laid out every detail he could remember from the moment Trevor French had fallen from the society's float, to his electrocution by doorbell, to his conviction that Brooker would lie under oath to implicate Leo Nelson who, in fact, was probably a man called Neil Leonard.

'Whoa!' Ridley held up his glass as though to stop the flow of information. 'First things first. Or rather last things first. Why were you in Brooker's shed? What were you looking for?'

'I never meant to look,' he confessed. 'I followed the bloke from work, thinking I'd doorstep him at home. Try to persuade him to give an honest account of Bonfire Night – I'm pretty sure Brownlow won't question anything the man chooses to say. But then I saw there was a gate to the back garden and, when I found it open, decided to take a look around before I knocked on his door. The shed, when I got to it, was unlocked and a quick search seemed a good idea.'

The inspector raised his eyebrows at this.

'I thought I'd be in and out in minutes,' Jack excused himself. 'It was when I saw the bag of tools that it came to me. A knife could be hidden there among the pliers and screwdrivers. As far as I know, the police have never found the murder weapon.'

'And?'

'There wasn't a knife,' he said sadly, 'just the tools of Brooker's trade. But then I caught sight of another bag and that one was padlocked – it seemed a definite possibility.'

'That was the padlock you were trying to hammer open?'

Jack nodded.

'I have to tell you there was nothing untoward in that bag either. Brownlow has searched the shed since your little adventure.'

'Trying to implicate me, no doubt.'

'Whether he was or not, he found no knife. You've been barking up the wrong tree, Jack.'

There was silence for several minutes until Jack suddenly broke it. 'I'm not sure you're right in that. Brooker could have got rid of the knife. Thrown it into the river on Bonfire Night, minutes after he'd stabbed French. The man had a strong motive to kill. He hated Trevor French; he was furious the man had supplanted him as chairman of Grove. *And* he was standing side by side with French on that float. He's ruthless, too – witness my electrocution. I'm certain it was Brooker who rewired Nelson's front doorbell to be dangerous.'

'Concentrating on Edwin Brooker means you're losing the bigger picture,' Ridley counselled. 'You can't assume, for instance, that this Nelson is the innocent you believe. *He* was on that float, too, standing side by side with French. He could have easily manoeuvred himself to be in the right place to strike the fatal blow. And apparently – I've just learnt from you – he could be masquerading under a false name. Why would he do that, if he's entirely innocent?'

'I think there's a reason. He was involved in an accident years ago – 1938 in Chichester. A mother and daughter were run down. I think both of them must have died. Nelson – or Leonard – was charged with dangerous driving but acquitted because the child ran out into the path of the car, followed by her mother, and he had no means of stopping in time. I guess he's changed his name to stay anonymous. He doesn't want people remembering.'

'It's still a lie.'

'It is and he lied as well about coming from Lewes. I don't think he ever lived in the town as he claimed. He was living and working in Chichester at the time of the accident. But that was part of his cover-up, I guess.' He paused. 'It doesn't make him guilty of murder, Alan.'

'It doesn't make him innocent, either. What do you know of him between the accident twenty years ago and when he turned up here?'

'Very little. He's been in Australia the whole of that time. He and his brother set up a hardware store, very successfully, I believe, in a small town there.'

'Hardware? So, he deals with knives.'

'And a host of other tools. I think he must have taken off for Australia after the court case. Is there any way you can discover when he actually left England?'

'I can ask for records from the port authority. He would have sailed from Southampton, I imagine. If you think it will help.'

'I'm not sure it will. I'm scrabbling around, that's the truth. I like the man, want to help him, but he's not very good at helping himself. Can you check as well when he returned? The date he landed back at Southampton.'

'You're going to be very disappointed if Brownlow turns out to be right about him,' Ridley remarked, drinking down the rest of his whisky and getting up to leave.

Jack walked with him into the hall. 'I don't like the way he pounced on Nelson. He seemed to single him out, decide he was the perpetrator, and only then start looking for evidence, presumably to support his theory.'

'If he did do that, it would be a serious matter. Let's face it, Jack, you just don't like Brownlow.' There was a short silence before he added, 'But then, neither do I.'

'When are you properly back to work?'

'Very soon, I hope. Brownlow is handing over the investigation, bit by bit, but it's tricky. He's not the easiest man to deal with and Norris has decided he won't co-operate. He likes the man even less. None of it helps.'

'I can only wish you good luck. And the dates...?'

'You'll have them, old chap, never fear.'

17

Flora walked through the gates of Riverdale school the following morning after driving from Abbeymead, to be met by several teachers and a stream of children, all walking towards her.

'The school has had to close,' Miss Timpson, the school's musician, stopped to tell her. 'It might just be for the day, but the pipes froze last night and the girls' toilets have overflowed.'

'School's closed, school's closed,' a chorus of small voices chanted as their owners rushed past Flora, making for the gates.

She was disappointed, almost sad. It meant an unexpectedly free day, but she had only a few more to spend at Riverdale and she'd been looking forward to enjoying them. Volunteering at the school had been the most satisfying aspect of her life in Lewes. To encourage young children in a love for books, one she hoped would last them a lifetime, had been a joy. Once back in Abbeymead, the All's Well would become her world again and it was doubtful she would find very much time to visit the town, let alone the school.

'Put your feet up for the day,' another teacher advised laughingly, as she made her way to a parked car. 'I'm going to.'

It was a tempting notion, to return to the college flat, switch on every electric fire that Cleve had supplied, and hunker down. This morning when she'd tumbled from bed, it had been so cold in the apartment that her breath had misted the bathroom mirror and, at breakfast, she'd been forced to blow on her hands before she could pick up the slice of toast she'd buttered. Jack never felt the cold – that could be infuriating – but even he, she noticed, had gone back to the bedroom for a second jumper. She could return to the flat, but on the other hand...

The other hand won. She would visit Lilian French. Jack had seemed keen that she did so, and it was time the woman was honest about what exactly she knew of Leo Nelson, her former beau. And both Jack and she had agreed that Lilian must know far more than she'd admitted.

From Riverdale school to the house in Glebe Avenue, at the western edge of the town, was a good thirty-minute walk, but the day, though very cold, was crisp and windless and, as she strode along encumbered by nothing more than a small handbag, Flora began to enjoy the chill on her cheeks and the warmth in her limbs.

Turning the corner into the avenue, she could see that Lilian's front garden was looking more desolate than ever, though the house itself remained attractively cosy. A family house, Flora thought, allowing her mind to stray to a new home for herself and Jack. One day, she decided, one day, but not just yet.

Walking up the front path, she hoped to see some sign of life. She had taken pot luck that Lilian would be at home today since she'd no way of contacting her to check. But the days until Christmas were growing ever shorter and there was a strong possibility that Lilian had chosen this morning to go shopping in town. Flora knocked and waited, then knocked and waited again. No answer. Annoyingly, she would have to pay a second visit, although, once school resumed, finding time could be a problem.

Turning to retrace her steps and make her way back to Cleve College, she had a chance thought that maybe Lilian was in her back garden – hanging out clothes perhaps. It was a good day for drying and would certainly be worth checking. But when she walked through the side gate and looked around the generous space, there was no Lilian and no washing. She glanced towards the house. Still no sign of life, and she was about to admit defeat when she noticed that the kitchen window – she presumed it was the kitchen – had panes that were very misted. Steam from a kettle? Then Lilian must be at home, just not answering the door.

Flora walked up to the window and, leaning across the flower bed that ran beneath, peered into the room. A heavy fog hung in the air, but the kettle sat to one side of the counter. What on earth was that cloud then? Her glance moved on. The oven door was open... how strange and... and there was something on the floor. A body? Oh good Lord, it was a body! It was Lilian!

She ran to the back door, a few yards to the left of where she stood, but it was locked and far too thick to break down. Frantically, she rushed back to the window and tried to prise it open but, without an exterior latch, it was impossible. She would have to break the glass. Looking around the garden, she spotted a rockery and raced to dig out one of the lightest stones, then panting heavily, lumbered back to the window and hurled the small rock with all the strength she could muster. Shards of glass fell tinkling into the sink and onto the draining board. A small hole had been created but it was nowhere large enough for Flora to reach through and grasp the latch inside.

Another swift survey of the garden and she spotted the washing line and the forked wooden prop used to support it. The prop might just work. It had to work.

Heaving the wooden pole to the window, she pointed the flattened end at the glass and systematically pounded it back and forth, knocking out more and more of the window until she had widened the original hole sufficiently to allow her to reach in and grasp the latch.

It was stuck fast. Her fingers were shaking. Why, why, wouldn't it budge? Again and again, she depressed the latch and tried to force open what was left of the window until, exhausted, she had to stop. It was then, looking more closely at the exterior frame, that she saw the paint. Thick paint splashed down both sides, effectively gluing the window shut.

No wonder she'd failed. But somehow she had to gain entry. If she went in search of help, it might be too late. Exposed to the gas that must be pouring from the oven, Lilian could die at any moment. Dragging the prop upright again, Flora began breaking more glass until almost one entire pane of the window gaped wide – wide enough, she judged, for her to pass through. Quickly, the prop was thrown to one side and, grabbing hold of the drainpipe that ran alongside, she hauled herself up onto the sill, finding there a precarious resting place. Very gingerly, she stepped through the shattered window and onto the kitchen counter.

Rotten eggs. The smell hit her immediately. An overpowering smell of sulphur. A hissing from the open oven had her move as swiftly as her shaky limbs would allow and, jumping down from the counter, she rushed over to the gas stove and turned the dial. It had been set at its highest mark, she noticed. The fog hanging over the room had slowly begun to disappear as fresh air had flowed in, but Flora knew she had to let more in and quickly. Already, she was feeling light-headed and there was a ringing in her ears.

The kitchen door! She ran to it and turned the handle. But like the window, it refused to budge. Desperately, she grasped hold of the brass doorknob, turning and pulling. Pulling,

pulling, but without success. Had the door been painted shut, too? Try to think, she told herself, think clearly, though it was becoming more difficult by the minute. Not painted, but locked from the outside. So, was the key still in the lock?

Hurrying back to Lilian, she felt for her pulse. The poor woman was completely unconscious, still breathing but with a heartbeat that was very slow. There was another smell now hitting Flora's nose, a sickly-sweet smell, strong enough to vie with the gas. But she couldn't think about that now. She had to get Lilian to fresh air.

Pulling her as best she could across the kitchen tiles, Flora managed to lay the woman's limp body beneath the gap in the window, hoping the air that was now pouring through would at least keep Lilian alive. Her own heart was hammering in its effort to cope with the toxic air, but she must ignore how bad she felt and find a way out. She had to get that kitchen door open.

Facing the locked door, she bent down and with one eye closed, peered through the keyhole and was met with a chink of light. If the door *had* been locked from the outside, the key had disappeared and there was no chance of retrieving it. No key, but could she break through the door as she'd done through the window? The chance of success seemed minimal – houses of this period boasted solid wooden doors, and what could she use? A kitchen chair as a hammer? Unlikely. Some other implement perhaps? Just as unlikely.

Flora stood back, trying to breathe slowly, trying again to think clearly. Her gaze swept the room – a washed plate on the draining board, a pile of laundered dusters on the counter, a newspaper spread across the table. Lilian must have been reading it when... what had happened here? But there was no time to speculate. There was nothing she could use, Flora saw, as her gaze came full circle.

Apart from doors of solid wood, a house like this, she knew, would most often possess a spare key for each room. So, where might that kitchen spare be? She stared at the door, willing it to open, her frustration turning to hopelessness: looking up, looking down, to one side and then the other. Up! There was a ledge above the door, she realised suddenly, and from experience she knew it could be a hiding place.

Rushing over to the table, she grabbed a chair and hauled it to the door. From this new height, she was able to run her hand along the ledge and, midway, struck the cold steel of a key. Scrambling down, she was praying hard. It must fit. It must fit. But her hand was shaking so badly, it took far longer than it should have done to turn the key. But turn it did. And the door was open!

She was breathing more comfortably now, though still feeling as if her eardrums might burst at any moment. But how was poor Lilian French? Would she even survive? How long had the woman been lying there, in a closed room with a deadly gas spewing into her lungs?

It took Flora a renewed effort, one she could barely make, to drag the still unconscious body out of the kitchen – Lilian unresponsive and floppy to the touch – and onto the carpet by the front door, hoping she wasn't bruising the woman too badly. It was slow, painful work, but they were in the hall now. For a moment, Flora was overcome with weakness, her arms and legs seeming to lose all strength but, in a final push, she reached up to grasp the front doorknob. The door opened like a charm and, at last, she could breathe freely.

Leaving the door ajar and the air flowing through the house, she walked out into the road to look for help. There had been no telephone in the hall and she hadn't the time to go looking for one. An ambulance would, in any case, take a while to reach them. But she dared not leave Lilian for long, certainly not to go knocking on the neighbours' doors, and was relying on someone seeing her from their house – or on a passing motorist who'd be willing to stop if she walked into the road, waving her arms in distress.

Five minutes later, a small van hove into view. They had been five very long minutes but, as soon as Flora spotted the white shape moving slowly along Glebe Avenue, she ran into the road and began jumping up and down, her arms waving wildly.

The driver came to a halt and wound down his window. 'That's a dangerous thing to do, girlie,' he said. 'Right in the middle of the road.'

'I need help. The lady who lives there,' she said desperately, turning to gesture at the house, 'she needs help. Can you take us both to the hospital?'

It was only when she turned back and looked properly at the face of the driver that she froze. Edwin Brooker! How could that be?

18

Several hours later, sitting beside Lilian's hospital bed, Flora calculated the odds that Brooker's van would be driving down Glebe Avenue at precisely that moment. He could have been calling at a neighbour's house, as he'd insisted was the case, his tone truculent, when she'd begged and pleaded for him to take both her and the unconscious Lilian to the Victoria hospital, a fifteen-minute drive away.

It would hardly take him out of his way, she'd argued, and he'd be free to return to whatever job, fictional or otherwise, he was supposed to have that morning. After precious minutes of wrangling, he'd eventually agreed, but with a scowl and muttering darkly.

Once Flora had relinquished her burden into professional hands, she had sunk, relieved, into a waiting chair, intent on staying at the Victoria until she was sure that Lilian would make a good recovery. Thankfully, the medical team had been upbeat.

'She'll have a zinger of a headache, and probably some nausea and shortness of breath for a while,' the young doctor had told Flora, 'but hopefully, nothing more serious.' He'd looked at her searchingly. 'It's a very good job you decided to call on Mrs French when you did. Much more exposure and we'd be talking brain damage or...'

He left the sentence unfinished, but it was clear he'd meant death. Had that been the plan? Flora very much feared it had, but not from the suicide attempt the doctor obviously suspected. When the matron had questioned her as Lilian was rushed away for treatment, she'd pretended an accidental gas leak which, she'd promised, was being reported, saying nothing of the open oven, the locked kitchen door and the painted windows. Not to the hospital staff, at least. But to Inspector Ridley? She would make certain that he knew.

For most of the morning, Lilian dropped in and out of consciousness, watched over by an attentive nurse, while Flora tried to clear her head and think clearly what might have happened before she'd walked up the front path of the house in Glebe Avenue.

There'd been a deliberate attempt to harm the woman, it was clear. Someone had lured her into the kitchen perhaps, or maybe she'd answered the front door and taken her visitor there herself. It looked as though Lilian had been relaxing, reading the daily paper, so maybe she'd invited the unknown person in for a chat. There had been no sign of a shared drink, though, Flora recalled. Either the visitor had refused one or Lilian hadn't offered. Because... she didn't like whoever it was? Didn't expect or want the visit to be a long one?

Then what? Somehow, this villain had rendered Lilian unconscious, since she would hardly have laid herself down in front of an oven belching gas. But how could that have happened? That second smell! It was the sickly-sweet odour of chloroform, Flora realised. That was how it was done. Then the gas turned on full and left unlit, and the door locked from the outside – in case Lilian should gain consciousness and try to escape? What had happened to that key?

The painted windows, though. How did *they* come about? They must have been tampered with – earlier – in order to allow the paint to dry to an unyielding mass. Another potential escape route blocked. A careful, wicked plan then to harm, probably to kill, the poor woman who lay, white-faced, in the bed beside Flora.

Sometime in the early afternoon, she saw Lilian stir, not with the restless fidgeting of the morning as she'd sunk in and out of consciousness, but calmer this time with her eyes fully open. The patient gazed around, her expression fearful. When she tried to sit up, she failed, collapsing back onto the pillows.

'You'd be best to lie still, Lilian,' Flora said softly. 'You're in hospital. You've had an accident' – in Lilian's present state, the pretence was necessary – 'but you're OK, the doctor says.

'I'm Flora Carrington,' she went on. 'I was the one who found you. We have met before, a few weeks ago. I called at your house this morning, hoping to talk to you, but you were... ill... and you needed to be in hospital.'

Lilian reached out for Flora's hand. The gist of the speech seemed to have been understood. 'Thank you,' she whispered. 'Thank you. But I am so thirsty.'

'Here.' Flora poured a glass of water from the jug the nurse had left. 'Sip it slowly, though.' Lilian raised her head slightly, taking the glass from Flora, and drinking gratefully.

She lay back on the pillow, smiling slightly and seeming more comfortable. Now might be the time to ask the most pressing question, Flora thought.

'Do you remember what happened?' Surely she would know her attacker.

Lilian shook her head but after a while began to speak, her

voice weak and stumbling. 'I went to the front door.' She nodded to herself at the memory. 'There'd been a knock, but when I opened the door, there was no one. I turned to shut it.' She screwed up her eyes, trying to remember. 'The door stuck – I don't know why. And that's all I remember.'

'All?' Flora queried, keenly disappointed.

'All... except for the smell. It made me feel sick.'

'A sweet smell?' she tried.

'Horribly sweet.'

Flora sat back, still holding the woman's hand, and allowed her mind to wander. There had been no invitation into the kitchen for her murderous visitor, after all. Lilian must have been attacked at her front door. Chloroform, it had to be. A figure darting out of the bushes maybe and stuffing a pad against Lilian's nose as she turned back into the house. That's why she had seen no one. And the door sticking? Probably a foot wedging it open, making sure this wretch had access to the house.

Lilian would have collapsed in the hall and it would need some strength to move an unconscious body from the front door to the kitchen. So a man? Yet she had done it, hadn't she? Albeit in the other direction. But if it had been a man, Brooker for instance, who was roving the area at the time, he was muscular enough to have scooped up his victim and carried her to the kitchen.

'There is one thing that struck me as odd,' she said hesitantly. One thing? a caustic inner voice queried. 'The kitchen door was locked, but I found a key on the ledge above.'

'We always kept a spare there. We did for all the doors. Trevor said it was "just in case".'

The would-be murderer could not have known that a second key existed – a single hiccup in an otherwise ruthless plan. But maybe there would be more.

'Every door in the house has two keys?'

'It's a 1930s house – they tend to,' she said, sounding apologetic.

'And the other key?' The one that must have been used to lock the kitchen from the outside.

'I don't know.' Lilian looked dazed. 'Wasn't it in the door? It should have been.'

It hadn't been, which suggested that the attacker had locked the kitchen door from the outside and either pocketed the key or thrown it away. But all of this was conjecture and she wasn't likely to discover more from Lilian. What she could discover, though, were answers to the questions that she and Jack had been asking for the past few days. But only if Lilian were strong enough.

'Would you like me to tell anyone you're here, once I leave the hospital?' she began, aware that she must tread carefully.

'I don't have anyone to tell,' Lilian said tremulously. 'Now that Trevor has gone.'

'Leo Nelson, perhaps?'

'I don't think so. I wouldn't want to worry him. Leo has troubles of his own.'

'He does? That's not good. I wonder... would those troubles have anything to do with the fact that he's changed his name?'

In a sharp movement, Lilian twisted her head. She looked startled.

'I'm sorry,' Flora apologised. 'I didn't mean to upset you. It was something that Jack and I discovered quite by accident.'

That was a lie, but she didn't want this sick woman to be more worried than she already was. Knowing people were probing Nelson's past and maybe her own would be disquieting.

'But *you* knew, didn't you?' Flora asked gently. It was evident that she must have.

Lilian rearranged her limbs before she nodded. 'He was always Neil to me,' she said, sounding a trifle wobbly. 'Not when Trevor brought him back to the house and we said a first hello. He's over fifty now and that's very different from thirty. His hair has thinned badly and his skin – it looks leathery – the Australian sun, I imagine.'

'You didn't recognise him at all?'

'I was puzzled,' she admitted. 'There was something so familiar about him, something that made me feel I didn't need to ask him questions. I already knew the answers. But I just smiled and kept quiet. Then Trevor told me his name and I thought I must be wrong, but I wasn't.'

'Did Trevor know he was once your boyfriend?'

She gave the slightest shake of her head, as though even that was too much effort. 'Trevor wasn't the most observant person. When Neil first saw me, his eyes lit up. They really did! He'd recognised me, even though I hadn't recognised him. It was what started me wondering. I never told Trevor the truth and neither did Neil. It would have meant revealing who Leo Nelson really was.'

'And you kept his secret from everyone else. Why did you say nothing?'

'Neil didn't want it known. He told me why that was and I understood, but I was terribly worried all the time that I'd give him away. He was always alert for someone from the past recognising him. That's why, when he came back from Australia, he settled in Lewes rather than Chichester.'

'And then he moved to Abbeymead.'

'He was nervous. I think he thought the village would be safer. He'd be less likely to be recognised there. He'd travel into Lewes for society meetings, but then scurry back to Abbeymead.'

It must have been why the man had been so twitchy when Charlie Teague called at Overlay House, but then realised that the boy was far too young to have any knowledge of a twenty-year-old event.

There were further questions needing an answer, Flora

knew, but she was concerned for the patient. Looking across at Lilian, though, she saw that her colour had returned almost to normal and she was looking a good deal brighter. Perhaps a few more might be possible.

'Did Neil decide to adopt a different name,' she asked, 'because of the awful accident he was involved in?'

Lilian nodded again.

'And did you know about the accident?'

'No, honestly, I had no idea until he told me. No idea what had happened to him. He said that time of his life had been terrible – the court case, being in the newspapers, and people outside his shop shouting abuse. Even throwing stones at him. I felt really sad hearing what he'd gone through.'

'And that decided you to keep his secret?'

'What else could I do?' She paused, sinking a little lower in the bed. 'That day when Trevor first brought him home,' she went on, 'and I had this odd feeling about him, I watched when he left our house. Watched him walk down the street and suddenly I knew for sure – knew who he was – and I nearly fainted. Trevor had introduced him as someone he'd met on the train and struck up a friendship with. Leo, he called him. Leo was going to join the Grove. I knew then that he'd be around plenty and that somehow I was going to have to cope with it. But how was I to behave? Trevor had no idea I'd known him years ago and it was clear that Neil hadn't told him.'

'Did Leo talk it over with you – privately?'

'He called the next day, when he knew Trevor was at work, and told me what had happened to him all those years ago and how he was trying to start a new life in Lewes. How he'd no idea that I was Trevor's wife – well, he wouldn't have, would he? – and he'd no idea how we should go on.'

'What a tricky situation.' Flora sympathised. 'But how did you decide to go on?'

'That we'd say nothing to Trevor, or to anyone, that we'd

known each other before. That I'd keep his true identity to myself. We're different people now, he said, not the couple we used to be. That's what we have to remember.'

'But the couple you used to be must still have lingered.'

'I suppose so. I suppose it was bound to.' The pale of her cheeks showed the hint of a flush. 'We were very close once and I never knew why Neil left without a word. And now I did. It felt comforting that it hadn't been my fault that he'd felt he had to get away. Had to travel halfway round the world.'

'And now? Now that you're a widow?' It was probably an indelicate question but it was important, Flora suspected, to understand how these two people actually felt about each other.

'It's different. It's bound to be, but I'm still very fond of him. He's been saying that he'll probably go back to Australia. He felt uneasy living in Lewes – it's why he moved to the village – but he feels uncomfortable there, too. And there's nothing for him in England, he said, except me.'

Was Leo – Neil – prepared to make a serious commitment to this fragile-looking woman? If that were so, why had he been phoning Thomasina Bell? Keeping that question to herself, Flora asked, 'Did he mention why he feels so uneasy?'

'Not really. I had the impression that he felt threatened in some way. It was why I said nothing to the police – when they called, after Trevor was killed. I told Neil he should be honest with them and tell them his real name and what had happened to him in Chichester. But he said the inspector in charge was quite hostile. He felt the man was after him and, if he confessed to living under a false name, his life could become even more difficult. He begged me to say nothing, and I did as he asked.'

'Before I go, we should talk about the police.'

Lilian looked blankly at her.

'They need to be involved. It wasn't Leo, or should I say Neil, that was threatened today, was it?'

Flora watched Lilian's face, wondering if she dared speak

the truth and was reassured. 'This morning, Lilian, someone deliberately set out to hurt you. You must know that. The police should know what happened. They need to find the culprit. Have you any idea who it could be?'

'No, and I don't want to think of it.' A sudden film of tears filled her eyes. It was plain that the subject was best left alone, at least for the time being. But then, unexpectedly, Lilian burst out, 'It's that wretched bonfire society that's behind it. Behind all the trouble. Trevor being killed, Neil feeling unsafe, and now me...'

Was that Brooker she was referring to? Flora wondered. 'Anyone in particular?' she asked.

'All of them. They're all guilty,' Lilian declared, subsiding wearily onto her pillows.

Flora left the hospital an hour later, having seen Lilian fall asleep once more. The nurse had told her at the ward door that Mrs French was sure to be discharged within the next few days and would be sent home in an ambulance. That was a relief. Flora had been puzzling how best to transport the patient home and, freed of the worry, she could concentrate on what had happened at Glebe Avenue this morning.

Who had come to Lilian's front door, a chloroform pad in their hand? Who had set the gas going in a deliberate attempt to kill? Someone who planned meticulously was the only answer she received. Someone who perhaps had spent the previous evening painting windows shut. Could she see Edwin Brooker doing that? Maybe. The fact that he'd been in the area at just the right time had to be suspicious. It was possible he really had been booked by a client, but there was no way of checking unless she walked the length of the road asking each householder.

He could equally have been driving around the neighbourhood waiting for Lilian to die. How long would that take? Not long, if the doctor's warning was correct. Driving around and waiting for the moment when he could use the key in his pocket to open the kitchen door and check that he'd been successful. That he'd killed her. What a truly horrible thought!

But why would he want to kill her? He had hated Trevor French for usurping the chairman's role, but Trevor's widow? What would be the point? Lilian had no involvement, no interest even, in Bonfire. Unless... she had somehow learned what had really happened that night, a truth that concerned Brooker, and he had decided to silence her.

And then there was Leo Nelson, Lilian's Neil. What game was he playing? Asking her to go to Australia with him, but to all intents and purposes courting Thomasina Bell. Could he be responsible for this morning's near tragedy? It seemed bizarre to think it, but if Lilian had become a little too clinging after the death of her husband, if Leo was regretting his invitation, even – though it was crazy to think it – if he suspected Lilian of working against him. After all, he was feeling threatened, she'd said. Uneasy in Lewes. Uneasy in Abbeymead.

And Lilian knew the secret of his identity. Was there more that she knew of his past that she wasn't saying? Or more that she knew of her husband's death on Bonfire Night? It was easy to forget, but Nelson was still a suspect for Trevor French's murder. Perhaps the invitation to Australia hadn't been offered freely – they had only Lilian's word for it. Perhaps it had been offered under the threat of discovery and Leo wasn't as enamoured with Lilian as he first appeared, seeing his future not with her, but with Thomasina. What would he do to get free? If Lilian really did spell danger for him, what would he do to save himself?

19

Two days later, a lone figure greeted Flora as she walked into the empty playground of Riverdale school, the children already hard at work in their classrooms. Thursdays meant a later start, Flora's first reading group not until after the morning break. As she drew closer, she saw the woman waiting at the school's entrance was Lilian French.

'Mrs French, how good to see you.' Flora held out her hands in welcome. 'And looking well.'

'Lilian, please. The hospital discharged me late yesterday and I wanted to see you... Flora... before you leave for Abbeymead. That is today, isn't it?'

'Yes, this afternoon,' she confirmed. 'But—'

A sudden thought gripped her. She hadn't looked ahead, had she, beyond leaving Lilian safely ensconced in a hospital bed? An abrupt realisation that this frail woman could still be in danger, came as a shock. Whoever had left her to die would soon know they hadn't succeeded. And would they try again?

A puzzled expression filled Lilian's face and Flora stuttered an apology. 'Sorry. Daydreaming.'

'I came to say thank you,' Lilian said. 'Not that I could ever thank you enough for what you did.' Her voice broke slightly. 'If you hadn't come to see me that day...'

'But I did come,' Flora said rousingly, 'and everything has turned out well.' It was a necessary lie. 'Except... have you been to the police yet, as I suggested?'

'No, I decided not to.'

'But why not?' She felt alarmed. 'They need to know what happened to you, Lilian. They can protect you in the future.' Whereas I can't, she admitted to herself.

'Please don't worry. I don't need protection. I'm sure nothing like that will happen again. And, in any case, I'm travelling up to Newcastle tomorrow, to be with my daughter. I'll be staying with her for the next few weeks – a kind of extended Christmas.'

That, at least, was a relief. Lilian should be safe all those miles away, but why was the woman so sure she would suffer no further harm?

'Can I ask you,' she began tentatively, 'why you think the attack was a lone one?'

'It won't happen again, I'm sure,' Lilian repeated.

'You said in the hospital that you had no idea who could have done that to you. Have you changed your mind?' It was a guess, but seeing an expression of concern flit across Lilian's face, she knew she had guessed correctly.

'You think it might be Leo Nelson, don't you?' Another guess.

Lilian gave a slow nod. 'If it was him, he didn't mean it. And I don't want to make things worse for him, Flora. If I go to the police, that's just what I'll do. He's already scared witless that they're trying to pin Trevor's death on him.'

And the police could well be proved right in doing so, but that was something she wouldn't say. Lilian's calm acceptance, however, that a man she had known since girlhood, a man who professed to care for her, could be capable of the most heinous crime, was astonishing.

'Why would Nelson do such a thing – and to you?'

'He was very upset and I don't believe he was thinking straight. He can be a very emotional man. I remember when we broke up, he behaved so badly...' She tailed off, then seemed to recover herself. 'And now, after all these years, it must have felt as though history was repeating itself. It was the day before you found me... I said no, you see.'

'Pardon?'

'I said no when Neil asked me to marry him. He said that he hoped I would but, if not, he still wanted me to go to Australia with him. He wanted me with him for the rest of his life, he said, and hated the idea of anyone else having me beside them.' She stopped talking, seeming overcome by the memory, while Flora waited patiently. 'I can't do it,' she said at last. 'I like Neil enormously' – she was using Leo's real name now, Flora noticed – 'but Trevor was my world. No one can replace him. And I don't want to live in Australia. This is my country and it's where I want to die.'

Where you nearly died, Flora added to herself.

'But to do such a terrible thing,' she exclaimed aloud.

'I would never accuse him directly,' Lilian said placidly, 'but I know Neil better than anyone, I think. Better than he knows himself. He can be impulsive, act rashly. I'm sure that if he *is* guilty, he will be tearing himself to bits with remorse.'

Flora struggled to find something intelligent to say – the situation was extraordinary. Eventually, she managed a sensible goodbye. 'I'm very glad you'll be leaving Lewes tomorrow. And I hope you have a really enjoyable Christmas with your family.'

'Thank you.' She leaned across to kiss Flora on the cheek. 'And... words are so inadequate... but thank you again for rescuing me.'

Flora walked slowly back into the old red-brick building,

making her way to the staffroom for a cup of tea before her class. She needed it. Lilian French had given her an enormous amount to think over. Most importantly, it was the knowledge that the woman would be safe in Newcastle for the next few weeks and, by the time she returned, the murder case would hopefully be done and dusted.

But her belief that it had been Leo Nelson responsible for the attack? If that were true, it would confirm the story Flora had told herself: that in his later years, Nelson had decided to leave Australia and return home to marry the woman he still loved, brushing aside any obstacle he might find – in this case, Trevor French.

Flora, though, was beginning to doubt her own story. Lilian had said that Neil, as she called him, could be rash, could be impulsive and swayed by emotion. But he'd have had to be half-crazed to do such a thing, she reflected, and nothing that she'd seen of the man, nothing Jack had seen – and he'd met and talked to Nelson a number of times – suggested such massive turmoil.

And what about the attack itself? That had been neither rash nor impulsive, but carefully thought through and planned to the smallest degree. Utterly cold-blooded. Perhaps Lilian didn't know Leo Nelson as well as she thought. Perhaps Jack didn't. So, who really *was* this man? And if *he* hadn't turned on the gas, someone else had.

∽

For an instant, Jack took his eyes off the road and glanced across at his silent companion. It was Thursday evening and they were heading for Abbeymead and a long weekend together but Flora, her hands clasped tightly in her lap, had spoken not a word since they'd driven past Lewes prison and out of the town. Now, having turned off the main thoroughfare, they were travelling along the narrow road that led to the village – and still she was silent.

He was worried. In the last day or so, he had learned a few details of what had happened that morning in Glebe Avenue, but Flora's account had been sparse and it remained a tale largely untold. He'd immediately recognised that his wife had been her usual courageous self, risking her life to save another's, but what had become apparent, too, was the distress she felt in talking of it. And it was no misplaced modesty at work, but true anguish. The realisation that someone could sink so low as to kill an innocent woman – and there was nothing to suggest that Lilian French was anything other than innocent – in such a cold and calculating fashion.

As they turned into Greenway Lane, Flora stirred beside him, appearing to have woken from a doze. Or had she, like him, been trying to think herself through this maze?

'Home,' she said brightly, as they came to a halt outside the cottage.

'Home indeed!' He forced himself to sound as bright. 'A few precious days in the village you love!' That he loved too, he realised, with a jolt. For the first time in Jack's life, it was somewhere he felt he belonged.

She smiled across at him, hauling her overnight bag from the back seat. 'How about you unpack and I make a start on supper?'

'Division of labour?' He smiled back. 'Sounds sensible.' And dragging his own bag from the car, followed her up the front path.

A few precious days, he thought, opening the familiar front door. Days tucked away in the cottage and, for Flora, in her beloved bookshop. She would be safe, and that's what he needed to know – the events at Glebe Avenue still sent shudders racing.

And tomorrow evening, as well, he'd be keeping Flora close,

the friends' customary Friday supper unexpectedly cancelled. Alice, it seemed, was up to her eyes in cooking for another gala dinner at the Priory and Kate had sent a message, via the college porter – Jack marvelled it had reached them – that she'd woken with a very sore throat that morning and was suggesting they meet again the following Friday. That suited him well. It was unlikely that Flora would come to harm walking to Alice's cottage, but keeping her safe was Jack's mission in life.

Jack had hoped that their first supper back at the cottage would lead Flora to talk of the near tragedy she'd been part of but, when she didn't, he decided he'd have to speak. They had washed up and were sitting together on the sofa when he began.

'I've been thinking.'

She looked up from her book.

'Wondering – could we be looking at two guilty people? One who tampered with the doorbell at Overlay and one who plotted to murder?'

Flora appeared to consider this for a moment. 'How would that work exactly?'

'Brooker could have done his worst at Overlay House and Leo used his position on the float to kill.' He'd deliberately not mentioned the attack on Lilian.

'Or it could be that Leo is responsible for it all.' She laid her book aside. 'I've been thinking that he could have rewired the bell himself – the man has run and owned hardware stores all his life and he must have gained more than a basic knowledge of electrics.'

'But why do it? It wouldn't be Leo who suffered damage, but a stray caller, so what would be the purpose?'

She pushed back her hair. 'It would enable him to play victim, if and when a poor unfortunate rang his bell. There's someone out there doing this to me, he could say, someone trying to make me appear a bad man. And the same thing is happening over the death of Trevor French. I'm being persecuted, unfairly accused.'

'There's a smidgen of sense to that theory, but only a smidgen. For most callers, the electric shock was unlikely to cause serious harm – my own experience was anything but pleasant, but crucially it didn't kill me.'

'So, a shock set at a level that fitted Leo's purpose.'

He laughed. 'The dangerous doorbell a simple ploy?'

'Why not? It would be a way to misdirect attention from whatever crime Leo had committed.'

'But to kill Trevor and then attempt to kill his wife?' He'd got to Lilian, at last. 'That's of an entirely different order.'

'Not if you believe that Leo came back from Australia to find the woman he once loved. That he engineered a meeting with Trevor French, making sure they became fast friends, and plotted to despatch the unfortunate Trevor at the first opportunity. Leo's field would be clear; Lilian would be a widow and ready to fall into his arms. When she didn't – he asked her to marry him, you know, and she refused – he went crazy and attacked her.'

'That's certainly one script, but what about a second to include Thomasina Bell?' Jack got to his feet and walked around the room for several minutes. 'Has she spoilt the plan?'

'If she has, Leo could have felt trapped. Maybe he found himself in love with the seamstress – unexpectedly.' Flora looked hopeful.

'That *would* be unlucky if you'd just invited another woman to return to Australia with you! It's possible, I suppose.' Men have done worse in the name of love, he thought cynically. 'But that would be to attribute immensely powerful emotions to Nelson and I just can't see it. I've talked to him at length several times and I know little more about him that when we first met.

The man remains a mystery – hardly someone bursting with uncontrollable feelings.'

'Lilian wouldn't agree with you, but there is one thing we *can* be sure of,' Flora said slowly. 'It was almost certainly the horrific accident all those years ago that sent Nelson hurtling across the seas to his brother and a new life.'

'And his return? Why did he come back when he did, if we discount the theory of a revived romance? It feels an arbitrary decision.'

'Nostalgia for his old life?' she suggested. 'A growing sense that the years left to him were diminishing fast and it was here in Sussex that he wished to die?'

'Possibly.'

It was what Leo himself had suggested, Jack recalled. Yet a niggle remained that something else had propelled this man to make what was another huge move at a time in his life when for most people staying put would be their first choice.

20

Alan Ridley's promised call came through the next morning, a few minutes after Flora had left for the All's Well. Eager to hear the inspector's news, Jack rushed into the house from waving her goodbye.

'Nothing much to tell you, I'm afraid, but here goes,' Ridley began. 'It took me a while to find our Mr Leonard, but find him I did: his name appears on a couple of shipping manifests. He's listed as sailing on the *Ormonde* which left Southampton for Australia in June '39 – luckily for him he was too old for the conscription that came in a couple of months earlier – and then he reappears some twenty years later as a passenger on the *Orion*. That ship docked in Southampton last November.'

'Thanks, Alan. A heroic effort! And it confirms what we thought,' Jack said slowly. 'He left for Australia the very same month he was acquitted, according to the *Chichester Herald*. He must have given in his notice as shop manager, packed a suitcase and left within days.'

'Just like that!'

'It looks as though he couldn't get out of England quickly enough. I can see why, but his return... the date fits with what I know of his turning up in England, first in Lewes and then here in Abbeymead, but there's no clue as to why he decided to leave Australia at that particular time.'

'He could have had family troubles,' the inspector suggested. 'He seems like a bloke who doesn't cope well with stressful situations. Maybe he and his brother fell out. But whatever the reason, it's not worth pursuing,' he warned. 'It's a minor point and we don't have the resources.'

Jack wasn't at all sure that it *was* such a minor point, but he had no way of following this line of enquiry himself and knew he'd have to stay content with speculation.

'Are you in charge now of the French case?' he asked hopefully.

'I take over on Monday. Officially.'

'And Inspector Brownlow? Is he happy with that?'

'Not too bothered, I think. He doesn't seem to have got very far and now he's other fish to fry. Trouble in Chichester, strangely enough, at a college teaching fashion of all things. The students have been rioting and Brownlow's trotted off to see what's going on there. It keeps him busy and, more to the point, off my back. He'll need a lot of tact – the Chichester station isn't at all happy having their men guarding the college full time – so that should be fun to watch.'

'A fashion college?'

'Yes, I know. What's the world coming to, eh?'

It had been a good day at the All's Well, several new titles unpacked, the accounts brought up to date – usually a Saturday chore that Flora wouldn't now have to face – and a steady stream of customers, all of them buying. After a difficult week, she felt far more at peace. In a very short while, she told herself, she would be home for good. She couldn't blame Lewes for the events at Glebe Avenue, but that day had become a dread she'd been unable to lose, and she'd be glad to say goodbye to the town. How close Lilian had come to losing her life! How close *she* had come to being overcome by fumes before she could save them both.

Starting to close down the till, she stopped midway when the shop bell rang. A late customer? Very late for a dark December evening. But it was Charlie Teague who shambled through the doorway, cycle clips in hand.

'Evenin', Mrs C.'

'You're an angel, Charlie, helping out like this. But are you sure you'll have the time? If necessary, you know, we can suspend the delivery service – until Mrs Lansdale is better.'

'No, 's'fine. Mrs...'

'Mrs Lansdale,' she reminded him gently.

'Yeah, Mrs Lansdale.' Charlie took off the peaked cap he wore, scratched a mass of floppy hair, then replaced the hat slightly askew. 'She's really keen on the books bein' delivered. To the oldies. And then other folks hear about it and want their orders through the door, too.'

'Like I say, it's good of you to come, but what about your chef's training? The deliveries will take you the whole evening.'

'I got the time, least for now. I don't go to the Nook no more, but they might need me at the hotel – it'll be Hector that needs me.' There was a note of pride in his voice.

'And the Farradays are happy you're no longer at the café?'

'They said they'll be OK.' He gave a cheerful grin. 'Shall I fetch up the books?'

'Yes, do, but Charlie – if you feel at any time you're doing too much, tell me please. Mrs Lansdale won't mind. Her back could be better very soon and she'll be able to ride Betty again.'

'She'll need to get a lot better,' he retorted. 'Betty's really cranky, now she's an old girl.'

'Respect, Charlie!'

He grinned again. 'OK, but she is. And with a load of books...'

He disappeared down the stairs to the cellar before she could again defend her beloved bicycle. Betty was only a little less precious to her than the All's Well itself. A few minutes later, Charlie reappeared, staggering up the narrow staircase with a stack of books in his arms.

'I'll have to go back. There's a second pile,' he said, slightly out of breath.

Had Rose been encouraging people to opt for delivery? Flora wondered. She might have to have a word. If, over the next few weeks, Charlie found his timetable at the Priory too demanding, as well he might, deliveries would have to wait until after Christmas. She could decide then whether or not to continue.

It had been her aunt Violet who had started the service, wanting to help those who found walking difficult. Flora breathed a small sigh. Aunt Violet was now long gone. She had tried to continue in the shop as her aunt would have wished but times changed, life moved on, and Alice was probably right when, last year, she'd urged her to let the delivery service lapse for good.

A second pile of books had arrived on her desk and Charlie with it. Expertly, he began to sort through them, arranging names and addresses according to the route he chose to ride.

'That's good,' he said with satisfaction. 'Nothin' for Overlay House this week.'

'Overlay? Have you been delivering there?' As far as Flora knew, Leo Nelson was quite fit enough to walk the short distance into the village and collect his own orders.

'Last week I did and I don't want to go there again.'

'He didn't shout at you, I hope,' she said, remembering the fate of Charlie's schoolfriend who had called at Overlay in the hope of a donation and been greeted by abuse.

'Nah, he didn't, but I don't like the bloke. And there was that woman there. I don't like her either.'

'What woman?' Surely not Lilian, she thought.

'She was here last Friday when I came to collect the orders, giving Mrs Law— Mrs Lansdale a parcel.'

Flora stayed puzzled.

'Mrs Lansdale undid it and it was some blouse or other. She thought it was wonderful, goin' on about how lovely it was. I reckoned it looked more like my mum's dishcloth.'

'As long as you didn't say that... was the woman Thomasina Bell? Very slim, very smartly dressed, wore a hat?'

'I dunno, but sounds like her. Then she was at Overlay when I got there later. And cuddlin' 'im.'

'Leo Nelson?'

'Yeah. Disgustin' it was. And they didn't like it that I saw them through the winder. Well, they shouldn't have been doin' it, should they?'

'No,' she said faintly, helping him carry the books out into the courtyard and into Betty's capacious basket.

It was then she noticed a thin red line on the boy's left hand, a cut that was still slightly open. 'Have you hurt yourself, Charlie? You should have told Alice and she'd have made sure it was treated properly.'

He looked down at his hand. ''S'all right. It weren't at the Priory, any case. It was that place again. Mr C's old place. I wish he was still there.'

'How did it happen?'

'I stuffed some paper in the bloke's dustbin. It was after I got told off for lookin' at 'em – can you believe they told me off, Mrs C? – and I thought to myself, well, he's rubbish so why not give him some more? There was a load of it in Betty's basket. I dunno what Mrs Lansdale does, but there was all this brown paper, bits of string and odd labels, and it was takin' up too much space. So, I dumped the lot in his bin. That's when I cut my hand.'

'On an open tin?'

He shrugged. 'Mebbe.'

'Or a knife?'

'Mebbe.' He shrugged again. 'I'll be off then.'

'Lock Betty up for the night when you get back,' she called after him, but Charlie was already on the bike and riding away.

21

Jack was unsure whether to call Ridley with the news Flora had brought back from the All's Well yesterday. The case against Leo Nelson for the murder of Trevor French was slowly and surely being built: a rejected marriage proposal, he'd finally learned from Flora, the intrigue with Thomasina Bell that his wife had guessed at, the possibility of a knife discarded in the dustbin. All circumstantial, he told himself. A completely different meaning could be attached to any of these events – it was interpretation that was key.

Or was he simply dancing on pins? Refusing to believe that Nelson could be guilty because he hated the idea that Inspector Brownlow – a man he'd disliked on sight – had been right from the start? That Nelson, having moved to stand on the left side of Trevor French, had taken advantage of the noise and sounds of Bonfire Night to slip a knife into his rival's heart.

The return from Australia, the adoption of a false name, the calculated move to Lewes and then to Abbeymead, might have nothing do with a wish to remain anonymous – after all, the accident, the court case, had happened over twenty years ago and who remembered them now? Instead, all of it could have been part of a deliberate lying low while Nelson planned a way to kill.

So... should he telephone Alan Ridley or not? Several times, he'd walked into the hall and picked up the receiver, only to replace it without making the call. In part, he suspected, his reluctance stemmed from an unpraiseworthy refusal to give Brownlow any credit. He wasn't proud of that. But if he made the call, he would be damning Leo Nelson, almost certainly, and he couldn't do it.

Finding it increasingly difficult to write, he pushed his typewriter to one side and walked down the stairs to the kitchen. Rather than waste the rest of the morning, he would make sandwiches, he decided and, when Flora returned from work, there would be a lunch to eat.

He had carved only a few slices of bread, however, when the knocker sounded. Annoyed, he packed the loaf back in the bread bin and went to answer the door, thinking it must be mail the postman had been unable to cram through the narrow letter box. But, surprisingly, it was Inspector Ridley who stood on the doorstep.

'Fancy a pint, old chap?' the inspector asked.

It was the last thing Jack fancied and his immediate response was to turn the invitation down. But Ridley was looking a little downtrodden, he noticed, and when the inspector followed up with, 'Got something to share,' Jack reached for his warmest overcoat – it was a cold day and there had been a covering of frost on the windows this morning. A pint would be a small price to pay if it helped him make up his mind whether or not to relate Charlie's tale.

He'd gone back to the kitchen to collect his keys when he heard Flora's voice at the door. She was home already from her morning at the All's Well, and greeting Alan Ridley. Where had the last few hours gone?

'We were just off for a quick drink,' he said, meeting her in the hall. He was annoyed with himself that he sounded sheepish.

Flora pulled a face. 'That's nice.'

'Do you fancy coming with us?'

Jack saw the inspector frown at his question, but did the man honestly expect him to walk out on Flora the minute she'd returned from work?

'Not really. I'm tired – it's been a busy morning – and I think I'd rather stay home.'

Feeling guiltily relieved, he was quick to say, 'I started to make sandwiches, but—'

'Then I'll finish them.' She reached up to kiss him on the lips. 'Don't fret, Jack. I'm happy you go for any number of pints.' She glanced towards the inspector who, shoulders hunched, had marched up the front path to the garden gate and was fiddling impatiently with the latch. 'And good luck,' she breathed into his ear, a wry smile lighting her face.

Lunchtime was exceptionally busy at the Cross Keys. But of course, Jack realised suddenly, it was less than two weeks to Christmas. So far this year, they had done little to prepare for the celebrations though it wouldn't be long, he was sure, before Flora had him climbing into the cottage roof space attic to retrieve the battered box of decorations handed down between generations of Steeles.

The pub had certainly splashed out on *their* decorations. Multicoloured paper garlands had been strung from oak beam to oak beam, interspersed with red and green paper bells. At strategic intervals. bunches of fresh mistletoe and holly had been pinned to the ceiling and a row of bright balloons hung across the bar. All good for business, he supposed, trying not to feel cynical.

'Sit down. I'll get them,' the inspector said, his tone unusually curt.

Something has happened, Jack thought. Something big that Ridley isn't at all happy about.

It was a good ten minutes before the inspector emerged from the scrum at the bar, carrying pint glasses of beer with a packet of crisps bulging from his coat pocket. Expertly, he weaved his way to the window table that Jack had managed to nab.

'Busy, busy, busy,' he muttered. 'But that's Christmas for you.' He gave an irritated sniff. 'Well, now we've got them,' he tapped the side of his tankard, 'best to drink up!'

Jack drank up. Then broke the long silence. 'You had something to share, you said?' The delay was putting him on edge.

The inspector looked fixedly at him before announcing, 'Leo Nelson is dead.'

Jack put his glass down with such a thump that beer foam splashed onto the wooden table, narrowly missing an arrangement of poinsettia and green pine.

'What!'

It was just about the last thing he'd expected to hear and it sent his mind into a whirl of speculation.

'Found this morning,' Ridley went on. 'The postie called it in. He was trying to deliver a parcel, couldn't get an answer and thought it was strange. Nelson, by all accounts, was a bit of a hermit. Always home. So the chap peered through the sitting room window and there he was, body sprawled across the hearth rug.'

The second peering through windows that had revealed a body, Jack thought, remembering Flora's frightening experience. This time, though, it had been one there was no saving.

'Have you any idea—' he began.

'None at all.' The inspector cut him off. 'But I thought you'd like to know. The postman had to walk to a telephone box before he could sound the alert. The ambulance attended a while later, but the man had been dead for several hours – the delay made no difference. He couldn't have been saved.'

'You've a forensic team at Overlay House?'

Ridley nodded.

'What does it look like to you? An accident? Suicide? Or—'

'Murder?' the inspector finished for him. 'Could be any of them. The post-mortem's this afternoon, which is lucky, seeing as every blighter seems to be taking time off at the moment. I'll let you know what it turns up.'

'From the position of the body, an accident seems unlikely,' Jack pursued.

The inspector spread his hands. 'It's possible. If he died last night, he could have been drinking, been in a haze and tripped over the hearth rug, then hit his head on the mantelpiece. That would have finished him off. It's one of those tiled jobs and they're pretty unyielding. But you know, you lived at Overlay long enough.'

'I never tried them out,' he said drily.

'As for suicide, do you know anything about the man that might lead to his taking his own life? Apart from the false name.'

He shook his head. But *did* he know anything? Jack searched his mind. Could it be guilt at what had happened long ago? Hardly. Nelson could have killed himself any time these last twenty years, if that were the case. Bad news from Australia? Maybe. The tangle he was in with these two women? Possibly, Jack supposed, but killing himself over a romantic mess? That seemed a little too dramatic.

Much more likely was guilt at Lilian's near demise, if Leo *had* been responsible for the attack. But this was something he'd promised Flora he wouldn't pass on. Lilian French had insisted that Flora say nothing to the police of the attack she'd suffered, and Jack felt bound to keep the promise he'd made. In any case, it was useless to speculate. The pathologist would tell them whatever there was to tell.

He took another long draught of beer and idly helped himself to a handful of the inspector's crisps. 'How is Inspector Brownlow coping with the Chichester crisis?'

'Still having trouble, poor chap.' There was a definite chuckle. It was a topic that evidently gave Alan Ridley pleasure. 'I could sink another pint. How about you?'

'Thanks, but I'd better be getting back.' He wanted to be home, wanted to talk to Flora. This was a startling development and she needed to know.

'I'll drown my sorrows on my own then,' the inspector said glumly.

'Dead?'

Flora stopped ironing the shirt she'd almost finished and thrust the iron back on its stand. 'Dead?'

'I was as shocked as you,' Jack said from the doorway and walked into the kitchen. 'I'd begun to think that Leo Nelson... But it doesn't matter what I thought. Not now.'

'Tell me what the inspector said.' She switched off the iron and pulled out a kitchen chair, sinking slowly into it.

'That Leo was found earlier today by the postman on his round. Barry Tubbs didn't get an answer when he knocked at Overlay and looked through the sitting room window to see the poor chap lying prone on the hearthrug. Then rushed off to telephone for an ambulance. Nelson had been dead for several hours by then, the inspector reckons. Other than that, I know nothing. And Ridley knows little more. He's waiting for the post-mortem.'

'I can't believe Nelson is dead. I was almost certain...'

'That he killed Trevor French? I was actually beginning to toy with the idea,' Jack admitted, 'and he still could be our murderer.' He sat down in the chair opposite. 'His death could have been an accident or even suicide.'

'It was murder,' she said firmly. 'I know it. Which means I've been looking in the wrong direction. I'd become so sure...' She tailed off.

'We don't know yet,' he counselled again. 'But if Nelson *has* been murdered, we still have a second suspect on our list. A strong suspect – Edwin Brooker! He's in the frame for killing Trevor French and for the attack on Lilian. He was driving around Glebe Avenue, wasn't he, at the right – or rather wrong – time?'

'I suppose so, but the love angle seemed so convincing, Nelson caught between two women, especially when Charlie told me about Thomasina and then the dustbin episode. But why would anyone want to kill Leo? Why would Brooker?'

'For the same reason that Trevor French is dead and that Lilian nearly met the same fate? All three are associated in some way or another with the Grove society and it's plain that Brooker has a very strong hatred for anyone who worked, as he sees it, to rob him of his crown.'

Flora screwed up her face. 'I'm not convinced. And I know you aren't either! Murdering, or attempting to murder, three people because you were deposed from your chairmanship seems way out of proportion.' She sat staring at the row of decorated wooden spoons she'd bought in Venice a few months previously. But then brightened. 'At least it proves that Inspector Brownlow was wrong!'

'It might not.' Jack put an immediate damper on her spurt of optimism. 'He could be right about Nelson. It's always possible that if he killed Trevor and tried to kill Lilian, someone else knew or thought they knew what he'd done, and decided to take revenge on him.'

'It's become too complicated,' she complained, getting up to finish the shirt and rumpling his hair on the way.

'It always does, but we get there in the end.'

The telephone call from Brighton police came through at teatime. They were sitting on the sofa, sharing a plate of scones and jam, when their peaceful snack was interrupted by a loud trill from the hall.

Jack went to answer and Flora strained to hear. From her husband's murmurs and one syllable responses, she guessed it was Alan Ridley with the post-mortem results he'd promised.

She had guessed right. When Jack came back into the sitting room, she knew from his expression what to expect.

'Murder?'

He nodded. 'Arsenic. Where from they're not sure, but enough in Nelson's body to kill.'

'Are they searching Overlay House?'

'A forensic team has been busy for hours. And Brownlow is on his way back from Chichester – to help out, Alan said between gritted teeth. Apparently, the students are quiet at the moment. Some kind of agreement has been cobbled together over the final exam they're due to sit, though I've a strong suspicion that Ridley is hoping they might start another riot.'

'The college is in Chichester?'

'Yes, do you know it? I'd never realised you could study fashion locally. But then why would I? Sussex is more go-ahead than I thought.'

Flora ignored the slight on her home county to ask, 'Do you know the college name?'

'No, but I don't imagine there'll be more than one. Why?' Jack's voice had taken on a note of wariness.

'Just something,' she said uncertainly. 'Something Thomasina Bell told me when I first met her. She was dismissive of London colleges and said she'd studied in Sussex.'

'Interesting – although why?'

Flora jumped up, sending her empty plate spinning across the woven rug. 'We should go, Jack! We should pay the college a visit.'

'Flora!'

'Tomorrow. Unless you've something planned for Sunday.'

'How about my starting a second edit of the new novel? And why on earth would we visit a college of fashion?'

'You could let the book slide for a few hours. Please, Jack.' She bent down to muffle him in an embrace.

'I'll drive to Chichester, if we really must, but why exactly are we chasing across the county to go to a college neither of us have any interest in?'

'*I* have an interest. I have a hunch – and don't groan. Let's talk to whoever we can find on the campus. See if they know Thomasina; if they remember her. There was something in her voice – her tone changed – when she mentioned the college. It was like a window into her feelings. A rare one. The place meant something to her. Presumably Leo Nelson did, too.'

Jack shook his head. 'I just don't see—'

'So far, we have lots of "buts" and very few positives. Thomasina Bell could be a positive. She seems to have been close to Nelson and also to Edwin Brooker – don't forget the bouquet the man sent her. And the card he wrote, hoping for something good in the future. Somewhere in that triangle, there's a clue, I'm sure, yet we know next to nothing about any of them. The college was part of Thomasina's young life, an important part, I'm guessing, and going there might help us build a picture.'

He said nothing but his expression had turned mulish, causing Flora to double down on her persuasion.

'Think how many times Chichester has been mentioned lately: Lilian French comes from the town, Leo Nelson or Neil Leonard ran a hardware store there, and Thomasina Bell studied at a Chichester college. Coincidence or something more? I think there has to be more, and a visit could take us an important step forward.'

'And if it takes us nowhere?'

'It will take us *somewhere*,' she objected. 'There'll be more scones, for a start! I know a cosy tearoom just around the corner from the cathedral.'

It was certainly a temptation.

22

Flora's enthusiasm had carried the day, as it so often did, although Jack remained reluctant to make the visit to Chichester. Not least because a BBC weather forecast had threatened snow for the south coast and, knowing from experience how easily the west of the county could be cut off, he had no wish to make what might prove a perilous drive. It was more than weather, though, that was causing him to drag his feet. Flora's latest hunch seemed to him freakish.

OK, Chichester, or Chi as its inhabitants called it, had appeared on their radar an unusually large number of times, and a fashion college in the depths of Sussex was unexpected, but still... how his wife could tie the city – and it was a city for all its small size – together with three very different people into one large bundle and suggest that this might be the solution to Trevor French's death was beyond him.

Sunday morning proved a disappointment. Secretly, he'd hoped to wake to a covering of snow – a useful excuse to dip out of an excursion he thought a waste of time – but the day dawned dry and bright, even sporting a pallid sun low in the sky. And when Jack turned on the wireless, it was to discover that the forecast had changed. The snow currently affecting the north of England would, as the day progressed, move down the country, the announcer said, reaching the Midlands by early afternoon. In the far south, however, they would be spared disruption. Slowly, he buttered a slice of toast. There was no escape: he was driving to Chichester.

The city was a good hour and a half's journey from Abbeymead but, apart from a hold-up in the centre of Worthing – the road passing the pier was always a pinch point – they made good time. Sitting behind a queue of cars on Worthing seafront and looking out on water the colour of gunmetal, Jack's spirits were low.

'I met Ambrose Finch's new secretary for the first time,' he said, trying to cheer himself up – he might actually know a snippet of village news that Flora didn't. 'Last Friday, at the fish and chip shop of all places, when I fetched our supper that evening. He seems to be settling into Abbeymead life.'

'He?'

'Yes, a male secretary. Very progressive. Robin Armitage, he introduced himself. A nice chap.'

'But why does Mr Finch need a secretary? He's been retired for years.'

'Perhaps he's begun working again. Restarting some of his old businesses. Maybe galvanised by the discovery that he has a son alive and well, who might come home. If he does, there'll be plenty of room for him at the School House. Apart from Armitage, and Finch himself, they've only a housekeeper living there.'

'The son – Lucas Finch – how did the detective find him? It *was* the private investigator who did?'

Jack nodded. 'The same man Finch has been employing for years. He finally struck gold. In Italy, I believe. The boy – well, man now – was working in a restaurant in Rome.'

Flora gave a small grunt. 'It will be a very different life for him – what a change, Rome to Abbeymead! I wonder how he'll cope.'

'Apparently, it was the boy who made the first contact so he must be keen to return to England.'

'That's unusual. If people disappear, they don't normally want to be found. At least, according to the newspapers.'

'Perhaps he'd had enough of pizza,' Jack joked. 'There was always a chance, I suppose, that it would happen. Finch has been advertising across Europe for years – in various newspapers – and the investigator got a call out of the blue.'

Flora said nothing, seeming to think it over. It was unusual, Jack conceded, but it was also miraculous news for Ambrose.

'Your hope of moving into the School House is well and truly gone then,' she said quietly.

'I never really had a hope.' He reached across to squeeze her hand. 'And I'm glad for Finch. It will be a New Year present for him. One I'm sure he deserves. Oh, we're off at last.'

The line of traffic had begun its crawl along the seafront and Flora settled down to enjoy the journey along the coast until, at Bognor, the road swung inland through mile after mile of flat pasture. Even from a long distance, the spire of Chichester Cathedral was clearly visible on the horizon.

Jack had consulted the telephone directory before they left home and felt pleased with himself that he'd found an address for the college, though not so pleased once they had driven into the middle of the city and become hopelessly lost in its narrow streets.

'We've passed the cathedral twice already,' Flora said unhelpfully. 'Shouldn't we ask for directions?'

'There's no need. I can find the college myself,' he said stubbornly. 'The town isn't that big.'

Suppressing a sigh, she continued to gaze through the window, finding pleasure in the mass of Georgian streets they were passing through, and surprised here and there by the odd remnant of Norman architecture still standing. Despite having lived in Sussex most of her life, Flora had never before visited Chichester and her first impression was that of an appealing city.

'We've arrived!' she realised suddenly. A stylishly designed name board had appeared on her right. St Clare's College of Fashion, it read.

'You thought I wouldn't find it, didn't you?' Jack asked tersely, then looked across at her and both of them burst out laughing.

'You did find it,' she agreed, 'and it looks good. There are only a few policemen today keeping watch.'

There were far more students than police, in fact, Jack saw, and some of them looking decidedly mutinous, but no major trouble, as far as he could tell. He drove up to the main entrance and looked around. Inspector Brownlow was nowhere to be seen.

Winding down his window, he spoke to the officer on duty, hoping he sounded authoritative. 'We're here to see the principal,' he told the man. But don't ask me a name, he said to himself.

The car, however, was waved through the gates and he dutifully followed signs to the car park.

'It's a splendid building.' Flora bent her head to look through the windscreen. The red-brick pile ahead of them, neo-Gothic in design, had a stately presence, towering imperiously over gardens that were plainly well-cared for.

Jack pulled into a vacant parking space and sat back in his seat. 'OK, Maestro. We're here. What next? I've a feeling the principal won't be that keen to see *us*.'

'Not the principal, no. But there should be a college office that deals with administration. There'll be files on the students who've studied here.'

'I'm not sure what a list of students is going to tell us – if indeed we get to see one.'

Flora set her lips. 'It's a start,' she said briefly.

But when they had walked through the ornamented entrance arch and into a wood-panelled hall, it was a desk rather than an office that faced them.

The woman sitting behind the magnificent spread of rosewood became aware she had visitors and, adjusting her spectacles to sit on the tip of her nose, asked, 'Can I help you?'

For a moment, Flora was struck dumb. Requesting details of Thomasina Bell felt awkward. Intrusive. Even suspicious. How could she phrase her enquiry without raising hackles or doubts over her motive?

'I have a friend who studied here,' she began, a trifle timidly, noticing that Jack had stood back seemingly with no intention of joining the conversation. 'Her name is Thomasina. Thomasina Bell.'

'Yes?'

'She knew I was coming to Chichester today,' she lied blatantly, 'and wondered... wondered if you had details of her studies here.' That was nicely vague.

'Details?' So vague, it appeared, that the assistant looked bewildered.

'Yes. She wondered... she wondered whether she could get in touch with any of her old student friends,' she finished in a rush. That, at least, sounded plausible.

'I'm fairly sure Miss Crawford wouldn't allow the college to supply that kind of information.'

'Miss Crawford is?'

'The principal,' the woman said crisply, now exuding a definite suspicion.

'Do you, by any chance, remember Thomasina?' The question sounded a little too desperate. 'She studied here in the 1930s.'

The woman blinked, her expression unsure as to whether or not she should be insulted. Behind the spectacles, she was a relatively young woman.

'I'm afraid not,' she began, when a voice behind Flora said, 'But I do.'

Flora turned to see a tall, elegant woman, dressed head to toe in draped black jersey, smiling at her.

'Patricia Crawford,' the woman said, holding out her hand. 'And you are?'

'Flora Carrington and this is my husband, Jack. We're sorry to call on a Sunday, but it's the only day we both have free.'

'Please.' The principal held up a manicured hand to wave away the apology. 'At St Clare's, we welcome visitors every day. The architecture, you understand, draws people here. But you know Thomasina, you say?'

'Yes, we've been living in Lewes and Thomasina has her studio there. She's making me a dress.' As a reason for asking meddlesome questions, it sounded woefully inadequate.

'I'm delighted to hear it. Delighted that a student of ours is working in fashion still. You will love what she creates, I'm sure. Thomasina was an excellent seamstress and a true designer.'

Flora felt embraced by the woman's warmth and relaxed slightly. 'I've heard how skilled she is at dressmaking but I had no idea she was a designer, too.'

'Yes, indeed. All my students have to take design along with cutting and sewing skills. Business classes, as well. They're not the most popular sessions, I'm afraid, but necessary for anyone intending to set up on their own. Please, why don't you come with me? I'd like to show you something. Your husband might find it interesting, too.'

The all-embracing smile had a hitherto silent Jack thank the woman warmly and follow in Flora's footsteps as she walked beside the principal's graceful figure down a wood-panelled corridor, its walls hung with a hundred photographs – former students? Flora wondered.

A procession of sturdy oak doors had Miss Crawford wave at them as they passed. 'Classrooms,' she said, 'and coming up is our biggest display space.'

Through an open entrance lay what Flora could only describe as a gallery, filled with costumed figures.

'This is our showcase. A testimony to the heights our most talented students can reach.' Miss Crawford beamed. 'Every year, we stage a show for our very best designs. You can see how good they are.'

Slowly, Flora walked along the row of papier-mâché mannequins: silk dresses, tweed costumes, velvet opera cloaks, the sheer variety astounding, and each individually designed and expertly made.

'Brilliant, aren't they? But you know, Thomasina's dress – it won that year's graduation award, of course – is still talked about today. In my opinion, it has never been bettered. And here it is.'

They had moved from one model to another and were now standing in front of an astonishingly beautiful ball gown. A wide V-necked sheath in ink-blue velvet with cascading ruffles and beaded short sleeves.

'What do you think?' the principal asked.

'Fabulous,' Flora breathed.

'Pretty amazing.' Even Jack seemed impressed.

'Thomasina was obviously hugely talented,' Flora said, and waited a beat before asking, 'Was she popular as well?' It was a very long shot, but there was a faint hope of possibly hidden conflicts that could have bearing on Thomasina's life today.

The principal thought for a moment. 'I wouldn't say wildly popular. Not that she wasn't liked, but she and Letty Reynolds were such fast friends I don't think they needed anyone else.'

'Letty Reynolds? The two of them were close?' The name

was new. But then, if Letty still lived in Chichester... or perhaps Thomasina had outgrown the friendship.

'You could say close!' Miss Crawford gave a gentle smile. 'Perhaps you noticed the photographs lining the corridor. Each year, we bring a photographer in for a graduation picture. You passed Thomasina and her fellow students. Let's walk back and take a look.'

They had retraced their steps halfway along the corridor before Miss Crawford stopped and pointed to a photograph, clearly much older than most, hanging in the centre of the middle row. Our 1930s graduates. There is Thomasina.'

Flora followed the principal's finger and felt Jack's breath on her neck as he strained to see. The young girl looking out at them, no more than twenty was Flora's estimate, was definitely Thomasina, ranged among a host of other young women and just one solitary man.

'And this is Letty.' Miss Crawford's finger moved one figure to the left. 'She was almost as talented as Thomasina herself. A formidable duo.'

'For such a close friendship, it's strange that Thomasina doesn't appear to have kept in touch with her.' Flora hoped she sounded casual enough. 'Such a shame.'

'Oh, my dear, there was no way she could keep in touch. Poor Letty has been dead these twenty years.'

'Dead? But she would still have been a very young woman.'

'It was a tragic accident, some years after she left the college. She was knocked down, her small daughter, too. They were hurrying to get to the child's ballet class. So utterly sad.'

Flora half turned to her husband and saw his eyebrows rise. This was the connection she'd hoped for, the hunch she'd gone with.

'They both died?'

'Letty died at the scene, I believe, but the little girl – she lived, just about – but her injuries were horrific.'

'Did it ever become known who was responsible?'

'There was a court case. A local man. I don't remember his name. Not his fault apparently, but all very distressing.'

'The daughter, I suppose, might still be alive?'

The principal frowned. Flora's curiosity seemed to have struck a false note.

'I believe she was taken to live in a nursing home,' she said shortly. 'She would have needed that level of care.'

'And the nursing home? Have you any idea where that might be?' She was now tempting fate, Flora knew.

Miss Crawford's frown deepened. 'I don't, but locally the Angelina Retreat is the most well-known. And has an excellent reputation.'

Flora held out her hand, feeling silent gratitude. 'Thank you so much for the tour, Miss Crawford. It's been extremely interesting and I'll be sure to tell Thomasina that I've seen her wonderful dress.' She was trying to regain the ground she had lost.

The principal gave a curt nod. 'I'm glad to have been of help,' she said smoothly, turning on a pointed heel and gliding back down the corridor to some hidden nether land of her own.

'I don't think she appreciated your questions,' Jack said drily, once they were out of the building and making for the car park. 'Your somewhat direct questions!'

'Maybe not, but we're coming away with the clue I'd hoped for. The connection between Thomasina and Leo Nelson. He was the driver of that car. We can check with Ross and the article he found, but I'm sure of it. So maybe...'

'Maybe?'

'It's not a romance between Thomasina and Leo Nelson. It's a tragedy they share.'

'Which means she knows who he really is.'

Flora gave a slow nod. 'She must have worked it out.'

'It also means that Thomasina must have kept in touch with

her friend after college. The accident would have happened seven or eight years after they graduated.'

Flora looked struck. 'That's true. Otherwise, she might not have known what happened to Letty. But the daughter? I wonder if she knows about the child.'

A silence fell as they climbed into the car, Flora looking straight ahead, her eyes beginning to sparkle.

'Don't tell me.' He started the engine. 'We're going on a hunt for the Angelina Retreat.'

Turning out of the entrance to the college, they passed the few policemen who still remained on duty, neither of them aware of the small van parked in the adjoining road.

'The nursing home can't be far away,' she said persuasively. 'And a visit won't take long. There'll still be time for scones.'

'No, there won't, not even for you, Flora. It's Sunday and the tearoom will close early. The scones will have to wait. We'll go tomorrow.'

'But I'm at the All's Well tomorrow.'

'Ring Rose,' he said firmly. 'She'll cover.'

And Flora knew that for once Jack wouldn't be persuaded.

23

'Before we make a trip to this nursing home,' Jack said, pulling up outside the cottage, 'we need to check with Ross Sadler. Check the article he found. Otherwise, it could be a wasted journey – and potentially an embarrassing one.'

Flora clambered from the car and started up the front path. 'I'll put the kettle on,' she said over her shoulder. 'Why don't you ring while I make tea?'

It meant calling his friend on a Sunday, one of the few days Ross might be at home with his feet up, but he knew that Flora wouldn't rest until she'd made this visit and had her theory confirmed.

Thankfully, Ross was his usual cheerful self when he answered the phone. 'I'm just lazing, Jack,' he said in response to his friend's apology. 'Reading the Sundays. Snacking on biscuits. How can I help?'

'It's about the stuff you dug up on the accident in Chichester. The article you quoted mentioned a date, I think, but not the names of everyone involved. Did the newspaper publish them?'

'Straight off, I can't remember.' There was a pause. 'Look,

I've still got the article, brought a copy home with me. Can you hang on a minute and I'll let you know.'

Flora had appeared at her husband's side, her eyes bright with questioning. 'He's looking,' Jack whispered.

'Hello? Jack? No names on that particular article, just the date and a few details of where it happened and who the driver was. But I did pull out several others while I was looking. Only small snippets but one of them – the one from the *West Sussex Times* – mentions the woman who was knocked down. Here it is. A Miss Reynolds. Does that ring a bell?'

'It certainly does. Thank you, Ross. It's just what we needed.'

'You should come back to the paper, old man,' Ross suggested with a laugh. 'You spend as much time investigating as you do writing those damn novels.'

'I'll think about it,' Jack promised, knowing that journalism was unlikely ever to see him again.

'Reynolds?' Flora queried, when he replaced the receiver. 'That was Letty's maiden name. And she was still using it. I wonder why.'

'Another puzzle, but we do have a confirmation that Letty Reynolds and her daughter were the victims of an accident and that the car was driven by a Neil Leonard, aka Leo Nelson.'

'So... the Angelina Retreat tomorrow?' she asked, reaching up to smooth back the flop of hair that refused to sit flat.

'Back to Chichester,' he confirmed. 'The scones had better be good!'

∽

Yesterday, they'd been lucky to alight on St Clare's College after several tours of central Chichester, but the Angelina Retreat was another matter. It lived up to its name – a retreat it was. By the time they'd stopped and asked several people, they'd gleaned the information that it lay south of Chichester, between the city and the sea, a mile or so from the village of Bosham. But having arrived in Bosham, and tried several credible-looking roads, they continued to drive in circles, each time arriving back in the village. It needed an old man, sitting on the seawall, contemplating the incoming tide while he puffed a pipe, to give them precise directions.

The Angelina Retreat was discovered at the end of a narrow track, itself an offshoot of a slightly wider lane which, in turn, had branched from a minor road. No wonder it had taken them the best part of two hours to find the home.

The large white stucco villa, Flora saw, had grown considerably from the house it had once been, extended on both sides and, no doubt, at the rear as well, to accommodate as many patients as possible. And she could see, too, why this would be a first choice for many relatives. The grounds surrounding the house had been professionally landscaped, not in any formal fashion, but in a way that allowed the unfolding of a natural beauty. Although the trees, planted in clusters throughout the grounds, were bare at this time of year, their leaves swept and burnt weeks ago, a mass of flowering shrubs provided vivid splashes of colour, a challenge to the grey of today's sky.

Jack pulled into the car park just as a nurse came hurrying towards them, car keys in hand. He jumped out to speak to her and Flora, winding down the window, caught the murmur of their voices.

'You're visiting a patient?' the nurse asked, dark splotches beneath her eyes. It must have been a long shift, Flora thought.

'It's our first time here,' Jack explained. 'Is there a particular entrance we should use?'

'Just the main door – it's actually at the side of the building. There.' She gestured a hand towards the eastern flank of the villa.

Jack was thanking her as Flora closed the Austin's door. 'Ready?' he asked. 'And do we have a story, by any chance?'

'I'll think of something,' she promised, hoping she could keep her word.

The interior of the home was as attractive as its surroundings. No institutional tiles for the Retreat, but a pale-yellow wallpaper and floral blinds. No bare floorboards either. Instead, a thick carpet of dark grey wool with chairs upholstered in a matching chenille, large and comfortable. A reception desk of polished rosewood lay ahead, a huge vase of white camellias to one side.

The woman behind the desk, however, seemed at odds with the decor and, as it turned out, could not have been more different from their contact of yesterday. Patricia Crawford had been warm and welcoming, this woman sharp-nosed and brusque in manner.

'We've come to visit a patient,' Flora began. 'A Miss Reynolds.' She hoped the woman wouldn't demand the young girl's first name. This was something Miss Crawford either hadn't known or hadn't wished to divulge.

Without a word, the woman pushed a blank writing pad aside and opened what seemed a large diary.

'Reynolds?' she checked.

'Yes. She's a long-term resident.'

'All our residents are long-term.' The woman's tone verged on the caustic as she ran a finger down the list of... names, Flora saw, squinting at the book upside down. Names and room numbers.

The woman smiled up at them, a smile Flora didn't trust. 'I'm afraid you're a little late. But you're in good company. So many of our visitors are – when they turn up at all.'

'Late?' Flora repeated blankly.

'Louisa Reynolds died last September. Well over a year ago.'

She tapped the desk calendar. 'A coronary embolism. Quite sudden. Painful, but mercifully quick.'

Flora, bewildered by the turn of events, turned to her husband for help and Jack obligingly took over.

'We've been abroad for some years and communications there have been poor.' Flora looked at him admiringly. He had learned to lie with as much fluency as she. 'We've only just returned to this country,' he went on, 'and we had hoped to see Louisa. We knew her mother, Letty.'

This was getting ridiculous, Flora thought. He sounded so convincing. He had been convincing. The woman's demeanour had subtly altered.

'I'm sorry to give you such sad news. Is there anything else I can help with?'

'No... I don't think so, except... I hope the Retreat wasn't left with unpaid bills.'

The woman stiffened and returned to her customary bite. 'Louisa's benefactor met all her bills, including her funeral.' Her tone was acid.

'I hope Louisa had *some* visitors,' Flora put in, coming to life at last, and feeling aggrieved at this woman's clear animosity. 'We weren't able to come ourselves but—'

'Just the one,' their tormentor said. '*She* was faithful. All the way from Lewes and never once missing a week.' The diary was slammed shut. 'Now, if there is nothing else—'

'We'll be going,' Flora said quickly, taking hold of Jack's hand and marching them out of the building, not pausing until they reached the car.

'What a dragon!' she exclaimed, her face pink with annoyance.

'But an informative dragon, nevertheless. Though I'm sure she had no wish to be. Let's go, sweetheart.'

'The tearoom?' she asked hopefully.

'Home,' he said firmly. 'Forget the tearoom – I'm too tired for another round trip of Chichester.'

They were making the turn onto the main Brighton road before she spoke again. 'I'm sorry the driving has been so difficult today.' Jack was looking tired, she saw. 'But I think it was worth it! Louisa had a faithful visitor, that horrid woman said. That was Thomasina?'

'It's likely. In fact, almost certain – who else would know the girl and be travelling from Lewes?'

Flora pulled off her woollen hat with a hard tug, combing her fingers through tangled hair. 'Was she also the person who paid the bills, I wonder?'

'That's something I'm nowhere near as certain about. The words the woman used, how she spoke – to me, it felt as though there were two different people involved.'

'Maybe. I'm not sure either. Let's think about it.'

And they did, on the long journey home.

'I'm sorry about the scones,' she said, making tea for them both several hours later.

'I shouldn't be. It's good we gave them a miss. Look what's on its way.'

They had felt the first flurry of snow as they'd opened their front door but now, glancing through the window, Flora saw the flakes falling more thickly and, though not settling yet, it was only a matter of time, she reckoned.

'I'm closing the curtains. We need to be cosy. Especially after the nursing home.'

'A very expensive nursing home would be my guess.'

'It doesn't matter, does it? Not really. However expensive, it can't make up for being so ill.

That poor child,' she went on, when they'd settled down to drink their tea and dunk ginger nuts. 'Horribly injured, her mother dead, and possibly only Thomasina as a visitor. Where was her father? She must have had one.'

'Miss Crawford never mentioned a father, I noticed. And Ross's newspaper article spoke of a Miss Reynolds.'

'He and Louisa's mother must have been estranged, but perhaps he was in the background, paying for her.'

'It's possible but my money is on someone else.'

Flora took a long drink of tea. 'Leo Nelson?'

'The same. I can see him insisting that the child had the best care possible, whether or not the accident was his responsibility. And when you think how much the Retreat must have cost over the years, I don't think Miss Bell would have had the funds.'

'She runs a successful business,' Flora reminded him.

'But that successful? And don't forget this happened when Louisa was a small child. She would be around six, so no more than seven or eight years after Thomasina and Letty graduated from St Clare's. Would Thomasina have built a strong enough business by then to afford the Retreat?'

'Whereas Leo Nelson, Neil Leonard, had built a highly successful business in Australia with his brother.'

'Exactly. And probably felt it was all he could do to make up for that dreadful day.'

'So... the nursing home would have told him that Louisa had died, otherwise he would have continued paying her fees.' She put down her cup, looking across at him. 'That has to be important.'

Jack nodded. 'It's crucial. I reckon if we compare the date of Louisa's death with the date Ridley gave me for Nelson's arrival in Southampton, we'll find the two events are only a few months apart. The Angelina Retreat tells Leo the sad news: Louisa Reynolds has died suddenly. And almost as suddenly he decides to sell up – he mentioned his brother was older than him so maybe *he* wasn't averse to retiring. Sell the hardware store, take the cash and book a passage to England. How's that for a theory?'

'It works,' she said, munching a second ginger nut. 'I wonder why it was so important to him to stay out of England until she died.'

'Who knows? Emotional distress? A psychological need for distance? The girl's death could have been a release for him, a signal that the trauma was finally over and that chapter of his life closed. He could emerge from his hiding place at last.'

'Not quite. He didn't go back to Chichester, did he? The call of Sussex was too strong, but he made sure he returned to a place a fair distance from his hometown.'

'And then he moved again, to this village. I wonder what the move to Abbeymead was all about?'

'Maybe he was still scared someone might recognise him.'

'He must have felt haunted. I feel sorry for the poor chap.'

'Well, he's not haunted now,' she said practically. 'He's gone beyond fear. At the moment, I can't see how the nursing home relates to Nelson's death, and even less to Trevor French's, but I've a feeling it does. We've done well, Jack!' She reached out to squeeze his knee. 'Are you going to pass on what we've learned?'

'I'll have to. Ridley might even be grateful! I've no idea where the police are with their investigation – Brownlow coming and going will have complicated matters – and they may have uncovered more than we have. But maybe not. We might be some help.'

24

On Tuesday morning, they drove to Lewes for the last time, the two of them keenly aware of change hovering on the horizon: this was Jack's final week at Cleve College and Flora's at Riverdale school, and both were leaving with mixed feelings.

The three days they would spend in the town, however, meant that Jack wasn't able to make the call to Inspector Ridley – their apartment lacked a telephone and he was reluctant to ask permission to use the one supplied by the college. The foyer was too public. What he had to tell the inspector was sensitive and he'd no wish to be overheard by passing students and staff.

It wasn't until they were again back in Abbeymead, therefore, that he made contact with the Brighton police. It was a Friday morning and Jack was hopeful he'd find Alan Ridley in his office sifting through what was bound to be a mass of paperwork, prior to the weekend.

When his call was answered, however, it was to find that Ridley was out and about and, in his place, Sergeant Norris, the inspector's trusted right-hand man, was holding the fort.

'Mr Carrington, good to hear your voice! Particularly good if you happen to have information!'

'The investigation not going well?'

'You could say that. Or you could say it's a complete mess. We've been going through Steve Brownlow's notes – he's now back in Norfolk – and it looks as though every bit of his fire-power was concentrated on getting one man convicted – Leo Nelson or Neil Leonard, whichever you prefer. Now the man is dead, the evidence Brownlow collected will have to be reviewed.'

'And that will entail?'

Norris breathed out heavily. 'A whole new raft of inter-views – fresh interviews, conducted with everyone who was on that float. Not that they're going to remember much,' he grum-bled. 'Bonfire Night was well over a month ago and memories fade. In my experience, very quickly.'

'Is that what Alan is engaged in today – interviews?'

'Spot on. He's out with several of the boys going through the original list, name by name. Tedious work but since we're back at square one, we've no option. Actually,' Norris paused, 'it's worse than square one – we've now another murder to deal with. Nelson's. And at present, we've not made the slightest dent in solving his killing, so anything you can give us will be very, very welcome.'

Jack painstakingly related their last two days of pokin' and pryin', as Alice called it, earning a low whistle from Norris after he'd absorbed their discoveries at St Clare's College and at the nursing home.

'That is interesting. Very interesting. It puts Thomasina Bell in a whole new light, doesn't it? She'll be a person of interest for us now. Definitely.'

'Miss Bell is mixed up in it somehow, but she wasn't anywhere near Trevor French on Bonfire Night,' he cautioned. 'As far as I can make out, she was standing at the rear of the float, too far away to wield a knife. And in the case of Leo Nelson, she appears to have been on the very best of terms with him. My young friend, Charlie, was disgusted by seeing them cuddling.'

Norris gave a grim laugh. 'OK, but from what you're telling me, Nelson was the man responsible for an accident that killed her best friend. She wasn't going to be too happy with him.'

'He was cleared of negligence. The accident wasn't his fault and, judging by the pair's closeness, it would seem Miss Bell accepted the verdict. You could say, I suppose, that in a sense she bonded with him over the tragedy.'

'Hmm,' Norris muttered. 'She's still worth talking to – at length, I reckon.'

'How has your forensic team fared at Overlay?' Jack asked, changing tack. 'Alan told me the results of the post-mortem. Arsenic poisoning.'

'It was, but where it came from is still a mystery. We've gone through the house but found nothing and the team is due to finish up today. They've only the garden and the shed left to rake through. On first sight, neither contains anything obvious. No cans of rat poison!'

It seemed unlikely to Jack that they would discover anything more in either place. But how could arsenic poisoning remain a mystery? The police were certainly on the back foot in this investigation.

'Has Alan chosen his interview victim for today? That's if you can tell me.'

'No big secret. He's starting with Edwin Brooker, if he can run him to ground. A bit of a shifty character, it appears. We've been checking the membership list of Grove against our files and his name came up – he was our one match. Charged with affray and fined very heavily, though he escaped prison. It was some years ago, but still...'

Jack wondered whether this was the moment to mention the attack on Lilian French – it was an incident of which the police were still unaware. Perhaps, though, he should pass it by

Flora first. Lilian, she'd said, had been adamant she'd no wish to involve the police, although her reason – that she might harm Nelson in helping to build a case against him – was no longer valid. A dead man couldn't be harmed further. But he would wait to speak to Ridley, Jack decided, discover the line of enquiry the inspector was following before he added more to the mix.

It was Alice's turn to host what had been a delayed Friday meal and tonight, as always, Flora was happy to be seeing her friends – chatting, laughing with them, catching up with news. This evening, though, felt especially significant. Spending half the week in Lewes as she'd been doing, and denied the kind of daily contact with the village that for years she'd taken for granted, she'd felt more and more that she was losing touch with the people she held most dear. Now, her world was changing again and the rhythms of an old life making ready to return. Tonight would be the beginning.

Her friend's cottage was ablaze with light, a glowing beacon as she walked towards it down the high street. The Chinese restaurant in the building next to Alice, over which her friend had felt so indignant, had traded for only a few months – Abbeymead, it seemed, had not been ready for food quite that foreign – and now the modern infill that had replaced a bomb-destroyed cottage was empty, awaiting a new set of tenants. Overlay House, too, Flora reflected, was once again empty. Who would move into Jack's old home, if anyone?

Alice came bustling to her front door, giving Flora a hearty kiss before she took coat and hat and threw them over the banister. The bentwood coat rack, a spindly effort, was already staggering beneath the weight of heavy wool. Kate had already arrived and so, it seemed, had Sally, taking a few precious hours away from the madness that was the Priory hotel at this time of the year.

'The others have beaten you tonight,' Alice said, walking ahead. 'We've the soup on the table already.'

'I can smell it.' Flora sniffed appreciatively. 'French onion? Yes, sorry, I'm a bit late. The switch to the oven has been playing up – somehow it's got stuck – and we've had to light the gas manually. Poor Jack doesn't have the knack. He's too tall to crouch! And *I* found it difficult.'

'It's about time you got yourself a decent cooker. That one in Lewes is a fright, too.'

'It is, or rather was,' she amended happily, walking into the room that served as both sitting and dining room for Alice.

Kate jumped up to kiss her on the cheek and Sally held out a languid hand. 'Sorry, Flora, I can't get to my feet. I'm absolutely exhausted and we've a week to go before the big day.'

Flora took the bowl Alice was handing her and suddenly felt very hungry. A basket of rolls was being passed around the table, murmured thank yous, and then silence as they ate. Their friend was the most sublime cook, Flora thought. Onion soup was onion soup but, when cooked by Alice, it reached a whole new level of tastiness.

'Have you left the college flat yet?' Sally asked.

'Last night, a final farewell! We've been moving stuff back gradually, but we still weren't able to bring everything that was left even though the Austin was crammed – I hadn't realised how much I'd taken to Lewes – but Jack will drive back in a few days and collect it all.'

'An evening for celebration then.' Sally glanced happily around the table.

'I should have opened the blackcurrant wine.' Alice looked cross with herself. 'I've a last bottle in the cupboard.'

'Keep it for Christmas,' Flora advised. 'For now, this scrumptious meal is my celebration.'

'So, you've left Lewes, but any news on Overlay House?'

Sally's question was addressed to everyone, but it was Flora who shook her head. 'It's empty, of course, and it will take time for the landlord to find a new tenant.'

'If he ever does!' Alice said, finishing her soup. 'There's not many who'd want to move into a house where someone has been murdered.'

Kate shivered slightly. 'It will have to be someone who knows nothing about Mr Nelson's death. Although the village will be keen to tell whoever moves in.'

'Then the house will likely stay empty and fall to pieces eventually,' Alice prophesied. 'It's halfway there already.'

Flora hoped not. She had never liked Jack's home but she knew how much it had meant to him at a difficult time in his life. To see it gradually fall into disrepair, the garden he'd lovingly tended become a wasteland once more, would upset him greatly.

'I always said there was somethin' wrong with that man. That Nelson,' Alice announced, bringing a dish of braised beef to the table. 'Now he's gone and got hisself killed.'

'You were convinced he was a spy,' Sally reminded her somewhat foolishly. 'If he was, he didn't do too well.'

'It's why he got hisself killed,' her aunt retorted. 'Probably. I walked that way a few days before he died.'

Everyone stopped serving themselves vegetables. 'Along Greenway Lane?' Flora asked. 'Not to see me, though.'

'You were in Lewes, my love. No, I was goin' to the Kettler farm. Dan Kettler told me he had a load of butter 'n' cheese goin' spare. His wife ran the creamery, but now...'

Three heads nodded in sympathy. Daphne Kettler had died several months previously.

'Anyways, I was passing Overlay House on my way there and guess what I saw?'

The beef continued to cool.

'I don't often speak ill of the dead but, whatever you say, Sally – and I can cope with your teasin', don't you worry – that Nelson was a wrong 'un. He didn't fit the village and he shouldn't have been here.'

'But what was he doing, Alice?' Flora asked, baffled.

'He was with that woman, the one your Rose goes to for her fancy get-ups.'

'Thomasina Bell?'

'That's her. Standin' in the front garden, pawin' at the man. And 'im lettin' her. In the middle of the day! What's this village comin' to, I thought. She was all giggles and coy looks. You're too old for that, miss, I thought. Much too old. It was downright embarrassin'. *And* she had a basket with her, too. Shoppin' for 'im. Mebbe cookin' for the man!'

'But how does that make him a spy?' Sally's lack of tact had Flora and Kate look at each other across the table, waiting for the explosion.

'It makes him stupid enough to be a very bad one,' Alice announced triumphantly. 'It was disgustin', that's what.' Charlie's very word, Flora recalled. 'Disgustin'.'

The amorous advances of Thomasina weren't news to Flora, but she wouldn't spoil Alice's story by relating what Charlie had seen two weeks earlier. Happily, the conversation moved on: to the popularity of the gala dinners Sally had begun at the Priory, to baby Sarah's attempt to pull herself to her feet and, finally, their plans for Christmas, the most pressing topic. It wasn't until they were halfway through a mincemeat and marzipan tart that the bombshell hit Flora. And it was Kate who dropped it.

'I was at the doctor's,' she began innocently enough. 'Sarah was there for her diphtheria vaccination and this woman came out of his office. I had to look twice. She wasn't anyone I knew from the village, but somehow I recognised her face. Then I realised I'd seen it in the paper. That man who was killed on

Bonfire Night. It was his wife, or his widow, I should say. The newspaper had quite a big article on his funeral – I think he was someone important in Lewes. That's why I noticed her. I wondered why she'd come to Abbeymead. Why she'd come to see Dr Hanson. And crying, too. I felt upset for her.'

Flora had never mentioned to her Abbeymead friends the drama at Glebe Avenue or her role in it, and she wasn't about to now. But Kate's news was disquieting, more disquieting the longer she thought of it. Lilian French was supposed to be in Newcastle but here she was travelling to the village to see a strange doctor? Crying to a medical man she didn't know? What did that suggest?

'Mebbe she'd rather not go to her own doctor,' Alice said wisely. 'Mebbe things aren't going so well with her and she feels she can't speak to someone she knows.'

'It's anonymity, isn't it,' Sally added. 'Everyone in Abbeymead knows everyone else, but this woman comes from Lewes and no one will know her here. Except Kate who reads the local paper! If you're having a crisis and need help, you might not want your neighbours to know.'

There was silence around the table. 'There's shame around not coping,' Kate said sympathetically. 'It's almost a disgrace if you don't. I know when Dad died, I felt I had to keep smiling. Pretend I was OK. And that lady has had a lot more to cope with than I did.'

'Hopefully, Dr Hanson will have sorted her out.' Alice collected their pudding bowls. 'Tea, everyone? I wouldn't want to hear the poor woman has followed her husband.'

It was then that Flora's heart did a full stop before she started breathing again. Suicide? The image of an open oven door loomed in her mind. Could Lilian have done that to herself? Could she have been the one to turn on the gas and lie down beside the oven, having thrown away a key, locked the kitchen door with the spare, and then hidden it from sight? No, that was a nonsense. Even if she'd had suicide in mind, why would she need to do any of those things? To make sure that she wasn't found, a whisper said. To make doubly sure.

'Are you all right, my love?' Alice had brought a tray of tea to the table and was looking fixedly at her.

'Yes, fine. Sorry – just planning. Thinking about the week-end. How much I can do in the garden,' she said, hoping she sounded genuine.

25

'Suicide?' Jack paused, toothbrush in hand, while Flora continued to brush.

She nodded, her mouth full of toothpaste.

'But why the elaborate preparations? Surely someone intent on killing themselves wouldn't go to all that trouble – painting windows, throwing away a key.'

'I'm not sure she did, but it's possible,' Flora responded, replacing her toothbrush in its holder, 'if she really meant business. I don't know how many visitors Lilian has every day, but if she knew she might be interrupted, she could have taken extraordinary precautions to get the job done.'

'Is that really likely, though? You assumed she'd been attacked by someone she'd made an enemy of, and that still seems the most obvious explanation.'

'Until Kate dropped her bombshell, it was. On the few occasions I've met Lilian, she's seemed a calm woman. Measured. A quite private person. Desperately upset by what happened to her husband, of course, but not someone who would ever think of suicide. And yet, she came to Abbeymead, a village she doesn't know, when she was supposed to be with her daughter in Newcastle, to consult a doctor she'd never met, and then cried in public – in full view of everyone in the surgery. That isn't calm or measured.'

'But when you saw her in hospital, right after the incident, she thanked you for rescuing her, didn't she?'

'She was hardly going to tell me that I'd messed up her plans, Jack. Not after I'd risked my life to get her out of the house.'

'I suppose not, but...' He turned the bathroom light out and walked back into the bedroom to pull down the eiderdown.

Flora followed, snuggling down in the bed and glad, on a perishingly cold night, to feel the weight of the bedclothes.

'Suicide is unlikely, I agree,' she said, half-smothered by a sheet, 'but it's a possibility that we've not considered before. It gave me a real shock when Kate told us what she'd seen – it could turn our thinking upside down. If Lilian wasn't the victim of an attack, her hint that Leo Nelson could be responsible – did she say that to disguise what she'd done? – is entirely wrong. Nelson couldn't have been responsible. And if, as well, he was innocent of Trevor's murder, which I think he was, that leaves us with just Brooker. Our sole suspect.'

Jack climbed into bed, twisting to wrap his arms around her. 'We can only hope that Ridley is getting on better than we are,' he said half-jokingly.

'I'm sure we'll get there.' Snuggling even further beneath the covers, she sounded dozy. 'We usually do.'

Jack yawned. 'I guess tomorrow is another day.'

'A day when I'm going to try on my new dress,' she remembered happily.

He lifted his head to look down at her. 'How's that?'

'Oh, I forgot to mention. Thomasina Bell rang the All's Well today to tell me the dress I ordered is ready for a first fitting.'

'Her studio is in Lewes, isn't it?'

'Yes,' Flora sighed. 'I thought I'd said goodbye to the town last night, but it seems not. I wished she'd let me know before we left the college.'

'I'll drive you over.'

'No, you won't. There's really no need, Jack. I can catch a bus and you have a book to edit.'

'Buses,' he reminded her. 'You'll have to catch buses.'

'OK, buses, but I won't have shopping to carry – it will be an easy trip. I'll forget lunch and leave straight after I close tomorrow morning.'

Jack was quiet for a long time and she thought he'd fallen asleep, but then, out of the darkness, he said, 'I think you should postpone the visit.'

'Why would I do that? I'm longing to see the dress. It's sure to be a marvellous creation! Initially, I wasn't keen on ordering it – in fact, I didn't think I ever would, it was just a pretence to talk to Thomasina – but now I can't wait to see what she's made.'

'Alan Ridley and his team are interviewing everyone who was on that float—'

'What! Again?'

'Again. It seems that Brownlow's notes have proved useless. The interviewees will include Thomasina Bell and Sergeant Norris intends to make a point of talking to her himself. She's become "a person of interest", he's decided.'

'Why is that? As far as I can see, the only possible crime Thomasina could be guilty of is the attack on Lilian. She does have a motive there – jealousy over Leo's friendship with his old girlfriend. And that's only if it *was* an attack and not a suicide attempt.'

'Nelson was responsible for the death of her best friend, have you forgotten? How's that for a motive?'

'A good one, except for the fact that he was found innocent of causing Letty Reynolds' death *and* he and Thomasina seemed to be on the very best of terms – and that's putting it mildly! It's not just Charlie who's reported the blatant canoodling. Alice was in great form this evening, outraged at the pawin', as she put it, going on at Overlay House.'

It was exactly the argument that Jack had deployed in his conversation with Sergeant Norris, but if he wanted to dissuade Flora from going to her dress fitting, it was best to stay silent.

'And as for any idea that she might have killed Trevor French,' she continued, 'where's her motive? Why would Thomasina risk everything to kill him? I think she probably resented Trevor taking over the Grove society, was angry maybe on Edwin Brooker's behalf, but as a reason to murder? I can't believe that. And it's not just why, is it? *How* could she have done it? How thrust a knife into a man's side from the back of the float?'

'I still wish you wouldn't go to her studio tomorrow,' he said doggedly. 'Leave it a few days. Let the police do their questioning first.'

'I've made an appointment and I can't cancel at such short notice.' Flora couldn't see Thomasina being too pleased if she rang tomorrow morning with the news that she wasn't coming to Lewes that day.

There was another reason, too, just as important, which she wouldn't spell out. Jack would see it as trivial. She would be working in the bookshop every day next week – Rose had asked to take a short break – and a trip to Lewes would be impossible. Rose and Hector were moving into the flat they'd finally managed to rent, and her assistant needed time to settle into the new property.

If she didn't go for her fitting tomorrow afternoon, she wouldn't make it to the sewing studio before Christmas. Now that she'd chosen the pattern, chosen the material, she wanted that dress. Wanted to wear it at all the Christmas events that were approaching fast. The dress would be perfect, Flora was certain, and equally certain that Thomasina as 'a person of interest' wouldn't stop her from enjoying it.

It was another dry but very cold day – there had been a run of them lately – and not unwelcome after the drenching that autumn had brought. The wind, though, was a new feature. It was blowing hard, an icy blast rushing in from the Channel and scouring the Downs and everything between. Flora made sure she wore the thicker of her two winter coats, a woollen hat and fluffy gloves. Waiting for a bus could be a cold business.

She was lucky. The Abbeymead service to Brighton had kept good time today and when she reached the Steine, leaving the bus at the mad palace that was Brighton Pavilion, she had only a ten-minute wait before another going to Lewes pulled in at the stop.

Twenty minutes later, on the outskirts of the town, Flora reluctantly left its cosiness to begin what was a lengthy walk to Thomasina's garden studio some way north of the main town. By the time she turned into Christie Avenue and was passing the pebble-dash exteriors of a row of matching houses, she felt thoroughly chilled. Perhaps she should have taken up Jack's offer of a lift. But no. He had work to do and this visit was pure pleasure.

She was halfway along the tree-lined road when she saw a van she thought she recognised. Focusing hard – the vehicle was still at some distance – Flora could just make out the word 'Electrician'. Brooker's van! Of course it was. She'd ridden in it as a passenger, when she'd more or less forced the man to take her and Lilian French to the local hospital.

For a while, she made no move, keen to discover Brooker's whereabouts. It was always possible the electrician was working in one of the houses in the street. Possible, but seemingly untrue. Making sure she stayed well hidden, Flora waited until she saw the figure of a man walk down the driveway of what she knew was Thomasina's house and cross the road to the waiting van. Brooker seemed pleased with himself, almost bouncing, if such a solidly built man could bounce.

She waited until he'd started the ignition, then turned her head to face away as he drove past. It was better the electrician knew nothing of her visit. As previously, Thomasina's house, as she drew near, appeared quiet. Empty. The woman would be at work, she supposed, and walking through the side gate, she made her way to the cedarwood chalet that filled a large section of the back garden.

Walking up the short flight of steps to the veranda, she spied Thomasina through the window, hanging up a garment she had evidently just ironed. She knocked on the glass of the sliding door and Thomasina looked up, her face flushed. Heat from the iron, Flora wondered, or the result of Edwin Brooker's visit?

'Come in.' The seamstress slid back the door, angrily pushing away a strand of hair that had come free of its moorings.

'Your dress, Mrs Carrington.' Thomasina pointed to a dark green merino wool hanging from a rack that had been fitted to the rear wall of the studio. 'I hope you like it.'

Flora walked over to the rack, marvelling at how truly special it was. 'I love it,' she said, stroking the soft material. 'You've done an excellent job. Thank you.'

'I should wait until you try it on,' her companion said abruptly, 'before you lavish too much praise.'

The dressmaker was not in the best of moods, it was clear. Not that their previous meetings had felt particularly warm, but one thing was certain: she could sew beautifully. Garments in various stages of completion were hanging from the rack as Flora reached for her dress, and all of them quite stunning. She turned to look for the folding screen, and from the corner of her eye caught sight of a small, square leather box sitting on the corner of Thomasina's cutting table. A jewellery box?

The seamstress brushed past her, scooping up the box into the pocket of the smart pinafore dress she wore. 'You can change behind here,' she said curtly, collecting the screen from its resting place and unfolding it in one abrupt movement.

The box, whatever it contained, was not for public display.

26

Bells were jangling loudly in Flora's head as she took off her skirt and the two jumpers she'd donned to keep out the cold. Plainly, Thomasina was upset, and the most likely thing to have upset her was the recent visit by Edwin Brooker. A visit which now appeared highly significant. Flora had managed only a brief glimpse but that had been a ring box that Thomasina had pocketed. An engagement ring? And a piece of jewellery, it seemed, the woman wanted no one to know of.

If there had been a proposal, why was the seamstress so troubled by it? The woman was unmarried and, as far as Flora knew, Edwin Brooker was just as single. There was nothing to prevent a wedding. And, if it was that Thomasina had no wish to marry, she could have turned him down. Gently. Perhaps, during these last few weeks, she'd encouraged him to believe she would agree, and had now thought better of it. Edwin Brooker wouldn't be happy with that. Angry, more like, Flora thought, aware of the man's uncertain temper.

But he *had* been happy. He'd been jaunty on that walk to his van. Flora was annoyed. If only she'd arrived a few minutes earlier, she might have overheard an interesting conversation.

Brooker evidently thought the encounter had gone well, but Thomasina? Had she agreed to marry and her abrupt manner simply a desire to keep the news to herself? Or not agreed, and was annoyed that she had been forced to placate the man in some way? By making promises, by keeping secrets? Flora would dearly have liked to know.

Slipping the merino wool over her head, she walked out from behind the screen for Thomasina's inspection. The dress-maker was busy rearranging the tools of her trade, her movements rapid and jerky, as though her life depended on their being in just the right place: needles, tape measure, scissors. It was plain to Flora that she was still greatly disturbed.

'Let me see,' Thomasina said, patting a pot of pins into place. 'Yes, it looks good.'

'It looks superb.'

'Hmm. Maybe an inch less on the bust, and I'll need to pin up the hem. What length do you like your dresses?'

'Just below the knee, I think.'

Thomasina bent down, a pincushion at her side, and began to shorten the hem to the length Flora had requested. Meanwhile, her customer, looking into the mirror, was spellbound, imagining the expression on Jack's face when she wore this splendid creation to the first of their Christmas events, mince pies and mulled wine at the vicarage. Magical, she thought dreamily. This whole studio was magical and, for a moment, she wished that she, too, could sew – her attempts so far had been scrubby at best.

But this was a special place, Flora decided, somewhere quite out of the ordinary: the air cedar-scented, the light crystal clear even in mid-winter, and its orderliness so satisfying – bales of material stacked neatly on shelves, boxes of buttons arranged by colour, a basket of trimmings, a whole raft of scissors.

Her gaze became intent. Scissors. Thomasina had a small collection and they all looked remarkably sharp. Flora remembered seeing them on her previous visit, slicing through material as easily as through butter. Wielded as a weapon, they could do damage, she reckoned. As much damage as a knife? Alan Ridley was looking for a knife – maybe the pathologist had suggested a certain kind but not suggested scissors. It could have been scissors.

Thomasina stopped pinning. The woman was watching her closely.

'Sorry,' Flora apologised. 'Daydreaming again.'

A last few pins and the seamstress got to her feet. 'I'll leave you to get dressed. I need to go back to the house – I'm expecting a telephone call, long distance – but I'll let you know when the dress is ready. I shall require payment on collection, of course.'

'Of course,' Flora said curtly, turning to walk behind the screen. Really, this was a woman she couldn't like. She would pay for her dress and make sure she never saw Thomasina again.

The image of a pair of scissors had stuck, though, commandeering her thoughts as she took off the special dress and gave it a last stroke. Could the murder weapon have been scissors – and scissors that came from here? Unlikely, she decided, although there were certainly enough from which to choose. But a pair of sharp scissors could come from a multitude of places and, in any case, Thomasina couldn't have used them. She had been in no position on that float to wield them successfully. But someone else could have borrowed them from here, Flora continued to argue silently. Someone who had been in the right position. Someone called Brooker?

She had struggled into her second jumper and was reaching for her coat and hat when she smelt the smoke. Hurriedly, she finished dressing and went to investigate. Pushing the screen aside, Flora was aghast at what she saw. An entire corner of the chalet was alight, a golden ball of fire creeping up the wall, the smoke billowing forth in small round puffs and slowly draining freshness from the room. A soft and camphorous smell filled the air – prickly, cooling. Like a mothball, she thought.

But this was no mothball and snatching up the dress – she wasn't leaving it to become cinders – she grabbed her handbag and made for the sliding door. Except... it no longer slid. Ineffectually, she tugged at the handle, but it remained firmly shut. Dropping bag and dress to the floor, she used both hands for the job, heaving at the door with every ounce of her strength.

The window frames on one side of the building had begun to buckle, the panes at first cracking from the corners but, very soon, deepening to spread from bottom to top, scarring the entire surface of the glass. As Flora watched in stunned silence, the wall of cedar was consumed by a pillar of flames, growing ever upwards to reach the roof and whipped to a frenzy by the fierce wind that had been blowing since daybreak.

But where was Thomasina? Surely, she must be aware of the tragedy unfolding – the noise and smell of destruction must be permeating the house. She would be calling the fire brigade, that was it. Unless... there was a jolt to Flora's heart. Unless the telephone call had been a ruse. Unless, while she had been dressing, the woman had crept back and set fire to a space she must love.

But there was no time to think of Thomasina. The smoke was becoming denser by the second. Flora felt her eyes sting and her chest tighten and tried to pull a jumper over her nose and mouth as protection. But her throat was sore and her breath becoming increasingly short. Surely not again, she thought frantically. Hadn't she already coped with this situation – poisoned by gas rather than smoke? It was as though some ghastly nightmare had returned to taunt her. And, just as then, she looked wildly around for a way to break out of her prison.

The side wall where the flames had erupted had almost

crumbled, but to walk through the yawning gaps would mean walking through fire. She couldn't do it.

The flames were spreading rapidly now, from the ruins of the outer wall to the shelves of material, and from there to the chair covers, the cushions, the paperwork on the desk. Hot ribbons of light, flying, leaping, a crazy life-threatening dance that would soon engulf the entire room.

Desperately, she made to grasp the handle once more, only to jump back, shocked. Pain seared its way across her hand. In that one minute, the handle had become scorching steel. And now the sliding door was buckling beneath a fiery onslaught. Jack had been right – she should not have come. But the idea that a dress fitting could bring with it danger had seemed so absurd, so outlandish, and yet the threat he'd somehow divined was happening, now, right now, and she was going to die in this inferno.

There was a sudden crack as the door caved in, forcing her to cower as melting glass fell to the floor. From the reeking void it had left behind, a hand appeared. A hand? What was she seeing? Dear Lord, she would die hallucinating. But the hand was real, reaching out for her, pulling her forward, through the doorway. And through the fire.

'Jack,' she spluttered, as he half lifted her over the threshold into fresh air, 'is that really you?'

'Don't try to talk. Let's get out of here.'

'But my bag,' she gasped. 'My dress.' And before he could stop her, she'd turned back and bending low, was feeling along the floor of the chalet.

'I've got them,' she said, fighting for breath.

Roughly, Jack pulled her to her feet and, with his arm wrapped tightly around her, they ran to the side gate. Behind them a heap of cedarwood, once a magnificent studio, was now a massive bonfire, its smoke and flames visible for miles.

'A dress!' he exploded, once they were through the gate.

'I had to save it. It's so beautiful,' Flora croaked.

His face cleared and he gave a crooked smile. 'Of course you did. But let me take it now.'

Gratefully, she handed it over. Adrenaline had kept her largely unconscious of the pain, but suddenly her hand was alight and producing flames of its own.

'Miss Bell is nowhere to be seen, did you know? I reckon she's—' he began, when Flora let out a gasp.

Hearing it, he frowned, and turning over her palm, saw the bright red swelling and the flaking skin.

'You're hurt! Badly, Flora. We must get help. Immediately.' He thought for a second. 'It's best we drive back to Abbeymead. The surgery will be closed, but Dr Hanson won't mind if we knock at his door. Not with a hand as bad as that.'

'I'd really like to go home,' she pleaded. 'I can bind up the hand myself.'

'No. Definitely no. You're seeing a doctor.'

Flora lacked the strength to argue, a crushing lethargy infiltrating her body. Her head, too, had begun to feel decidedly strange, hardly seeming to belong to her. Overcome with dizziness, she allowed Jack to shepherd her down Thomasina's driveway and into the road beyond where the Austin was patiently waiting.

And parked just behind, Inspector Ridley in an unmarked car.

'Jack Carrington, of all people!' He'd clambered out. 'Hello there, and Mrs—' The inspector broke off, his eyes fixed on Flora. 'What the—'

'Thomasina Bell,' Jack said crisply. 'You need to get hold of her. I'm almost certain she's responsible for this. I think she may have a penchant for murder as well as arson, or she knows someone who does.'

'The dressmaker?' Alan Ridley looked incredulous. 'But I'm here to speak to her.'

'You might need to go looking,' Jack said, as a massive crash sounded from the rear garden.

The remains of the studio, Flora thought brokenly.

Without waiting to say more, the inspector dashed across the road, up the front drive and through the side gate, a surprised police officer following closely on his superior's heels.

Jack meanwhile had tucked his wife into the front seat, a blanket around her knees, before making sure the precious dress had pride of place at the rear.

'How did you get here?' she asked, as he climbed in beside her.

Her voice had almost disappeared from the smoke she'd ingested and she spoke in little more than a whisper, but it was a question she had to ask. A question that until now she hadn't considered.

Jack tapped the dashboard. 'As you see. On four wheels.'

'No, I mean, why, how, did you turn up when you did?'

'I wasn't happy,' he said, taking hold of her good hand. 'I was going to leave you to it, but then I couldn't. I had to drive here, see for myself you were OK.'

'You're amazing. You always are. You came at just the right time.' She turned her head to kiss him on the cheek.

'Not so amazing. In fact, really quite simple. I had a hunch,' he said cheekily.

27

It took some time to run Dr Hanson to ground. As expected, the surgery was closed and knocking on the doctor's front door – the house was attached to his work premises – they were told by Mrs Hanson that her husband had been called out to an expectant mother and was currently helping a baby into the world.

'That's far more important than me,' Flora said quickly. 'Let's go home.'

'Matthew will be back soon, I'm sure,' the doctor's wife said. 'It's bound to be a quick birth. It's Mrs Perry's fourth.' Her gaze fell on Flora's damaged hand. 'Look, why don't I open up the surgery and you can wait there?'

'That's very kind, Mrs Hanson. We'll do that.' He took hold of Flora's arm, steering her firmly towards the surgery door.

Alone in the waiting room, they sat on plastic chairs facing each other. 'Don't be cross.' He gave her a droll look. 'It's important that you see Hanson. You need that hand looked at, otherwise you could be in trouble and you really wouldn't want that over Christmas.'

Flora wouldn't. She had events to go to, a party or two to

attend, and best of all a new dress to wear. With only a small sigh, she subsided onto her chair and waited.

Mrs Hanson had been right about a quick birth, the doctor returning home within half an hour, and a few minutes later calling them into his office.

'You did right to come,' he said, after he'd examined Flora's swollen palm. 'That is one very nasty burn. Have you run it under cold water?'

'It's not been possible,' Jack replied for her. 'Flora was caught in a fire.'

The doctor tutted. 'Cold water is the thing, you know. But let's see what we can do.'

Very gently, he cleaned the wound with mild soap and water, then patting it dry, reached into one of the cupboards that lined his office wall and took down a small jar. 'An antibiotic cream,' he told them, 'that should stop any infection setting in. I'll bandage the hand, but the burn will have to be washed daily and the dressing changed. Can you manage that?'

'Yes,' Flora breathed painfully. The washing had not been easy.

'And take something for the pain,' the doctor added, seeing her expression. 'These should do the trick.' A handful of tablets was transferred into an empty pot. 'And if you've been in a bad fire, I should listen to your chest as well.' Jack was grateful that Hanson's interest was in Flora's health rather than the details of the fire she'd escaped. That could have been difficult to explain.

'No, really, I'm fine, Doctor,' she answered quickly, and gave the two men what she hoped was a convincing smile.

Once back at the cottage, Jack insisted on helping her from the car and up the path, before returning to lock the Austin and cover its bonnet with a thick blanket. Temperatures were due to fall again and this night was forecast to be even colder than the last.

In the kitchen, Flora was trying inexpertly to fill a kettle one-handedly. 'You're excused chores,' he said, taking it from her. 'I'll make the tea, but first...' and, putting a hand beneath her elbow, he guided her into the sitting room and pushed her gently down onto the sofa.

'I'll be back,' he said, making for the staircase and returning a few minutes later with the unused patchwork quilt they kept in the airing cupboard.

'Jack,' she protested, as he tucked it round her. 'I'm not an invalid and you're not to wait on me.'

'That's just what I intend to do. You need cosying.' He bent down to light the fire. 'Let me get this going and then I'll bring tea and biscuits.'

'You're spoiling me.'

'I am, but I don't often have the chance, so indulge me!'

'I shouldn't have gone,' she said in a small voice, pulling up the quilt so that only her face and neck were visible. 'You warned me not to.'

He paused at the door. 'In your defence, my love, it wasn't exactly a warning. I had a dim sense of worry, that's all.'

'Which turned out to be anything but dim. I should have listened.'

'The day you do that, I'll paint it on the pavement outside the All's Well – in big red letters,' he joked. 'Seriously, Flora, I can't blame you for not taking notice. On the surface, what was there to fear from a dress fitting?'

'Actually, I don't think there was. Not initially. Not until Thomasina seemed suddenly to realise that I'd worked it out. Well, half-worked it out.'

Jack frowned. 'I want to hear every detail of what went on in that studio, but first the tea.'

The fire had now well and truly caught and a warm glow

was filling the hearth, the smell of applewood sending Flora, left alone, into a comforting doze. How very different, she thought sleepily, from the flames that had been set to destroy her. The terror of being trapped in that inferno remained with her and, physically, she felt utterly weary – her body's reaction, she imagined, to the trauma she'd put it through – but also strangely relaxed. The painkillers Jack had insisted she take, and whatever Dr Hanson had done to her hand, had eased the pain considerably. And she was home. She was safe.

It was a while before Jack returned and she saw that he'd unpacked a new box of shortbread biscuits to accompany the tea.

'I was saving them for Christmas,' she said, pulling herself upright.

'Christmas starts now. It's official. A shortbread a day keeps the doctor away.' He offered the open box to her and she chose her favourites, the fan-shaped ones.

'Now tell me what happened.' He settled down beside her, pouring cups of tea for them both.

Flora paused, shortbread in hand, and tried to clear her head. Tried to clear the smoke from her brain. It was important she gave Jack a true and detailed account.

'I'd gone behind a screen,' she began, 'and put on the dress – it's so elegant, Jack. Oh! Where is it?'

'Keep calm – all is well. I've hung it by the window to air. But it's not looking too good. I don't think it's completely finished.'

'It isn't. It still has pins in the hem, but I can probably sew that for myself. It was when Thomasina was pinning...'

He looked expectant.

'Sorry, I'm not making a very good fist of this, am I?' With her good hand, she brushed away the crumbs. 'Thomasina asked me what length I wanted the dress and it was while she was bent down pinning the hem that I looked around the studio.

Really looked. I was thinking how fantastic it would be to have a space like this just for yourself, to do in it whatever you chose. A kind of woman cave. I have the bookshop, of course, but that's a shared space, isn't it? Customers coming and going, and now Rose working there, too. But Thomasina's studio was special.'

Jack drank his tea, waiting patiently for the crux of the story.

'Anyway,' she went on, 'I was looking around at how everything was so neatly ordered and my glance fell on the scissors block. The scissors were different sizes, slightly different shapes, and I suddenly thought how sharp they must be. I remembered when I visited the studio before and saw Thomasina cutting material, slicing through it.'

'And you thought why not a pair of scissors rather than a knife?'

'Exactly,' she said gratefully. 'I must have been staring hard at them, trying to work out what might have happened on Bonfire Night, but when I looked down I saw Thomasina staring at me in a strange way. I can't describe her expression, but I think now it was when she realised I'd somehow guessed her gruesome secret.'

'And decided that you couldn't live to tell the tale.'

'It *must* have been Thomasina who set the fire going – when she made an excuse to go back to the house. There's no way it could have started so suddenly and been so fierce unless it was deliberate. In that moment, when she saw me looking and thinking, she must have been overwhelmed. Crazed. Made desperate. To destroy that glorious room, a hugely expensive sewing machine, all those materials – all of it worth a fortune – and...'

Flora closed her eyes. Flames were burning bright behind her eyelids and she couldn't go on.

'I agree she must have been desperate,' Jack said, 'but why?

She can't be guilty of the murder – she couldn't have used the scissors herself.'

'That's what I thought. You would have to be close to your victim to kill with them.' She gave a small shudder of disgust. 'If her scissors *were* the weapon that killed Trevor French, they could have been borrowed, couldn't they? Or stolen from the studio.'

'You're thinking of Brooker?'

'He's the obvious one, particularly now. I think he may have asked Thomasina to marry him. Today. There was a ring on her cutting table.'

'Really?' Jack puffed out his cheeks. 'Then they're a good deal closer than we thought – despite the advances she made to Nelson. But it's odd that she suddenly twigged you were on to her. Did she already suspect that you knew something?'

Flora drank down her tea and tried to steady herself. 'She might have, I suppose, though I don't remember asking anything to make her uneasy. A few questions only.'

'They might have been enough to start her wondering. If she's harbouring such a wicked secret, she'll be suspicious of everyone – but to do such a wild thing. Literally send her future up in smoke! She must have had more than a suspicion that we were poking around. But what?'

'I wonder if we'll ever know. She must have run away as soon as she was sure the studio would burn to the ground.'

'And you with it,' he said grimly, packing their cups onto the tray.

'But not only me. There's Lilian and, even worse, Leo Nelson and Trevor French. If Brooker is behind those attacks and Thomasina knows it...' she said slowly, 'no wonder she was upset by his proposal. If she was married to him, she would be silenced for good. A wife's evidence wouldn't count.'

'You think she saw it as a ploy to keep her quiet?'

'Maybe. And practically, if it ever came to saving *herself*, she could never tell what she knew and be believed.'

'Whatever the truth of it, it's up to the police to track her down and take her in for questioning. Ridley will have put a call out and there'll be police in every county looking for her. It shouldn't be long before they have her under lock and key.'

Flora idly reached for another shortbread from the still open box. 'She has a van,' she said. 'I don't think it was parked in the road when we left. She could be a long way away by now.'

'A van that is particularly noticeable – sprayed pink with a large pair of scissors painted on the side!'

They relapsed into silence, Flora shuffling closer and tucking her good hand through his arm. It was the ringing of the telephone that woke them both from the warm doze they'd fallen into. Jack jumped to his feet and walked swiftly out into the hall.

Flora could hear his muttered responses through the open door. They were brief and intermittent. Whoever was on the other end of the line – and she guessed it was Inspector Ridley – was doing the talking.

'That was Alan,' Jack said, walking back into the room and flopping down on the sofa again. 'I expect you guessed.'

'About Thomasina?'

'Good news. She's under arrest.'

Flora looked relieved.

'And, surprise, surprise – along with Edwin Brooker.'

'Really?' She allowed the quilt to slip.

'It seems that after the pyrotechnics, it was to Brooker she fled. Brooker's shop, in fact, which he promptly shut and bundled her back to his house. The problem with that little plan was that one of Ridley's men was already there, waiting to interview the chap as part of the inspector's decision to take new statements from everyone who'd been on the Grove float.'

'Both of them are in police cells then,' she said wonderingly. 'Brooker for concealing Thomasina?'

'Probably, and much the best place for them. Right, now's the time for you to find your bed. If you're hungry, I can bring up supper, but if not, you can sleep. You're almost asleep now.'

Flora's eyes searched for the clock. 'But it's only just past six.'

'Bed,' he said inexorably. 'And you'll sleep in tomorrow. I'll get breakfast and we'll go to the Cross Keys for lunch. They can't do much harm to a ploughman's.'

'But I had plans for Sunday.'

'Whatever they were, forget them,' he advised. 'You'll have to. You've only one usable hand. If you're very good, I might let you take a short stroll with me! Oh, and sometime tomorrow I'll be calling on Rose. Next week, she can deputise for you at the All's Well.'

'She and Hector have just moved into their new flat,' she protested. 'There'll be boxes to unpack—'

'They can wait for a few days. Rose won't mind.'

28

It seemed that Rose didn't mind, saying that over the next few evenings she could unpack all that she and Hector had brought from their individual lodgings. In the circumstances, she assured Jack, she'd be happy to look after the All's Well for the week. Friday, her usual day at the post office, was Christmas Day and not even Dilys, Abbeymead's fearsome postmistress, would expect to see her assistant at work.

'Rose can hold the fort tomorrow,' Flora said severely, when she learned of the arrangements, 'but after that, I'll be back. Where I belong – among my books. In a couple of days, I won't even be wearing this wretched bandage.' She gave her damaged hand a wave in the air, the once pristine white covering already a dingy shade of grey. 'And I can't stay in the cottage for days, Jack, it will send me mad. I'm feeling so much better.'

'You're still short of breath. I heard you breathing hard just pulling on a jumper this morning! You need a few days' rest.'

Flora's mutinous expression had him offer an olive branch. 'You could come with me tomorrow. Only a drive to the college but it will be a change of scene.'

'You're picking up the rest of our stuff?'

He nodded. 'I don't think we left much – just enough to fill the Austin's boot. I know you were glad to see the last of the apartment, but will you come?'

'It's better than looking at four walls, I suppose,' she said a trifle grumpily.

It turned out to be a lot better than looking at the cottage walls. Jack had carried to the car the few belongings that remained in the flat – a suitcase, two lamps and some pots and pans from the kitchen cupboards – when Dr Summersby, the new college principal, appeared at the side of the Austin.

'Jack, good morning,' she said, sporting a professional smile. 'And your wife?'

'Good morning. Yes, this is Flora.'

'I'm so happy to meet you, Mrs Carrington. Your husband has been such an asset to Cleve.'

An asset that you're happy to be rid of, Flora thought, while shaking the hand Dr Summersby offered her.

'Classes have finished and everyone will be making for home later today, but we're having a small pre-Christmas get-together in the staffroom. I was hoping you'd join us for a sherry – or two. I did telephone your home number, but you must have been on your way here.'

Jack glanced uncertainly at his wife.

'How kind,' Flora replied, adopting the same gracious manner. 'Thank you, we'd love to. It will be a pleasant way to say goodbye.' There was just the slightest edge to her voice.

'There'll be quite a few goodbyes to say. I have a whole new vision for the college – I'm sure Jack will have mentioned my plans – and that means big changes, particularly for the staff. But I intend that all the tutors I've asked to leave will be properly compensated.'

That was news, and news to Jack, Flora saw. 'It gets better

all the time,' he whispered. 'I'm free of a job I was beginning to find irksome and now I'll be paid for my freedom!'

The sherry party, as Flora thought of it, was as genteel as she'd expected, but it gave Jack the chance to say a proper farewell to colleagues he'd enjoyed working with, a few of whom had become good friends. The principal's decision to make big changes to Cleve was understandable and Flora knew that Jack had been undecided whether or not he wished to stay, until the decision had been taken for him. Now, it seemed, he was being paid to leave! And for *her* future? She would be back in Abbeymead for good, something she'd craved during the months they'd spent in Lewes. Right now, it seemed, their lives couldn't be better.

Or could it? Sitting in the car on their drive home, Flora felt oddly restless. Today had marked the very end of a chapter and should have heralded the beginning of a new, but somehow it didn't feel that way. Rather, it felt more of the same. And faintly dissatisfying. She scolded herself. It seemed she was never happy, yet that inkling of discontent – she'd felt it before and pushed it away – hadn't disappeared. A prompting maybe that she and Jack should think beyond the old life. That, together, they should be bolder. But how, exactly?

A letter was on the doormat when they walked through their front door. An official-looking letter, which pushed any other thought from her mind. Jack picked it up and she followed him into the kitchen.

'From the police?'

He nodded. 'I reckon it's... yes, it is,' he confirmed, tearing open the envelope and spreading flat the single sheet of paper. 'An invitation to attend Brighton police station. Tomorrow, if possible. To sign our witness statements. How's your left hand at writing?'

'I'll manage. But think how many statements we've signed over the last few years, Jack.'

He took her undamaged hand in his. 'At a rough guess, I'd say too many.'

They woke to a day of bright sunshine and a sky of deep blue. Appearances were deceiving, however, as the temperature overnight had once again plummeted and a thick frost coated every surface it could find: grass, trees, hedges, roofs. It took Jack twenty minutes of scraping the Austin's windows before he felt confident he could drive safely.

He was glad to see that Flora, walking towards him down the front path, had piled on the clothes, her face hardly visible beneath a squashy woollen hat, an upturned coat collar and a huge scarf that her aunt Violet, he remembered being told, had taken two winters to knit. What Jack could see of her complexion still verged on the ashen and he cursed the necessity of making the trip to Brighton in such arctic weather.

They wouldn't be staying in town, Jack was determined – no walks on the promenade, no fish and chip lunches. Instead, he hoped, a few minutes spent reading their statements before signing them off, and maybe a few more speaking to Alan Ridley, if the inspector had time. There were questions they both wanted answering and by now Ridley was likely to have the answers. But after that, they'd be on their way home. Before breakfast this morning, he'd made sure the fire was ready to light and a basket full of logs sat at the hearthside.

When they arrived in the town mid-morning, it was to find Brighton very busy, but then when wasn't it? Today, though, there seemed even less parking available than usual and, leaving the car as close to Bartholomews as he could, they set off for what became a twenty-minute march to the town hall and the police station housed in its basement. By the time they walked down the steps to its entrance, Flora had begun to cough badly. Jack wondered if he dared suggest that she see Dr Hanson this afternoon – there was a surgery around teatime – but it was a brief thought only. She'd insist that she was fine and had no need of the doctor. The bandage, he noticed, had already been discarded and, though her damaged hand was considerably less swollen than yesterday, it remained an unsettlingly bright red.

Walking up to the reception desk, he was surprised to find the sergeant on duty was expecting them and, instead of showing them to the row of waiting chairs, escorted them straight away to Inspector Ridley's office. The inspector looked up at the sergeant's knock, pushing aside the spectacles he'd begun to wear and reaching out to one of the tottering stacks of files that littered his desk. As usual, his office was half submerged in paper and Jack wondered, as he always did when he walked through this door, how on earth Ridley ever found anything amid the permanent confusion in which he appeared to work.

'Knew you'd make it today!' The inspector got to his feet, walking out from the desk to greet them. 'But thanks for coming in, folks – on a day like today, as well. This shouldn't take long, though, and I'd advise you to get home as soon as you can. I wouldn't be surprised if we had snow before nightfall. The clouds are already gathering.' He glanced through his window at a sky that, in the last hour, had become mottled, a layer of featureless grey despoiling the blue.

Jack wouldn't be surprised either and had every intention of making it back to Abbeymead before the first flakes fell. The file Alan Ridley had selected from the crumbling stack lay open on his desk, two closely typed pages, Jack saw, with each of their names heading a document.

'We went ahead with the statements,' Ridley said. 'It saves time – for you and for us – and I didn't reckon there'd be a lot more to say. We've typed up what you told me in Lewes,' he looked from one to the other, 'so, unless either of you have anything to add, it won't be a lengthy read.'

Jack was pleased. There *was* nothing more to say and the less time they spent in Brighton, the better. Flora, he noticed, signed her statement after only a cursory scan, almost as if what had happened to her at the Bell studio had happened in another world. And to another person.

'Interesting that you've arrested Edwin Brooker as well as Miss Bell,' Jack said. 'Are they both in your cells?'

'We've got Brooker, but Miss Bell has been transferred to the female wing of Holloway.' The inspector looked across at Flora. 'Based on her attempt to burn you alive, she's classed as a dangerous prisoner.'

'She'll be charged with attempted murder?' Jack asked.

The inspector beamed. 'That's the least of it. Two attempted murders, in fact. *And* two actual murders. We've got a real beauty here!'

Jack felt his mouth drop open and, twisting his head to look at Flora, saw that she was as shocked.

'Thomasina Bell?' he checked. 'She was behind it all?'

The inspector beamed. 'Got it in one.'

'But Brooker?' Flora stammered.

'His offence is relatively minor and he'll get bail when his case is heard later this week. Apart from aiding and abetting a fugitive, all we have on him is tampering with a doorbell – the one that floored you, Jack – deliberately rewiring it to be dangerous. But even that charge was difficult to prove until he spilt the beans.'

'He's been willing to talk?'

'Singing like the proverbial canary! Both of them, in fact – though from different cages. Edwin Brooker, you could say, is a disappointed man. It seems he had hopes of making Thomasina his wife, even bought her a ring and proposed. On the day of the fire! Though there's no sign of the jewellery.'

'The ring was in the studio, on the cutting table,' Flora put in. 'But then I saw Thomasina slip the box into her pocket. She must still have it.'

The inspector looked surprised. 'It wasn't on her person when she was arrested, so who knows? It could have burnt with the rest of the building, I guess.'

'And Brooker is disappointed because…?' Jack asked.

'He feels he's been shafted. Sorry, Mrs Carr— sorry, Flora. Feels he's been manipulated. Miss Bell appears to have been encouraging, pretending she was keen on him and would welcome a proposal. Once he was locked in a police cell, though, the truth seems to have dawned and he started to realise what she'd been up to. How she'd used him as part of her grand plan.'

Jack ran a hand through his hair. 'And part of the grand plan was to make the doorbell dangerous? It was Thomasina who asked him to rewire it?'

'She did and the idiot did just as he was asked. Watched Overlay House for when Nelson went for his walk – it seems he had a pretty regular routine and stupidly left the door on the latch – giving Brooker the chance to nip in and do the business. It took him only minutes to alter the wiring.'

'He did as he was asked and no questions?' Flora's face was paler than ever, Jack noticed.

'Miss Bell told him some rubbishy story about Nelson being a threat to her as long as he remained in Sussex – hinted it was something dastardly from the past. She managed to convince Brooker that she wouldn't be safe until Nelson had gone. Until he'd been run out of the county.'

'How exactly would tampering with the doorbell get rid of Nelson?' Flora pulled her coat more tightly around her.

The office was cold and getting colder. Not too many more questions, Jack thought.

'Anyone who rang the Overlay bell would be injured,' the

inspector replied. 'As Jack found out. That wouldn't go down too well with the village, Thomasina reckoned, and if it happened too many times, there would be voices raised against Nelson. She hoped he'd be hounded out of Abbeymead.'

'But did she really believe that?' Flora screwed up her forehead. 'We thought it was a possibility but as a plan to get rid of him, it always seemed insubstantial. There's no way she could know how the village would react.'

'I reckon she was casting around. She wanted to do Nelson harm. Any harm she could. At this point, she'd failed to kill him on Bonfire Night and the bell was a little something she could hit him with – until she succeeded. Who knows, he could have had an accident and electrocuted himself.'

'She wanted to harm him because she blamed him for her friend's death,' Flora said with certainty, now hunching shoulders against the cold.

The inspector nodded. 'And for maiming the little girl for life.'

'Even though the man was judged innocent,' Jack put in.

'The court's verdict appears to have had little influence on Miss Bell, its judgement holding no weight for her. Neil Leonard would always be guilty. It didn't matter either that the chap had paid for the child to be cared for all these years – I don't know if you knew that. In fact, his taking on the responsibility seems to have reinforced Bell's conviction that he was guilty.'

'So, he *was* the one who paid the nursing home fees,' she said wonderingly. 'I thought it might be Thomasina. Or the child's father.'

'*He* went AWOL shortly after the little girl was born and has stayed away ever since. A shotgun wedding, I reckon. It took place only a few months after Letty Reynolds graduated from St Clare's. As for Thomasina, the nursing home fees would have been far too expensive. Give the woman her due, she visited the home every week until the girl died, but it was Nelson or Leonard who paid up. Now, how about a cup of tea before we finish?' he suggested brightly. 'It's so damn cold today.'

They were quick to refuse the offer. The cold they could cope with but police tea was another matter.

'After the daughter died, things would have stayed calm, I reckon,' Ridley went on, forgetting the tea. 'Bell's visits had stopped, Nelson no longer paid fees. But then Trevor French suddenly brought a new man into the Grove society. When Miss Bell first saw him, she's told us, he seemed vaguely familiar, but it took her a while before she realised why. After all, she'd last seen him twenty years previously and then only his photograph in the paper and his fairly brief appearance in court. She worked it out quite quickly, though. "He was the man who killed the best friend I ever had and maimed my dear goddaughter." Those were her very words in this office a few days ago.'

'And as soon as she realised who he was, she decided to kill him?' Jack asked.

'Pretty much.'

'You said that she tried to kill and failed at the Lewes bonfire.' Flora was puzzled. 'But the scissors... I felt so sure the scissors had been used as a weapon that night. And such a strong feeling that she'd guessed my suspicion.'

The inspector looked across the desk at them, his eyes bright with the knowledge that he had this case sewn up. 'She used them all right. But on Trevor French. He was killed by a sharp object which we've never found and which, if Miss Bell's testimony is true and it *was* a pair of her scissors, we're never going to. They'll have gone the same way as the ring.'

'That's the double murder,' Jack muttered. 'Leo Nelson and Trevor French. But why kill French?' His face expressed bafflement.

'Oh, she has an easy answer to that. It was a mistake!'

29

'How on earth could it have been a mistake?' Flora asked. 'And how could she have wielded a pair of scissors from the back of the float?'

'She couldn't, that's the simple answer. She's explained it all. Like I said, the lady has been singing. I get the feeling that for Miss Bell the world has nothing left. The people who were dear to her are gone, and the man she hated has gone, as well. Killing Nelson was a badge of honour, if you like. Twisted, I know, but now she can relax. Mission accomplished.'

'But Trevor French?' Flora pursued.

'The short answer?' Alan Ridley grimaced. 'He wasn't supposed to die. Thomasina didn't like him – mind you, she doesn't appear to have liked anyone very much – and she was cross that he'd taken over as the Grove's chairman when, because of him, she'd lost the costume prize the year before. Even crosser when French brought Nelson into the society and she realised who he was. But as for killing him...'

'Yes?'

'It was an accident. A simple case of mistaken identity. She pushed the wrong man off the float. There were five or six chaps standing at the front, among them French, Edwin Brooker and Leo Nelson. At some point, they must have moved their positions slightly and French and Nelson from the back were very similar – the same height, the same build, even much the same haircut, although both were wearing some fancy headgear. But the costumes, of course, meant they were almost identical.'

The inspector stroked his moustache, seeming to think himself back to that night in Lewes.

'The procession provided an excellent opportunity for Thomasina to kill,' he continued placidly. 'The noise, the crowds, the darkness. And so, when the float jolted over an uneven section of the road – when *is* the council going to fix those potholes – she took her chance and pushed from behind.'

'And it was French who fell off the float, not Nelson,' Jack muttered.

'Exactly.'

'But she couldn't have expected a fall to kill the man. Or could she?'

'It might have killed him – it would have been her good luck if the fall *had* been fatal – but she wasn't expecting it.'

'Which is why she'd brought her sharpest pair of scissors,' Flora put in.

The inspector nodded.

'But how did she do it? From where she was standing on the float, it would be impossible, surely.'

'Impossible,' Ridley agreed. 'So... she pushed her victim off the float, then jumped down herself, supposedly to tend him. At that point, we reckon French must still have been alive – in pain with a broken ankle, but otherwise breathing normally.'

'She was pretending to care for the man,' Flora said, her voice shaky, 'holding his hand, asking for water, while all the time...'

'While all the time she was bending over him and murmuring sweet nothings in his ear, she was thrusting the blade of a razor-sharp pair of scissors between the rib bones. As a seamstress, she has a good awareness of the human body – she spends her days dressing them – and she calculated correctly. The scissors went in...' Flora was looking quite sick, Jack saw with alarm, 'pierced the chest and hit the aorta. The bleeding that followed was so swift and so extensive, death was almost instant.'

There was a stunned silence for several minutes.

'She must have believed she had killed Leo Nelson,' Jack said.

'It wasn't until you lifted the mask from the dead man's face, Jack – to help with his breathing? – that Thomasina saw she had killed the wrong man.'

'That must have been quite a moment for her.'

'Quite a moment,' the inspector agreed. 'It made her rethink her plans, certainly. Bonfire Night had given her the perfect opportunity for murder; the crowds and the confusion meant she had a good chance of avoiding suspicion. But after failing that night, she was forced to wait for a new opportunity, and that wasn't obvious – Nelson hardly left his house so killing him quietly was difficult. In the meantime, the waiting seems to have spurred her into making even greater efforts to ruin his life.'

'And she was willing to confess to this?'

'There wasn't much point in her keeping silent. Not after it was clear she'd set fire to the studio knowing Mrs Carrington was inside. She'd go down for that and for Lilian French, so why not allow herself to boast of all she'd done? Tell us how clever she'd been.'

'Lilian?' Flora wriggled to the edge of her chair. 'It was Thomasina who attacked her?'

'We've managed to lift fingerprints from Mrs French's

house. Thomasina will be convicted for two attempted murders, that's a certainty, which means a very, very long prison sentence. And my feeling is that Miss Bell much prefers to hang – hence the detailed confession.'

Flora took a long breath. 'I thought there was a chance that Brooker might be responsible for attacking Lilian. He had some kind of motive – in his view, at least. Lilian's husband had stolen his position. She had nothing to do with Bonfire, of course, but it's clear that Brooker was consumed with anger and he seems the kind of man to wreak revenge far and wide. *And* he was there that day, driving around Glebe Avenue. The day Lilian was gassed.'

'There at Miss Bell's request, apparently,' the inspector said. 'She'd told him yet another tale, a complete nonsense: that she was going to talk to Lilian French and would Brooker drive around the area to make sure she stayed safe. Be there for her if she needed him. She'd heard that Mrs French had a hot temper and was a little scared of confronting her, but she'd be brave and do it if *he* was in the background.'

'What! He believed that? There was no talking!' Flora said. 'I'm fairly sure Lilian was chloroformed at her front door.'

The inspector threw up his hands, presumably in despair at Brooker's naivety. 'She twisted the bloke round her little finger, that's the truth. Told him that Lilian French was conniving with Nelson to hurt her – by badmouthing her, spreading rumours, losing Thomasina clients. All part of the pretend threat she'd concocted. She was going to see Lilian, she told Brooker, meet her face-to-face, and ask her to stop the harm she was causing.'

'And Brooker accepted that?' Jack found it difficult to believe how stupid the man must have been.

'To be fair to Brooker, he'd seen them together, Lilian and Nelson,' the inspector said judiciously. 'Realised they were close or had been in the past. And, let's face it, he wanted to believe the woman. In reality, of course, Thomasina wanted him there, wanted him to be seen driving around Glebe Avenue, for a very specific reason. It would provide the police with a possible suspect, if we ever got to know of the attack on Mrs French. Which we didn't.' He fixed Flora with a severe expression.

'Lilian didn't want the police involved,' she defended herself.

The inspector gave a small shrug. 'You should have reported it,' was all he said. 'Of course, if we *had* been made aware of the attempt on Lilian French's life, Thomasina would have been ready to swear to us that she'd seen Brooker in Glebe Avenue just before she knocked on Lilian's door and got no answer. She would have wondered, all innocence, at why he was in the area.'

'And you believe Brooker's account?' Jack asked.

'We have the proof. Many of the fingerprints we've taken from windows and doors at the French house are a match for Miss Bell's. Far too many for a single visit supposedly made for a few minutes' talk.'

'This woman is an arch plotter! I could do with her input for my next book,' Jack said, and earned himself a deep frown from Flora.

'Fiendish,' the inspector agreed. 'The window frames had been painted over to make sure they didn't open. You must have seen that... Flora.'

Flora nodded, but didn't respond. She seemed subdued, Jack thought. As well she might. It was a catalogue of violence, of which she'd been a victim, too.

'We found a matching paint in Miss Bell's garden shed – the one that didn't burn – and forensics have confirmed the match. The tin was half empty and bearing the same serial number. Mostly the fingerprints had been wiped, but there was one that wasn't quite obliterated. It might not be sufficient to stand up in court, but it was enough to convince Thomasina that her killing spree was over.'

'She painted the window latches and the hinges? But when could she have done that?' Flora, it seemed, was finding the inspector's account difficult to credit.

'At night, apparently,' Ridley said calmly. 'When Mrs French had gone to bed. The garden is accessible and round she went.'

'But what was her purpose?' Jack asked. 'Why go for Lilian French?'

'Was it jealousy?' Flora's voice wavered a little. 'I remember how she reacted to a phone call she took from Leo Nelson and I didn't think it was all pretence. But I suppose,' she said, thinking aloud, 'if she hated Leo so very much, would she have been jealous of another woman?'

'Not jealous.' The inspector sounded certain. 'But plainly vindictive. She worked out how Nelson felt about the woman. Wheedled it out of him that he'd known Lilian as a young man, had been in love with her and wanted to marry. Thomasina guessed that he loved her still, a vulnerability she could exploit. So far, she'd failed to inflict the final blow, and torturing him in whatever way she could was satisfying. Killing Lilian – an easy target – hit the spot. She would kill Lilian first, allow Nelson to suffer the pains of bereavement, then finish the job by murdering him. She actually told me that she'd come to think killing was too good for him. Making him suffer before he died – the village turning against him, losing the woman he loved – was far more satisfying. It was closer to real justice.'

Jack's appalled expression mirrored his wife's.

The inspector let the information sink in before he spoke again, tapping his pen against the desk in a kind of victory tattoo. 'That paint was a good discovery but, luckily for us, it wasn't the only thing we found in a shed.'

Two pairs of eyes were trained on him.

'Rat poison,' he said succinctly. 'Arsenic.'

'That's how she killed Nelson? But how, exactly?' Jack was

as bewildered now as Flora. They had never had a case so intricate, he thought, and a murderer so devious. 'Your team searched her house from top to bottom.'

'The clue wasn't in her house or her garden. It was at Overlay – in the shed. Apples. She took Nelson apples, and he'd lined them up neatly along a shelf in *his* garden shed. It's what you do to preserve apples over the winter, but you'll know that. The only problem for Nelson was that a good many had been injected with arsenic.'

'The basket,' Flora said suddenly. 'Alice mentioned seeing Thomasina at Overlay, in the front garden, talking to Leo Nelson – and being very friendly,' she murmured.

'The "friendliness" was to dupe the chap into thinking that Miss Bell cared for him. She was very good at cozening men.'

'Alice noticed a basket at Thomasina's feet,' Flora said slowly, remembering what her friend had said. 'She thought the woman had been doing Nelson's shopping, or worse – she was quite scandalised – that Thomasina had actually been cooking for him.'

'Nothing so homely.' Ridley's face was expressive. 'It wasn't shopping she was bringing to Overlay House, it was death. She fooled Nelson as easily as she fooled Brooker.'

'I'm not sure he was entirely fooled,' Flora said. 'Lilian told me that Leo felt threatened, although she didn't know why or where it was coming from. She thought it was probably the reason he moved from Lewes to Abbeymead, hoping to remain unknown and so safer.'

'If he did feel threatened,' the inspector said, 'it wasn't from Miss Bell. She seems to have convinced him that she was on his side.'

'I can see that he might believe her!' Flora exclaimed. 'There was a link between them from the past. Thomasina had been Letty Reynolds' best friend and he'd been Letty's accidental killer. Maybe he felt he could talk to Thomasina in a way that he couldn't to others. Share with her his feelings about the accident.'

Ridley nodded. 'Absolutely right. She used that to get close to her victim, get him exactly where she wanted. Able to offer him apples that would kill. According to the post-mortem, Nelson had eaten an apple, among other things, and, when the pathologist took a second look, there was the arsenic. Just a speck, but enough to kill.'

Stunned by the stream of revelations, they sat for a full minute in total silence until Ridley cleared his throat. 'Parked near here, are you?'

'Yes, sorry,' Jack apologised hastily. 'It's time we went. I think we must be shell-shocked.' He knew he was speaking for Flora as well.

'I'm not surprised. So were we. Norris had to take the rest of the day off, after questioning the woman. But we've had some time to assimilate it. Thomasina Bell is an unusual murderer. Clever, clinical, and hardly a mistake. Except for Trevor French and, of course, that final conflagration.' He turned his head to speak directly to Flora. 'You know, if you hadn't spotted those scissors...'

'I still don't understand how she worked out that I *had* spotted the murder weapon.'

'She was already suspicious of you. Suspicious of you right from the start, I can tell you that. She didn't truly believe you wanted a dress made but decided to play along. Your assistant, Rose...'

'Rose Lawson, or rather Rose Lansdale.'

'That's her. Smartly dressed woman, by all accounts, and a good customer. So Bell went along with Mrs Lansdale's request, but kept her eyes open.'

'Was she watching us?' Jack asked suddenly. 'There was one time... when I was walking back from Overlay House after seeing Nelson, after the doorbell incident... I sensed something, a movement in the trees or behind the hedge. At the time, I put it down to a bird or a small animal, but it could have been someone watching me.'

'Watching both of you,' the inspector confirmed. 'I reckon at the time you mention, she was watching Nelson's house. After all, it was him she was plotting to kill. Then she saw you and thought you could be a problem if you got too friendly with the man. Particularly when she realised that Flora was your wife, and out of the blue Flora had got in touch with her. More than enough to make her suspicious.'

'Maybe, but still fairly nebulous?'

'This woman is nothing if not thorough!' the inspector said drily. 'She was keeping an eye on you for several weeks, you know. She says it was when she saw you at St Clare's that she really started to worry.'

'She was there, too?'

'Parked outside the college, apparently, and saw the pair of you leave. A stroke of bad luck for you. In actual fact, she was at St Clare's to collect her friend's old portfolio, and it could have been one of those coincidences that don't matter except...'

'Except?' Jack queried.

'That your wife spotted the scissors and realised their significance. If she hadn't, Bell might have got away with it.'

'And Flora might not have been half-choked to death,' he said sharply.

'Well, there is always that,' the inspector agreed.

Flora got to her feet, holding on to the chair for support, Jack noticed. Bending down to collect her handbag from the scuffed wooden floor, she suddenly jerked upright.

'When she killed French by mistake,' she burst out, 'when she realised that she'd killed a man who had nothing to do with Letty Reynolds' death, it never gave her pause?'

'It doesn't appear to have deterred her in the slightest. In her view, Trevor French was corrupt, so why shouldn't he die?

He'd cheated her of a prize that should have been hers *and* displaced her friend, Edwin, from a position that was rightfully his. Even worse, he'd polluted the Grove society by bringing an evil man into their midst.'

There was another long silence.

'Sure you won't have that cup of tea?' the inspector asked.

30

On their way back to Abbeymead, Jack drove slowly. As he'd expected, it began to snow as they left Brighton, the deep blue sky of early morning long disappeared. The flakes initially sparse and insubstantial, were gradually thickening as the fall became more rapid with the passing minutes. By the time they neared the turn-off to the village, a cushion of white had settled on the landscape, every hedge and tree, every blade of grass, wearing its wintry dress.

He took care in navigating the narrow lane, grass banks on either side now invisible but, in any case, his mind was too full of what they'd learned from Alan Ridley to travel faster. Flora had barely spoken since they'd left the police station and he could understand just how shocked she must be feeling. He would wait for the conversation they needed to have.

It wasn't until they turned into Greenway Lane that she spoke. 'I don't think I'll ever wear that dress,' she said. 'I don't think I can.'

The dress was the last topic Jack had expected, but he rose to the challenge. 'You *must* wear it.' He hoped he sounded encouraging. 'You love it, and you shouldn't confuse the dress with its maker.'

'But she'll always be there. The hands that sewed the dress are the same...' She broke off, her voice lost.

He took his own hand off the driving wheel and wrapped it round hers. 'If you feel that badly – don't wear it. Put it in the next village jumble sale. No one will know where it came from. And at least you haven't paid for it.'

'I haven't,' she said, brightening, but then a frown followed. 'Do you think I should?'

'How would you even do that? And after all that's happened, I think you can be excused.'

She nodded and breathed a small sigh of pleasure as he brought the Austin to a halt outside the cottage. 'We're home, Jack.'

'We are and you need warming. Your hands are ice cold and that burn is looking badly inflamed. Time to unearth the brandy bottle, I think.'

It was the sitting room fire, though, that demanded their attention first, the logs taking a while to burst into flame and even longer to warm the room, small though it was. But, once a blaze was nicely established, Jack went in search of tumblers and the half bottle of brandy he'd tucked at the back of a kitchen cupboard.

'You've been hiding that,' she said accusingly, as he found a space for it on the occasional table.

'Just as well I did. Here.' He poured a generous tot of amber liquid into a tumbler and handed it to her. 'I know you're not keen, but hold your nose and swallow and you'll soon feel a lot better.

'Well?' he asked, once she'd taken a few sips.

'A lot warmer,' she agreed. 'But completely wrecked, if that's the word for it.' She took another slow sip. 'I had no idea what a truly dreadful woman Thomasina is and I think it may have taken a toll. Until that moment in the studio, if I had any suspicions about her, it was that she was a dangerous flirt, out to hurt two rather stupid men. Even when the scissors suddenly arrived in my head, I thought that maybe it was Brooker who'd borrowed them to kill Trevor French. French was his enemy, after all.'

'And after she tried to kill you? We should probably have talked about it, prepared ourselves, at least a little, for what Ridley told us today. But you've been too poorly and too upset to have much of a discussion.'

'I don't think we could have ever guessed how truly wicked the woman is. And we can talk now, I suppose, though it's a little late.' She stared into the fire. 'We've not done too well this time, have we? Just scratched the surface, no more. And any hunches I've had haven't been much use either. I've been way out, Jack – actually toying with the idea that maybe Thomasina sacrificed her magnificent studio to protect Brooker, if he'd been the one to use those scissors. How stupid. I couldn't have been more wrong. In reality, she was planning to incriminate him. Shift the blame onto him for Lilian's death – if she'd succeeded in that murder.'

'It's been a lesson, I guess.' He raised his glass to the firelight, the liquid a golden glow. 'Teaching us not to get too big for our boots. We're not the super investigators we thought.'

'No one else was either,' she said, sounding a newly assertive note. 'You heard what Alan Ridley said – until Thomasina was prompted into the madness of that fire, no one had a clue she was behind both killings. It was the fire that set new enquiries going. The pathologist looking again at his findings, for instance, looking for a particle of apple that might contain arsenic.'

'All true,' he said lazily. 'But it's over, thank the Lord, and all we have to worry us now is Christmas – it's almost here and we've barely noticed. Why don't we make the cake tomorrow?

There won't be many wanting to buy books in this weather and Rose can look after the All's Well for one more day.'

'It's a bit late for a Christmas cake. It should have been made weeks ago.'

'It's never too late for cake. *Another Way to Die* can go hang for the morning. You can measure and I'll stir.'

When Alice rang the following morning, it was to invite Flora for supper that evening – a break with tradition.

'Katie and I have been talkin',' she began. 'We didn't want to miss another evening, which we would, Friday bein' Christmas Day, so I said I'd cook tonight.'

'Are you sure, Alice? You cooked last time and you must be so busy at the Priory.'

'Run off my feet,' she said cheerfully, 'but I'll bring the soup and a couple of desserts back from the hotel. We're drownin' in food there – and that'll just leave a main. How about chicken and dumplings?'

'It sounds perfect. The chicken is from the hotel, too?' she guessed.

'Well, when can *we* afford poultry? And it's just slices left over from the carvery. So, seven o'clock? You're feelin' better now, I hope.'

'Much better,' Flora said as convincingly as she could, though she wasn't sure it was true. 'And looking forward to supper already. I'll bring my presents – it's close enough to Christmas to open them!'

Fortunately, she'd shopped for gifts at the beginning of the month – and there were never that many to buy: a prettily worked satin cushion for Alice, a bath set for Kate that had a sumptuous smell and, for Kate's husband, a book on wetland birds. Much to Jack's amusement, Tony had developed a keen interest in the native wildlife, even buying himself a pair of high-powered binoculars which, because of his busy life, he had yet to use. As for Jack, a framed print of the Cornish beach he'd loved was hidden deep inside her wardrobe.

Apart from the picture, the presents remained unwrapped and stacked in a small pile in the spare bedroom that Jack used as an office. For days, Flora had been meaning to tackle the task of wrapping and decorating, but time had trickled through her fingers and since Saturday's near-death experience, she had lacked the energy – and the dexterity. Today was beginning to look busy, but busy was good. It would keep her mind off events she'd rather not think of.

31

Alice had gone to town on the Christmas decorations this year, with brightly coloured balloons a hazard at every doorway and ceilings criss-crossed by handmade paper chains. A row of pipe-cleaner Santas lined the mantelpiece.

'It looks amazing,' Flora exclaimed, walking into the sitting room. A tiny artificial tree, sprayed white and dangerously over-loaded with glass baubles, sat in one corner. 'Even a Christmas tree!'

'*And* I found some paper napkins with them reindeers all over it. What do you think?' She gestured to the dining table covered in prancing animals. Flora duly admired it. 'I had to do somethin',' Alice said, 'or I'd have no Christmas at all.'

'You're working on Christmas Day?' Flora was sympathetic.

'To be honest, I don't mind. It will be busy but it's fun, like a big party. And I'll be with Sally, she's workin', too. But—'

A knock on the front door had Alice scurry to answer it. Mutters in the hall, footsteps on the floor tiles, and Kate, looking radiant in a new woollen skirt and jumper, walked into the sitting room. For an instant, Flora regretted her banished dress, but only for an instant.

'*You're* not working on Christmas Day, I hope?' she said to Kate over the oxtail soup.

'Oh, gosh, no. Tony wanted to close tomorrow but I've persuaded him to stay open until lunchtime. We're doing a Christmas Eve special for the older residents. His mum and dad don't arrive until the evening, so we'll have time to get the house ready.'

'They'll be amazed when they see how Sarah has grown.'

'Thrilled to bits, I imagine. It should be a wonderful few days. I know Alice is working but how about you, Flora? Do you and Jack fancy joining us?'

'No.' Her refusal came rather too quickly and she rushed to smooth over any awkwardness. 'Thank you, Kate, but this year we thought we'd have a quiet holiday.'

'Quiet is what the girl needs,' Alice said, appearing with the chicken and dumplings at just the right moment.

The meal was a dish to savour – weren't they always when cooked by Alice? – and one enjoyed with the minimum of chatter. Only the barest of Abbeymead news was exchanged over the dumplings and it wasn't until everyone had eaten a second slice of plum pudding that presents were brought out and the unwrapping began. Flora found herself the lucky recipient of a matching wool scarf and gloves, knitted by Alice, and a bottle of perfume from Kate and Tony.

'And looking at you now,' Alice said, fixing her gaze on Flora over the small pile of presents, 'I'm thinking you need more than a quiet Christmas. Peaky, that's what you look. You need time away from that dratted bookshop. Get Rose Lansdale to cover until the New Year.'

'I've *had* time off,' she protested. 'All week. I know Rose will help if she can, but she's still working a few days a week at the post office and she's just moved into a new flat. She'll have stuff to sort out there. She's been very good, helping me out this week at short notice.'

'Helping you out because you got yourself into trouble – again,' Alice scolded. 'I've a mind to speak to that husband of yours. He should be puttin' his foot down on all these goin's on.'

'All I did was order a dress,' she protested. 'I didn't know I was asking a psychopath to make it for me.'

Alice huffed. 'It's strange that it's always you in the wars, though, isn't it? You don't see me gettin' set fire to, or Kate, or anyone else in Abbeymead.'

Flora looked appealingly at Kate who rallied to the rescue. 'That meal was one of your best, Alice, and so much lovely food this season. It's difficult now to remember all those years of rationing. We made do, but... Did you know that Charlie cooked a batch of chocolate yule logs for the Nook – actually two batches? They've been walking out of the café. I'd ask him to bake more, but he must be up to his eyes at the moment.'

'We all are,' Alice said, clearing the table. 'But the lad pulls his weight, I will say that.'

'He's got over his passion for coffee bars?' Flora smiled to herself and followed Alice into the kitchen.

Charlie had caused consternation this summer, his newfound independence encouraging him to spend every penny he earned in places his mother and Alice considered dubious.

'It was a phase,' Alice said comfortably, stacking their dishes in the sink to wash later. 'But he best make sure he doesn't do it again. Right cheeky, he became. Anyways, Hector is keeping him far too busy to go rovin' round Brighton, or anywhere else he shouldn't.'

'I'll be going to the vicar's party after the carol service tomorrow,' Flora said, carrying a filled teapot and cups back into the sitting room. 'And hoping I can persuade Jack to come – I don't suppose either of you will make it.'

'No time, my love,' Alice answered for them both, 'but what

we will do is meet for a drink on Boxing Day. I'll make sure I get an hour or two off. How does that suit you?'

'It sounds good.' By then, she and Jack would have enjoyed a whole day alone together.

'And then there's this big party,' Alice went on. 'Some time in the new year. I reckon most of the village will be invited to that.'

'A party at the School House?'

'Ambrose Finch's housekeeper – you know the woman, Dottie Harte – was in Houseman's the other day buyin' her veg, and she told me that Finch has been workin' on an order for a ton of food and a ton of drink, too. She thinks, when he's got a date, he's goin' to order from that fancy place in Steyning.'

'Have you seen the prodigal son yet?' Flora asked.

'Not yet, but I'm on the lookout.' Alice wore a determined air.

Flora looked across at Kate and together they suppressed their smiles.

Despite Flora's protests as she'd left home, Jack had insisted that he would walk her back to the cottage and, as the hall clock struck the last chime of ten, he was at Alice's door, swathed in a long scarf and wearing his trusty fedora. Hastily, Flora donned hat, coat and gloves while he stamped up and down on the brick path trying to keep warm, but turning down the offer of more tea. A linen bag was found to hold Flora's presents and, after a flurry of kisses and goodbyes, she was out in the cold, still air, the brightness of an almost full moon lighting their way. There had been no further snow, but a deep frost had set in and, crossing the high street into Greenway Lane, the crunch of their footsteps sounded loud in the silent streets.

'I think I'll go back to the All's Well straight after Boxing

Day,' she murmured, holding tightly to his arm and wary of slipping on the ice.

'Really? That soon?'

'It's unfair to ask Rose to give up more of her time. And I'm perfectly well now. Look, I've even got pink cheeks.'

'That's the cold speaking. But if you feel you must...'

'I do. I'm pining for my books!'

'I can't say I'm pining for mine, but a few more chapters to edit and I should have wrapped this last one up. *After* Christmas, though,' he said with emphasis. 'Did Kate invite us for Christmas Day? I thought she might.'

'She did and I said thank you, but no. And Lilian has left for Newcastle at last. She'll be with her daughter for the day. Far better medicine than anything Dr Hanson can prescribe.'

Jack gave an audible sigh of relief. 'So, we really are on our own for Christmas?'

'We are and how lovely is that!'

She went to walk on, but Jack came to a halt and pulled her close. Then, reaching across the ditch to the hedge, he broke off a small twig of mistletoe, a rare find.

'How fortuitous there happens to be a bush of mistletoe at just the right place.' He laughed, holding the sprig of white berries over her head.

'You didn't, by any chance, notice that on the way to Alice's?'

'I might have. And since I did, let's make the most of it.'

And beneath a crystal clear moonlight, he did just that. He made the most of the mistletoe.

A LETTER FROM MERRYN

Dear Reader

I want to say a huge thank you for choosing to read *Murder by Firelight*. If you enjoyed the book and want to keep up to date with all my latest releases, just sign up at the following link. Your email address will never be shared, and you can unsubscribe at any time.

www.bookouture.com/merryn-allingham

Although the small town of Lewes has featured in a number of Flora and Jack's adventures, it's normally a calm and friendly place. But on the fifth of November, it offers an entirely different scene. The town's bonfire celebrations are probably the largest in England and follow a tradition laid down over two hundred years ago. As well as celebrating the defeat of Guy Fawkes and his intention to blow up the Houses of Parliament, Lewes bonfire goes further – it blows up anyone the various bonfire societies dislike. The event is noisy, rowdy and pagan in nature – all those burning crosses! It's also the perfect setting for a murder.

If you've enjoyed the mystery Flora and Jack uncover, you can follow their fortunes in the next Flora Steele novel or discover their earlier adventures, beginning with *The Bookshop Murder*. And if you really enjoyed the book, I would love a short review! Getting feedback from readers is amazing and it helps new readers to discover one of my books for the first time. Do get in touch, too, through social media or my website – I love to chat.

Thank you for reading,

Merryn x

www.merrynallingham.com

 bsky.app/profile/merrynwrites.bsky.social
 facebook.com/MerrynWrites

PUBLISHING TEAM

Turning a manuscript into a book requires the efforts of many people. The publishing team at Bookouture would like to acknowledge everyone who contributed to this publication.

Audio
Alba Proko
Melissa Tran
Sinead O'Connor

Commercial
Lauren Morrissette
Hannah Richmond
Imogen Allport

Cover design
The Brewster Project

Data and analysis
Mark Alder
Mohamed Bussuri

Editorial
Lucy Frederick
Melissa Tran